Misbehaving

KATHY
RODGERS

GW00690175

POOLBEG

This novel is entirely a work of fiction. The names, characters and incidents portrayed in it are the work of the author's imagination. Any resemblance to actual persons, living or dead, events or localities is entirely coincidental.

Published 2003
by Poolbeg Press Ltd.
123 Grange Hill, Baldoyle,
Dublin 13, Ireland
Email: poolbeg@poolbeg.com

© Kathy Rodgers 2003

The moral right of the author has been asserted.

Copyright for typesetting, layout, design
© Poolbeg Group Services Ltd.

1 3 5 7 9 10 8 6 4 2

A catalogue record for this book is available from the British Library.

ISBN 1-84223-115-4

All rights reserved. No part of this publication may be reproduced or transmitted in any form or by any means, electronic or mechanical, including photography, recording, or any information storage or retrieval system, without permission in writing from the publisher. The book is sold subject to the condition that it shall not, by way of trade or otherwise, be lent, resold or otherwise circulated without the publisher's prior consent in any form of binding or cover other than that in which it is published and without a similar condition, including this condition, being imposed on the subsequent purchaser.

Cover Designed by Slatter-Anderson
Typeset by Patricia Hope in Goudy 11/14.5
Printed by
Cox & Wyman
Reading, Berkshire

www.poolbeg.com

About the Author

Kathy Rodgers lives in Longford with her two sons. Currently she is working on her second novel *Boomerang*. She also has written the final chapter of *Goldsmith's Ghost*, a novel which involved ten writers from three different counties (Longford, Westmeath and Roscommon) and was published in 2002.

Acknowledgements

I would like to thank the following people for their help and support.

Firstly, Paul Perry, former writer-in-residence in Longford Library, Fergus Kennedy the Arts Officer, Mary Carleton-Reynolds and the brilliant staff in the library especially Grainne and Isabella (not forgetting her daughter Sarah).

Thanks to my fellow writers and poets in Longford Writers group.

In the day job I work with some wonderful people and thanks to each and every one of you that I share a laugh with – you make my day. A special thanks to Tom Swanick and Cora for sorting out my PC problems! Also to the girl that loves the big cheese.

When authors praise the team at Poolbeg in their acknowledgements they're telling the truth – they're really great. They make you feel so special – so a very big thank you to Gaye Shortland for the great job in editing and to Paula Campbell and her team for the brilliant cover. To my agent Ger Nichol at The Book Bureau for her support and enthusiasm.

I'm blessed to know Stephine, – she reads my work, listens to my moans and still returns my calls – you're a gem. Thanks to Mo who cheered me up on a bad day when she told me she loved the first three chapters and couldn't wait for more.

Thanks to my parents Jo and Joseph and to my mother-in-law Anna for the baby-sitting and all that comes with it. To Gerard and Paul, thanks for treating us so well when we're in Dublin. To Henry, Janet and Maeve for all their kindness. To Dolores for the marathon phone calls.

To my sister and very best friend Anne, thanks for always being there for me – not forgetting her husband Thomas and their three beautiful daughters, Kate, Aine and Maeve. To the O'Sullivans – Oliver, Catherine, Conor, Oisin and Finn in London and to Pat, Karen, Erin and Emer in Sydney, I hope this makes up for all the Christmas cards I forgot to send.

To Eamon for the great holiday in Westport.

I'm blessed with two wonderful sons, Kevin and Shane, and I thank God for them.

You're all very special people to me.

In memory of Martin

Chapter 1

It was lunch-time and it was like rush hour in my head. I had a list of things to do and less than one hour to do them. I was in my local supermarket, like I am every day. I grabbed a basket and made for the baby aisle. Usually I tried to do a big shop once a week, on a Saturday morning, but it never worked out that way. I was always back shopping again the next day.

"Write a list," my husband Gary suggested, when I moaned to him that I knew the supermarket better than I knew my own home. At least I had a better chance of finding what I was looking for in the supermarket. Yet I was grateful for his suggestion. Those days Gary and I couldn't hold down a conversation for two minutes without one of us yawning. We blamed it on parenthood. Other parents reassured me that it got easier as the kids got older.

A quick glance at the checkouts made me grow more irritable – each one had a queue. Even the express looked sluggish today. In the distance I could see my mother-in-law. I turned down an aisle to avoid her. I hadn't time for a quick

1

chat. Kathleen would want to know if Jack's ear infection was better? Did he sleep the night? Did he eat his breakfast? That's the one thing Kathleen has in common with my mother: they need to know everything.

I stopped halfway down the aisle, bewildered. They'd moved the contents of the aisle. It used to be the toy aisle; now it had pots and pans grinning down at me. My armpits were damp with sweat. Outside it was cold and raining, inside it was like a tropical forest. I felt cheated. A loyal customer like me should be informed when they're going to move things. Didn't they realise how confusing it was for me? I raced up the aisle. There was no need for me to glance at my watch and find out the time. The clock in my head was tick-tocking the minutes down for me. All I had to do was keep in time. I'd done this a thousand times. First, I'd run into the supermarket to do a quick shop and get a sandwich. Then, I'd do some other errands before dashing back to work with only seconds to spare.

I headed for the baby aisle and thankfully it was still there. I picked up a packet of nappies. I still had to go to the bank. And, I had to collect a prescription for my baby. Another sleepless night loomed ahead of me. That's the thing about me: I'm good at predicting the worst outcome.

Gary and I weren't childhood sweethearts, but we grew up together. We never engraved our names on a tree or kissed when no one was looking. I let Gary have a peek at me doing a pee when I was five. He was curious as to how girls actually did a pee without a willy. Then, Gary had to go off and play cowboys and Indians with the boys, while I stayed with my best friend Eleanor and made tea in my white and red tea set.

My feet took me back to the sandwich-stand. I scanned the selection on display: chicken, tuna, ham. I read the labels and tried to make a "quick" decision.

Right now I could be in the pub with the girls from work having our usual Friday lunch of chicken curry and chips instead of standing in Tesco.

"Hi, Michelle," a voice said from behind me.

I turned around and saw Amanda in her school uniform.

"Hi, Amanda, how are you?"

"I'm fine. I've got a French test this afternoon and I'm not looking forward to it," she said, a slight tremor in her voice. Her mother minds my son for me, while I spend my day answering calls from customers.

Amanda's mother had told me she'd ring me if he didn't settle down for her. All morning I'd waited for her call and, when it didn't come, I called her hoping he'd be missing me so much that I'd have to leave work. I wanted to be with him and I longed for a few hours of blissful sleep.

"See ya," Amanda said.

"Did you go home for lunch?" I couldn't help myself, I had to ask.

Amanda shook her head. "I tried to do some study." She walked away from me with a chicken sandwich, her head full of thoughts of the dreaded test.

The tuna sandwich looked like the healthy option, so I picked it up. Being sleep-deprived I'd forgotten that I didn't like tuna.

My life was just busy, ordinary busy. Filled with the everyday things of being mother to a baby boy and wife to Gary.

A familiar face smiled at me and I smiled back as the

woman walked past. I live in a small midlands town. It's like a goldfish bowl: you're bound to bump into the same people again and again.

"Michelle," a voice said.

I turned to look. My heart missed a beat. He was standing inches away from me.

I stood motionless. The tuna sandwich slipped from my hand into the basket.

"Michelle."

My mouth dropped open. Inside I could feel my chest tightening, I couldn't breathe. It felt like I was under water. I was aware that things were going on around me, but everything was a blur.

"Damien," I managed to say, and then I gulped for breath. It felt like I had plunged into the deep end and I needed air quickly or I'd drown. "Hi," I muttered. The muscles in my face stretched into a weak smile. The sort of smile you saved for people you don't like, but have to be friendly to.

It was five years since I'd inhaled the Damien smell, that heady mixture of expensive aftershave and body odour. It excited me, made me go all tingly inside.

His soft blue eyes never left mine.

He broke into my thoughts by saying, "It's good to see you." A dreamy smile formed on his handsome face.

Damien's voice opened up the past. Its soft sensual timbre made my heart race. He hadn't changed. If anything he looked better, but then, you don't meet many attractive men in my local supermarket. At least I'd given up looking – after all, I was a married woman.

"It's good to see you." I echoed his words as I couldn't think of my own. I'd been well-schooled to keep my feelings to myself, a family tradition that I've never managed to shake off. I felt stupid, as I stood there tongue-tied and breathless.

At work we have steps that we go through to deal with difficult customers. I longed for Agent Clarke to pass the clipboard to me now. Rosemary and I liked to call ourselves agents. We worked for a company called Express Couriers. It was up to us to help our customers with any problems they had. We labelled ourselves Agent Clarke and Agent Kenny, just for the fun of it.

Damien towered over me. I noticed his face was lightly tanned. I avoided making eye contact. I couldn't help but notice threads of silver woven through his light-brown hair. A part of me longed to reach out and touch him, to see if he was real. Instead I looked down at my list. Yoghurts, milk, bread.

Silence fell on us. I knew he was looking down at me with those blue eyes that always had the effect of making my legs go weak. The shopping list made no sense. I felt like I was being transported to another place, to a time when I was a different Michelle.

"Shopping?" Damien said.

I nodded and then filled the silence by saying, "Yes."

"I know this is a shock . . . me turning up like this, but I needed to see you." He moved closer to me as he spoke.

I ventured to look up from his chest and meet his eyes again: they were the same devilish eyes, full of mischief. Dormant feelings surfaced. A feeling of warmth spread through me, making me blush. Was I falling in love with this man all over again? Could someone from your past just walk into your life and tilt it so that you lost your direction? My thoughts swayed.

I was sure of one thing, that I was certain of nothing. It dawned on me, then, with brilliant clarity, that things would never be the same again. The floor seemed to move beneath me, then steadied itself.

"I know it's been a long time," he said, in the cultured tone that once was as familiar to me as breathing.

Five years, I wanted to say. Five years, one marriage and a child later, you turn up – like a bad penny, as my mother would say.

"I – I –" I heard myself stammering. I wanted to cry and laugh at the same time. My hands gripped the shopping basket for support.

"I can explain. Perhaps we could have lunch together?"

A long time ago I'd closed my mind to Damien. I'd locked the door to that part of my life. I never thought about him, dreamt about him, wondered what he was doing now. Nothing. It was like he'd never existed, that our time together had never happened.

By some accident my mind was playing tricks on me. I'd opened the wrong door. This was not Damien, this was me – having a nightmare in the middle of the day. All I had to do was pinch myself and I'd wake up.

I reached out my hand and touched his arm. He was real – I was not dreaming.

"I have to do my shopping." I replayed the words I'd said to the girls thirty minutes ago: "I haven't time for lunch. I'm going to have a sandwich at my desk."

"Michelle," he said, his voice almost a whisper, as if he was afraid of other shoppers hearing.

I loved the way he said my name – it was like a caress. I quelled a longing to reach out and touch him again.

"I know you've got a new life and the last thing you want is to meet an old lover, but I need to see you."

Two girls from work passed by.

"Hi, Michelle," they said in chorus and then they sped down the aisle giggling.

"I know you're married," he said.

Those simple words conjured up a picture of my son and Gary. A family portrait, but I was missing.

"You've got a son," he added.

"Yes," I found myself saying. A tingle of joy ran through me. At least I could still speak.

"Jack," he said.

I attempted to smile, but the muscles in my face were frozen. Damien smiled for me.

"Michelle, I was thinking it was you!" came a familiar female voice.

I smiled feebly at my mother-in-law Kathleen. She turned to look at Damien.

He picked up a sandwich and walked purposefully towards the magazine section.

"How is Jack?"

"Fine," I said.

I glanced at my watch, saw the time, but couldn't make myself move from the spot. I was way behind schedule. I should have collected Jack's prescription already and be on my way to the bank.

"Michelle, you look terrible," Kathleen said. For once her eyes were full of sympathy for me. I knew she'd never considered me good enough for her only son.

"I don't feel well."

I stole a glance at Damien. He was standing at the

magazine-stand. The cream raincoat that he wore might have looked ordinary on another man – on him it looked tailored and perfect.

"Michelle . . ."

I heard Kathleen say my name. I felt irritated and found my face falling into a frown as I turned to look at her.

"Is there anything I can do to help?" she asked with an arched eyebrow. She had a pleasant face and, unlike my mother, she always seemed to be smiling.

I attempted to tune into her wavelength. I needed to get rid of her as fast as I could. Delving into my bag, I pulled out the prescription.

"You could collect Jack's prescription from the chemist for me."

She took the prescription from me. "Of course, I'll drop it in this evening."

That was the last thing I wanted Kathleen to do because she always forgot to go once she'd "dropped in". I saw her face brighten, then she turned and headed for the exit.

He was gone. I looked around and he was nowhere to be seen. Not at the magazine-stand, not at the express checkout, nowhere.

My head was spinning. I wanted to cry. Where the hell had he got to? And what did he want with me? I didn't need this, not now, not today.

I had shopping to do, a job that I had to get back to and baby Jack to think about. I was stopped in full flow as I watched him materialise with a bunch of flowers in his hand.

"For you, Michelle," he said.

For some unexpected reason my heart swelled with joy. This was the Damien I had fallen in love with. He bought flowers not as a peace offering or to negotiate with, but because he wanted to.

"Thank you," I said. Tears were filling my eyes, making him quiver in front of me. "There . . ." words failed me. "There . . ." I attempted to speak but couldn't.

"Let's go somewhere quiet. We need to talk."

I shook my head. "I can't."

"Michelle, I'm really sorry about this. I've handled it so badly. I should have phoned you or written to you, but I was afraid that you'd turn me away."

Habit made me look at my watch.

"I have to go – if I don't I'll never make it back to work on time."

Damien nodded.

I picked up my basket. My legs shook uncontrollably as I joined the queue for the express checkout. For once I didn't care if it took forever. He stood alarmingly close behind me.

An aching started in my belly and ran all the way down to my toes. I wanted this man. I inched myself a little away from him. He moved closer. While not actually touching, it was enough to excite me.

A part of me wanted to turn around, look into those electric eyes of his and ask him, 'Where are you taking me?'

"Hi, Michelle."

"Hi, Susan." I smiled at the girl on the checkout. She lived two doors down from me. She eyed Damien curiously. Quickly I moved away from him.

"Terrible day out," she said.

I nodded. I saw her stealing another glance at Damien. He was used to it, thrived on it. In fact, he'd probably die if women didn't stare at him.

"See ya," Susan said.

While I was pushing my nappies into the carrier bag, Damien was paying for his sandwich. A great sense of shame and guilt rose inside me. Even though I'd done nothing wrong. But I wanted to. I longed to. My fingers trembled as I picked up my shopping and ran for the exit. I ran all the way to my car. When I gave a quick look back, I realised no one was chasing me and felt disappointed.

The flowers scented the car, reminding me of when I was a little girl. I loved to pick buttercups and daises when I went to visit my granny. As I inhaled the sweet smell, I was again watching my brother Vincent running down the hill. His supple body moved speedily and with little effort, skipping over the long grass. It's a picture I've always held in my mind.

"You can't catch me!" he shouted and laughed at me.

I waved at him and started to run down the hill, knowing I wasn't as fast as he was, but enjoying it all the same.

Right now, that is what I wanted to do: run. I didn't want to think about my past with Damien or my present with Gary. And the last thing I wanted to do was go back to work.

Deep down I knew that I'd see Damien again. My stomach rumbled nervously. If I was honest, I knew I wanted to see him again. I wanted to sit down and listen to him, to hear his refined voice and be seduced by whatever he had to say. My head was spinning with the crazy picture I was dreaming up.

Chapter 2

I just made it back to work with one minute and thirty-three seconds to spare. Agent Clarke eyed me suspiciously.

I sat down and put on my headphones, just as a call was coming through.

"Good afternoon, Michelle speaking, how can I help?" I sang off my little rhyme.

I pretended to listen and thought: how the hell could I give anyone help? I needed help myself. The afternoon stretched out ahead of me like a vast desert of time.

Fog had held up our courier service in France. Three customers would be looking for a refund. Eleanor was going to love that. She might be my best friend but she was also my boss. It was a well-know fact that she hated parting with money. Even when it wasn't her bloody own. I clock-watched for my break.

"Michelle?"

I sat up to attention. Agent Clarke, or Rosemary, had actually addressed me by my name. Rosemary's hair-colour was mood-driven: it went from golden to honey on good weeks and on bad ones it looked a very bleached blonde. Maybe it was the office lighting, but it looked very bleached today. She took off her glasses and threw them on the desk. I sensed she was annoyed about something.

"What?" I said, my face contorted into a question mark.

Rosemary smiled and then said, "I'd like to take my break now. Can you manage on your own?"

Of course I can manage on my own, I wanted to say, but the words failed me. "Sure, no problem." I found myself wilting back in the chair.

I watched her open her bag and take out her purse with a flourish.

Over the past few weeks, I had observed a change in Rosemary's behaviour. Usually she ate fruit on her breaks or cardboard crackers or diet yoghurts – now she was breaking out and going to the snack-machine regularly. This led me to believe that there was something wrong with her.

I was tempted to ask her if she was alright? Yet I felt she'd volunteer this information if she wanted to. I was worried that all my favourites would be gone out of the snack-machine, if she didn't return to her rigid diet soon. I found myself typing this on the screen and then I realised I shouldn't send it to Rosemary because she'd given up reading my e-mails. She said she hadn't time to.

There were no privileges in this office. She had the same amount of time as I had. What the hell had happened to her? Since I came back from maternity leave, she'd been acting strange with me. The phone rang, as it usually did when I was absorbed in something else.

I attempted to help a customer find his package. It had

been sent to London instead of Birmingham. About a thousand calls later, I got it redirected.

Then I clock-watched and went to the ladies' where I spent almost five minutes looking at a hair that was growing on my chin. Every day I kept promising to cut it when I got home, but then I'd forget or couldn't be bothered and, the next day at work, I'd keep thinking everyone was looking at it.

I thought of Damien suddenly, and my face turned red with embarrassment. I hoped he hadn't noticed my hairy chin.

I stood back, looked at my reflection and cringed. I uttered a few swear words under my breath. "Bastard – why didn't he ring me? Why did he have to see me looking like this?"

Back at my desk, the first thing I did was book an appointment to get a facial. I was aware that Rosemary was listening in, so I didn't mention my hairy chin.

At last, I reached the final hurdle. Thirty minutes to go and then it was home time.

I was looking forward to seeing my little son again. I rang Gary and told him to get milk and a bottle of wine. We would have a liquid supper.

"You were spotted taking to a very attractive man in the supermarket," Rosemary suddenly said.

"Man?" I said, hoping I looked baffled. "What man?"

Rosemary thumped my back a little too hard. I pretended to lose my balance.

"You heard me." There was a slight edge to her voice.

For once, I wished my phone would ring.

"My lover," I said.

"Ha ha," Rosemary said, her brown-rimmed glasses sliding down her nose. She pushed them up again.

I pulled my face into a false smile. Her phone rang and she answered it in her usual sing-song voice.

"What man?" Eleanor asked. I turned around to see that she was standing by the door.

"Rosemary heard that I was talking to a man in Tesco's and she wanted to know who he was."

Rosemary laughed at something a customer said to her. Eleanor leant against my desk. We exchanged knowing looks – Rosemary was a bit on the nosey side.

It was tempting to tell Eleanor about my meeting with Damien. Eleanor knew "almost" everything about me. But there were things you didn't tell even your best friend and this was one of them.

"Can I have a word?" she said. "In my office." She gracefully removed herself from my desk and left the room. As usual she was dressed in a dark business suit, her slight frame belying a tough personality.

I turned to look at Rosemary who was humouring a customer as she lolled back on her chair with her head-set on. My eyes narrowed to slits as I threw a dirty look her way.

Eleanor and I had been friends since we were children. She had lived with her parents and two brothers at the end terrace. Their house was always calm and welcoming, so unlike my own. As children we complemented each other well: she did the thinking and I did the talking.

Eleanor's office was a place of order. On the wall was a flow chart with employees' names marked in and colour-coded for sick days, holidays or maternity leave. A lot of blue squares were coloured in against my name. I didn't have to ask what they were: I knew they were sick days.

She joined her thin ringless hands together and was about to say something when I butted in. "What has she been saying about me this time?" I didn't fold my arms or cross my legs. I was going to be wide open for this conversation.

"That you're not pulling your weight." She leaned back in her executive chair. Behind her dull eyes lay a microchip of information, waiting to be retrieved when necessary. "We need to resolve this. Rosemary, you and me. This has to be sorted out."

"Fine."

"Could you stay back this evening?"

I met her cold stare and said in my most diplomatic voice, "I'm sorry, Eleanor, I'd love to meet with you this evening and talk all this through, but you didn't give me any notice. I have to collect Jack from the baby-sitter's."

Her mouth thinned to a disapproving line.

I longed to stick my tongue out at her and say, "Na, na," like we used to do as children, but I hadn't the energy or the nerve. We might be friends, but she was still my boss.

"There are plenty of girls in tele-sales that would love your job."

"Eleanor –" I started to say and then stopped myself.

"I know you're tired and you don't need this, but in the work place I can't have favourites – you do understand?" She wanted to finish on a positive note as was her policy.

I nodded and felt like I was a child again, listening to her give out to me because I had done something wrong.

The big hand on the clock reached five and I knew it

was time for me to go. I was free of this place until Monday.

"Have a nice weekend and I'll see you on Monday," I said, my hand on the door handle.

Rosemary was still on the phone when I returned to our office. I picked up my bag, switched off my computer and left without a backward glance. That would teach her. She took it badly when her colleagues didn't at least mouth a goodbye to her.

Chapter 3

Outside, the rain had stopped. Silver drops dripped down from the leafy trees onto the ground.

Damien was in my head. I replayed our meeting. I couldn't help it. I knew it was wrong.

"Stop it, stop it," I told myself.

I was going to collect my son and his father, my husband, would be home soon. With my eyes closed I willed myself to see Jack. My arms ached to hold him. Once I'd got my son in my arms, I would be me again. Seeing Damien would be put into perspective.

Why the hell did it take him five years to come to find me? My heart was racing again. I could see his face swirling in front of me. A smile of sheer pleasure was pasted across my face – it was like I'd just had the best shag ever, I felt so fucking contented.

"Stop this! Stop this!" I muttered out loud. My stomach gurgled in a language of its own. I was ravenous with hunger. I hadn't eaten all day. The scent of the flowers was overpowering. I rolled down the window to let in some fresh air. A lump like lead swelled in my throat and it hurt to swallow past it.

At last I arrived at the baby-sitter's. I couldn't wait to see my baby. I felt my day was beginning, yet it was ending. I was exhausted.

"Mama," Jack said and snuggled into me when I picked him up. I gave Rose the flowers, as she deserved them. It also saved me having to explain to Gary where they had come from.

All the way home in the car, we sang "Ten Green Bottles Standing On The Wall". It was Jack's favourite. I thought he'd never make an accountant like his godmother Eleanor: he kept losing count.

As I turned the key in our front door, I could smell cooking.

"Damien." I found myself saying his name as I walked down the hall towards the kitchen. Slowly I turned the handle.

"Surprise!" Gary said.

I realised my face had turned a guilty red.

"I decided to take the evening off and cook dinner for my two favourite people!"

"That was nice of you." A great surge of unreasonable anger rose inside me. "But you could have collected Jack and spent the evening with him. You spend so little time with him as it is."

Gary raised his hands in the air in exasperation. "Michelle, I thought it would be nice to surprise you with dinner!"

"I surprise you with dinner every evening *and* look after

Jack." The words were out before I could have stopped them, cutting through the air like daggers. It was only then that I realised how like my mother I sounded.

My heart was beating a little too quickly. He was dressed as usual in T-shirt and old jeans. His dark hair was still damp from the shower. Gary was well built, with rugged hands from working on the building site all day. I noticed he had washed the breakfast dishes.

I smiled my thanks, more for the chores being done than the fact that he was home early. He was standing at the cooker, his head bent. I wanted to wrap my arms around his back and thank him, but I couldn't. I had known Gary all my life. I never had to explain myself to him – he always seemed to understand. I had to admit Gary's mother had done a good job: he was a caring loving, family man.

I stood in the kitchen and stared at nothing in particular. Jack was crawling around the floor. I noticed how dirty it was. Irritated, I picked Jack up and announced that I was taking him into the sitting-room.

Tears sprang into my eyes when I saw that Gary had lit the fire and tidied away all Jack's toys. The polished floor looked remarkably clean. Even in candlelight I could see he had wiped the coffee-ring marks off the table. I took off my shoes. This was where I belonged, with my family. I sighed and, for the first time all day, I felt I could breathe. At last I was home.

I could forget about Eleanor and Rosemary and the office politics for the weekend. Tomorrow, I would do the grocery shopping. The bathroom needed cleaning – it was a mess. Visit my mother. I couldn't possibly forget about my facial. Was Saturday going to be long enough for all I had to do?

Gary came in with a tray: two plates of chicken stir-fry, rice and chips and one small plate for Jack. He put it down on the coffee table.

Damien would never eat like this. He'd set the table with real linen napkins, heavyweight cutlery and crystal glasses that would sparkle in the candlelight.

"Do you mind if I switch on the TV?"

I noticed the black rings under his eyes. "Of course I don't mind," I said automatically. It was easier than talking to him.

All my life I had felt like an outsider looking in and tonight I felt no different.

Eleanor had her career that she loved, but she'd like this: children and a nice steady man like Gary, someone to share her success with. We had reached our second bottle of wine, or rather she had when she confessed this to me. I had just come home from the hospital after having Jack. I was breast-feeding. It was the first time in my life that I watched someone get tipsy while I stayed stone cold sober. I was bored rigid listening to her. I should have been able to sympathise, but I couldn't. I just wanted her to go home and let me continue wallowing in the bliss of motherhood. Of course it wasn't all bliss, far from it. But I loved my son so much.

I could sit all day and watch him in awestruck admiration. I knew this would bore someone like Rosemary – she didn't have any babies, she wouldn't understand what I was talking about.

You can't put an old head on young shoulders was a saying my mother used to spin out to her friend Lil when they were chinwagging about some terrible deed a neighbour's child had done. In our neighbourhood it was easy to start the chain of gossip going: it was the only thing mothers had to alleviate the boredom. My mother made me well aware that I had anything but an old head on my shoulders. But I always felt I had a sad one. There were always events going on that upset me.

Like my brother Vincent. He was always in trouble. He just couldn't help himself. I spent my childhood fretting on his behalf. When I turned twelve I realised it wasn't cool to worry. So I faked it. I pretended not to care. Vincent hated clingy girls, so I became ultra-cool and found out it was the best way to get boys interested in me.

The phone rang. Gary and I exchanged looks. We always did when the phone rang.

"I'll go," I said and jumped up off the sofa.

Jack started to whinge.

"Come here, son," Gary said and picked him up.

My heart pounded against my ribs as I ran into the hall to pick up the phone. I had a feeling it was Damien.

"Hello," I said in my best phone voice.

"I got fed up waiting for you to ring me so I rang you," my mother said, her voice razor-sharp.

"I'm going to see you tomorrow so I decided not to ring you today."

She grunted. "How's Jack?"

"He's fine."

"Is Gary there?"

"He is."

I could hear her inhaling deeply on a cigarette.

"Are you going out tonight?"

"No."

"Is Gary?"

"No, Mother, he isn't. Any more questions?"

"Vincent rang from New York today."

"How is he?"

"You know, he's too much like his father to be any good."

I bit my lip. My head started to throb. I massaged my forehead with my fingers. Vincent was my only real ally in this world.

"There is nothing wrong with Vincent," I said in protest. I never allowed anyone to say anything bad about him.

"If you say so," my mother replied, her voice resigned.

"I'll ring him tomorrow."

"Don't bother. He's never in at the weekends. Leave it until Wednesday night – he'll have all his money spent by then. Maybe you could talk some sense into him. I can't."

"Bye, Mother, I have to go, Jack is crying," I said. The lie slipped easily from my mouth due to years of practice.

Vincent was a good-looking man with vibrant blue eyes and a good sense of humour. I found myself saying my brother's name over and over again in my head. I was willing him to be safe and well and to get another bloody acting job before he drove us all mad.

Vincent was going through a bad patch: he was out of work. That feeling was all too familiar to me; of reaching so low that you find there is no lower. That's when Gary came along and picked up what was left of my shattered self and put me back together again.

Love was in short supply in our house in my childhood. I grew up hating *Little House on the Prairie* and *The Waltons*, but I watched them with fascination. I knew they were only acting; in real life people didn't kiss and hug and exclaim their love for each other.

In the sitting-room, Gary and Jack were playing together. This was a picture I saw in front of me all the time. My husband and my son playing together; and yet a part of me kept thinking this would not last. This would all end.

"It's time for bed," I said.

"Ah," said Gary, "I don't want to go to bed."

Jack laughed at his father.

Gary tickled him.

"Don't, Gary, you're overdoing it and I'll never get him settled."

Gary looked at me, a little hurt. "Sorry," he said.

There I go again, sounding just like my mother. My father never played with us. When he left work in the evenings, he went straight to the pub.

Some nights the sounds of our parents arguing would waken us. Other nights, we'd lie awake waiting for the action to begin. We'd feel disappointed if we fell asleep and missed it. It was our way of dealing with the shouts, the blows, the crash of furniture, the screams and then the dead stillness afterwards. That unnerving quiet. Our hearts thumping as we sat huddled and wondering, in our own childish way, if he had finally killed our mother.

Sometimes we wished he would kill her, because we knew that tomorrow she was going to take her anger out on us. On and on it went, until he keeled over and died in the pub one January morning.

As my father often said, she could be a bitch to live with and, boy, did she prove him right when he died! Secretly, Vincent and I were relieved when he died. Like the song said: things could only get better. Vincent was fifteen, me a year younger.

We thought our mother would have been pleased that he'd finally been taken from us, but to our surprise she wasn't. This we found confusing. We couldn't believe she could cry so much. From early morning until she finally retreated back to bed around midnight she cried for the loss of her "dear one", as she started to call him. Up till then he'd been a bastard and the world's worst provider; death had given him a new identity. She just ignored us. Of course she told the neighbours we were a great comfort to her. She played the part of the grieving widow and the doting mother to perfection. In fact, she played it so well that she probably believed it herself.

Sometimes I felt my past was the same as my present. I couldn't rid myself of all the old feelings. Even though I was in control and Gary was nothing like my father or my mother for that matter. I still felt it was temporary, it wouldn't last.

"Mammy's worried about Vincent," I said to Gary.

I felt Gary's eyes on my face. I knew what he was thinking: that we should send Vincent more money.

"I wish he'd get his bloody act together," I said. Tears were welling in my eyes.

"He will in his own time," Gary said.

How the hell would you know? I wanted to say. But the last thing I wanted was a row, even though one had been brewing in my head all evening.

The magic of make-believe. I wanted to slip back into that childhood world where Vincent and I had spent so much of our time. We could create the most fantastic landscape, full of our hearts' desires, exclusive to us. Sometimes I felt sorry for my parents and begged Vincent to let them enter. He seldom agreed to include them and when he did he only gave them bit parts.

"I love you," Gary was saying in a goofy voice like Barney used on TV.

Jack's face lit up, his chubby legs danced with joy. Father and son were communicating. Something like jealousy rose inside me. I couldn't put my finger on it.

Gary bathed Jack and I helped dress him for bed.

I loved Friday evenings. It was wind-down time. I loved Gary and Jack as much as I loved Vincent and yet all evening I had waited for Damien to phone me. Damien: the man who had chewed me up and then spat me out when he was done with me. Damien the bastard. The man who dumped me for another woman.

I knew the day I met Damien that we were worlds apart. He was not for me. We were opposites. But opposites attract. He had gone to college and was a computer programmer. I was the office temp. Eleanor and I had just arrived in London; we were sleeping in Vincent's spare bedroom. Vincent had landed himself a big part in an Irish play.

I was standing by the photocopier when a tall man stopped beside me.

"Hi, I'm Damien," he said. I knew he was Irish. He had a refined accent that was enviable. His handsome face reminded me of some actor I'd seen on TV.

"Hi," I replied. I felt myself blush.

"So you're our new temp?"

"Yes," I replied. I wished I had my brother's gift of the gab.

"If you follow me, I'll show you what I want done next," Damien said.

I picked up the pile of papers that I'd photocopied – thankfully I didn't drop them. The last thing I wanted was for him to see how nervous I was.

We walked down the corridor, joking about how hard it was to get a reliable temp. They're all foreigners, he said, laughing at his own joke.

Instantly, I felt we had made a connection and were on our merry way to bonding.

Damien left me with a pile of insignificant work to do. Bloody photocopying. Which I hated doing. I wanted to show off my newly acquired word-processing skills. But while I spent the next few days photocopying, it gave me plenty of time to watch Damien.

I couldn't help myself. I tried, I really did. I wanted to play it cool, to be aloof, to have him running after me. But every chance I got I'd be looking in his direction. Taking in every detail. The way he flicked the hair off his brow. The way his handsome face would frown when he was studying something. The graceful way he reclined in his chair when he was on the phone. And his eyes. He often made eye contact with me and I'd find myself holding my breath. His blue eyes were like magnets drawing me towards him.

Work at the advertising agency was always exciting. At least I thought it was exciting because Damien was there. I'm sure I wouldn't have been so keen if I hadn't been so smitten with him. I was aware that the other girls in the office found him attractive too – I overheard them talking about him in the canteen. The girls in the office looked and dressed to perfection. There was no way I could compete with them. I had to content myself with day-dreaming about him.

"Oh no, not another Damien story," were always the first

words out of Eleanor's mouth when we'd meet up after work.

I would try not to talk about him, but I couldn't help myself. I wanted to get to know him; I wanted to know about his past and be part of his future. There was so much about this man that intrigued me. I realised I had fallen head over heels in love with him. This was fairytale stuff. He wasn't going to fall in love with me. He couldn't. Things didn't work out like that. I had nothing but a mattress on my brother's floor while other girls in the office had apartments, cars, friends with villas in the South of France.

"You've got to find out where he goes at the weekend," said Eleanor.

"Who's going to tell me? I'm only the *temp*. All the girls have their eye on him – they're not going to tell me."

"We'll think of something!"

"What is wrong with me? Why am I acting this way?" I hated myself for wanting this man so much.

Eleanor looked at me, a glint of mischief in her big brown eyes. "There's nothing wrong with you." She paused and added with a smirk. "You're in love."

"Don't be daft, Eleanor, how could I be in love with him? I hardly know him."

Eleanor opened up her books. She was going to night classes and she was hoping I'd shut up.

"Let's go out," I suggested.

"I've all this study to do."

"Please," I begged.

Eleanor had become a bore. She never wanted to go out – all she wanted to do was to go to night classes. She wanted another qualification to hang on her office wall. She couldn't afford her own apartment so she had to stay with us. Vincent didn't mind because he was never there, but I did. For the first time in our miserable little lives, Vincent and I felt we were somebodies and that we were going somewhere. I was twenty-one, had Eleanor as my friend for a lifetime and I wanted out.

With Eleanor tagging along I couldn't shake off my old skin and grow into a new one. And I wanted to rid myself of everything that reminded me of home, of the miserable life that I'd left behind.

"Why don't you ask Damien to Vincent's play?" she said. "You've got tickets and they're like gold-dust. Everyone wants to go to it. My boss is going to it on Friday night – he said he's really looking forward to it."

Eleanor was really trying to be helpful, and I loved it.

"But *you're* going with me," I said.

Eleanor shrugged. "I'm not pushed." The corners of her mouth dropped slightly. This was the first time in Eleanor Skelly's life that she found herself in second place and she didn't really like it. Me, I was used to it. But this was one opportunity I was not going to let slip through my fingers.

"I can't just go up to him and say, 'Would you like to come to a play with me?'! He's my boss – so to speak!"

If handling people could be turned into an art form, Eleanor would be up there ranking with the best of them. She tilted her head as she thought.

"Mmm," she said.

I left some advertising literature belonging to the play on my desk, like Eleanor suggested. We were all Irish and the play was the talk of the town. He might be interested. I was even tempted to leave the tickets on my desk, but I thought someone might steal them.

I attempted to read about the play myself. But I felt I was out of my depth. I knew that Vincent had a key role – he was the black sheep in the family. After years of travelling the world he returned to the old sod and created havoc. Vincent loved the part; he felt he could really get under his character's skin.

I was back at the photocopier when Damien stopped to talk to me. As usual he had a bundle of papers in his hands.

"Did you go to see *Back to Ballymole?*"

"My brother is in it," I said. I felt my heart drumming against my chest.

I saw the look of surprise on his face.

"Tomorrow night is their last night. They're going to New York next," I said.

"I've tried to get tickets," he said, "but they were sold out."

It was on the tip of my tongue to say, 'You can come with me,' but I was determined to play it cool.

"So what part does your brother play?"

"He's Patrick the troublemaker."

"Really? He got great reviews." He then asked casually, "Are you going tomorrow night?"

"Yes, I am." I thought about what I had blocked out for the past few weeks. Vincent was leaving London and I didn't know if I could cope on my own. "I'm going to miss Vincent when he goes to New York."

"Is this your first time away from home?"

I nodded.

"London is full of Irish – come to think of it, so is New York." He gave me a quick assessing look and then said, "You look like a girl who won't be lonely for long."

I narrowed my eyes to slits and glared at him. "I don't

know how I'm suppose to respond to that comment." I regretted the words the minute they were out. Inside my stomach gurgled like it always did when I was nervous.

"I mean, you're pretty, you won't have many nights in." His brow was furrowed as he attempted to explain himself. "Unless," he said, his hand raised in the air, "you want nights in."

After days of observing him, I knew he wasn't acting like his usual self. I was tempted to laugh, but didn't. I felt my heart swell: he'd called me pretty.

"We should go for a drink this evening, us both being Irish – we could get to know each other," he suggested.

Every pore in my body dilated and oozed perspiration. I could feel it and worse I could smell it. A quick glance through the office told me I wasn't being paranoid: all the girls were watching us.

"You look hot. Are you okay?"

"I'm fine," I said a little breathlessly.

"Would you like go get some air?"

I ventured to look up at his blue eyes and found myself sinking.

He led the way to the fire escape. Outside, the sun was beaming down.

"Lovely," he said.

I was amazed to see he wasn't looking at the view of London but at me.

"Where are you staying?" he asked.

"With Vincent in Ealing."

"What are you going to do when he leaves London?"

"We're going to keep the apartment," I said, knowing how evasive I sounded.

Damien nodded. He shuffled from foot to foot. "Feeling any better? Would you like me to get you a drink of water?"

"I'm fine," I said.

"I bet you had no breakfast – up, shower and out the door."

"Three of us live in a space the size of a shoebox – we have to walk sideways not to bump into each other!"

Damien laughed and then said, "Can I ask who is the third person you're sharing with or will I be told it's none of my business?"

"My friend Eleanor," I said primly.

"I used to share with friends from college until I could afford to get my own place."

We both looked down at the passing traffic. I broke the silence by asking, "Do you like London?"

Damien nodded his head. "I sure do, but sometimes I miss my father."

"And your mother?"

"She's dead," he said and looked directly at me.

"I'm sorry."

"She died a long time ago. When I was twelve. I'm used to being without her."

"Would you like to come to the play with me tomorrow night?" Again my heart started to beat loudly, but I didn't care. He'd just blessed me with another of those charming smiles of his.

"That would be great," he said. "We'll meet later in the pub and arrange it." He glanced at his watch. "Shit! Sorry, excuse the bad language – I'm late for a meeting."

Below me I saw the traffic stopping at the traffic-lights. I could just imagine the heat inside the cars. For once I was glad to be me. I was happy to be standing on the fire escape, getting to know this man. I felt excited by the evening that lay ahead.

My thoughts drifted to my mother; it was not easy to think about her without feeling guilty. She was at home in our dreary house with nothing to look forward to and, thanks to my father, no pleasant memories to recall. I was living. It was nice to feel the sun on my face and the gentle breeze cooling me down.

In the pub, I had expected to have Damien all to myself. I didn't realise that almost everyone from the office would be there. Damien was talking to the Managing Director. There was no way I was going over to him. He was so cool, he didn't look in my direction, not even once.

Thanks to Eleanor, I'd got my date with Damien. I knew she'd be waiting for me back at Vincent's apartment.

As I was leaving, I heard Damien call my name.

"Going so soon?"

"Yes."

"Where to?"

"Back to Vincent's apartment."

Damien opened the pub door and I stepped out onto the pavement.

"Sorry about this evening," he said. "I had to talk to Big Joe."

Minutes passed while people pushed past on their way home from work. I stood waiting for him to continue. Eventually he said, "Big Joe is taking myself and the marketing team out to dinner this evening."

I shrugged it off. I was trying my best to play it cool and I knew I wasn't succeeding. I felt like my whole world had just caved in. I had imagined us having a wonderful evening together. Now, all I could see was endless cups of tea with Eleanor and then out to our local in Ealing around ten. She didn't like going to the pub after work – she thought it was such a waste of time and money.

"We could go for something to eat before the play – my treat." He stopped walking and so did I. "If you haven't other plans?"

"Sounds lovely," I said, not able to keep the excitement out of my voice.

We stood close to each other. Two glasses of white wine had me floating. Damien moved closer, bent his head a little and kissed me gently on the lips. The kiss, in daylight with people passing by, sent shivers of excitement through me. I'd been kissed before, but never like that.

"I've been longing to do that all day," he said.

I smiled a big thank you and we walked on holding hands.

"So where are you from?" he asked.

"The arse-hole of Ireland."

Damien laughed. He walked me to the tube station and waited with me until my train arrived. I thought it was the most romantic thing.

I hated rush hour, especially in the morning. I always vowed to get up early so I could avoid the rush, but I never did. Seeing all those people crammed together like ants made me feel so small, so insignificant. This was one time when I didn't notice all the pushing and shoving and people trying not to stare at each other.

"Where were you?" Eleanor asked, her face like thunder, when I breezed in later.

"We went to the pub after work."

"Did Damien go?"

I nodded.

"It worked for you." Eleanor crinkled up her face like she used to do as a child. I knew I couldn't leave her in the flat on her own, while I went out with Damien. There was no way out: I was going to have to get another ticket for Eleanor. I wasn't looking forward to begging another ticket off Vincent. He had gone up in the world and felt that we really should pay to see him perform.

"It did. Let's go out, my treat." Damien's words echoed in my ears.

"If you insist," Eleanor said.

* * *

Jack had fallen asleep on his father's chest. I finished my glass of wine and found myself wondering what Damien was doing now. Was he married? Surely he had a girlfriend? I couldn't imagine Damien without a girlfriend.

I refilled my glass of wine. Tomorrow was Saturday – no work. Mentally I ran down the list of things I had to do. Then I shrugged them away, not caring if I did them or not.

Chapter 4

In my mother's house the ceiling was full of cracks. Lying in my bed staring at the ceiling had been one of my hobbies while Eleanor went swimming or perfected her Irish dancing. There had been no point in asking my mother if I could go. I knew the reply. It was like a mantra that she chanted out every day: "We can't afford it."

Gary and Jack were downstairs having breakfast together. Normally, I joined them. I lay in bed, motionless, staring at the ceiling.

I willed myself to get up and talk to Gary before he went off to work. He's a building contractor, running his own business. I lay with my eyes fixed on one spot, unable to move.

We had plans, Gary and I. Maybe they were more dreams than plans. We wanted to build our own house. Our heads were pollinated with ideas. We had spent hours discussing what we'd like and more practically what we could afford. Then, we'd like a little brother or sister for Jack. Maybe I could give up work and help Gary with the business.

Cobwebs were hanging from the lightshade. They swayed indifferently as the breeze from the open window ran through the room. Suddenly the room was bright with sunlight. It dawned on me that I had no work today and a tiny ripple of excitement ran through me. I got out of bed and pulled on my dressing-gown.

"Good morning, sleepyhead," Gary said and grinned at me.

As I'm not a morning person, he switched on the kettle. "Coffee?"

I nodded my reply. He tossed my hair like he does with Jack. I put my arms around him and hugged him close.

"I love you," I muttered into his chest.

He patted my back. "Does that mean you'll help me do my accounts?"

I nodded.

He kissed the top of my head. "I've got to go."

"Ah, so soon?"

"I'm afraid so." He picked up his old denim jacket.

"Bye, Gary!" I was filled with indecision. Part of me wanted him to go to work and part of me wanted him to stay.

I watched him kiss Jack. "Bye, son," he said. Jack looked up at him and started to whimper. I picked Jack up and tried to distract him.

"Daddy, Daddy!" he wailed.

Gary made a quick exit. Tears streamed down Jack's flushed face. To distract him, I took him out to our back garden.

White clouds drifted across a light blue sky. We strolled down the garden. Nothing grew in our garden. I had attempted to set some flowers in the dark earth, but they never bloomed. Jack kicked his little legs – he wanted to get down.

I sipped my coffee and watched him as he played. For a brief moment, I thought about Damien and quickly blocked out the thought. I endeavoured to make a list like Rosemary does. Every time a Damien thought drifted into my head I blocked it before it got a chance to anchor itself.

* * *

Why was it that Saturdays went so quickly? Even a Saturday when it's pissing rain and Jack is being really difficult still goes quicker than a weekday. The day was almost over and I felt like it was only starting. I had ticked everything off my list as I did it.

I had ironed, washed the kitchen floor, cleaned the bathroom. Now I could tilt my hairless chin up – I had even fitted in my facial while Jack slept in his stroller beside me. The only thing that then remained was to go and see my mother.

As I sat in my mother's kitchen, I felt guilty for not wanting to be there. She was busy making tea for me. A ghost of my former self draped over me, making me sullen and depressed.

I was my mother's miracle child. The doctor had told her I'd never live, but my mother was determined to prove him wrong. She probably did it out of spite. My father's name was Michael so they called me Michelle after him. I was twice blessed: once to be alive and secondly to be called after my father.

If I had died, Vincent would have been an only child. Vincent was a handsome child with lively blue eyes, and a roguish grin that he never lost. All my life I lived under his shadow. Sometimes my mother forgot that I existed. Now, I reason that she never wanted to get too close to me in case I would die.

The truth was my mother never liked me because I looked like my father. Though, unlike my father, I had shoulder-length curly hair. His was missing. Friends and neighbours never stopped telling her that I was the spitting image of Himself. This always made my stomach churn. I'd listen to my mother's false laugher, as she'd agree with them. Later, I knew, some cutting remark would be passed that would bring me down to size.

"How are you?"

"Fine," I said, taking the mug of black tea from my mother. "Why do you ask?"

"You look," my mother paused, a worried expression crossing her lined face, "sad."

"I'm just tired," I said. I sipped some tea. It was too hot and I burned my mouth.

"Sorry, I should have put a drop of cold water in it."

We both turned to look at Jack. A wedge of sunlight beamed in the kitchen window, the buttery light highlighting the shabby cupboards and faded paint.

"He looks so like Vincent," she said.

"Do you think so?" I said. Glad of the easy conversation.

Jack looked nothing like Vincent: he was dark with hazel eyes like his father.

"I could do with getting this kitchen done up. It's only when the sun comes in that I notice how dirty it is."

I nodded and smiled at Jack who was pushing his Thomas The Tank Engine across the kitchen floor.

"Maybe in the summer we'll paint it," I suggested.

My mother grunted. "Why bother? Sure it will be the same next year."

"I suppose," I said and sipped some more tea.

It took a lot of restraint on my part not to suggest to my mother that she should get her hair done. It looked dreadful. I willed myself not to look at the kitchen clock.

"Are you sure you're all right?"

"I'm fine," I replied and bit my lip to hold back from saying, "Of course I'm all right."

"Did you ring Vincent?"

"No, I'll ring him tomorrow."

"I can tell you're worried about him."

I was preoccupied with other thoughts. It struck me then that I never should have returned home. I couldn't wait to get away. So why at the first sign of trouble did I run home? The thought was so surprising it took me a moment to ponder on it. I spilled my mug of tea down the sink. Spending too much time around my mother always had a strange effect on me. I was the one who cleaned up after the dinner, who went to the shop for messages. When I tried to protest about how little Vincent did, I was told to stop being cheeky. I could never win. My opinion didn't matter. I didn't matter. All the suppressed memories came bobbing to the surface.

"I'd better go," I said, and found my chest was tightening as I attempted to hold in my temper.

"So soon," she said.

When I lived in this house, I lived in my head. I spent my time staring at the ceiling in my bedroom. My thoughts were my own. When I tried to share them with my mother she never wanted to know. Now, the tables had turned. I was aware of her loneliness, but I couldn't help her; nor did I want to.

"If you like I'll baby-sit for you this evening, if you want to go out."

I cringed at her efforts to be included.

"No thanks," I said as I picked Jack up off the floor.

"Train! Train!" he said, pointing.

My mother picked up the train and handed it to him. "Good boy, Jack," she said and patted his head affectionately.

* * *

"Morning, Rosemary."

She raised an arched eyebrow and smiled at me. It was too bright a smile; she was not a morning person. I felt I was heading for a day of antagonistic exchanges, polar looks and prolonged silences. And I had only just sat down at my desk.

Rosemary was wearing a new orange top. "That top looks great on you," I said.

"This?" she said with mock irritation. "I've had this ages."

"It's lovely, it really suits you." I hoped I sounded convincing.

She was shuffling through papers in her in-tray.

"How was your weekend?" Truth was I didn't care how her weekend was, but I pasted a smile to my face and faked interest.

"Fine," she said.

"Do anything exciting?" I probed.

"Mm." She considered my question. "No." She studied her longest fingernail.

My phone rang.

"That's for you," she said, a little too sweetly.

"Good morning, Michelle speaking, how can I help?" I asked with indifference.

"Good morning, Michelle," the voice said in hushed tones. "It's Damien."

My heart missed a beat. All weekend I had waited. The agonising and wondering had ended. I felt my insides tingle with excitement.

"Did you have a nice weekend?" he asked.

"Fine, thanks." I stopped myself from smiling. "So how can I help you?"

Silence. I heard his gentle breathing. I wondered where he was? He could be parked outside.

"I presume you can't talk," he said.

"Yes, that's right."

"Could we meet for lunch?"

"Fine," I said, hoping I sounded casual.

"Where would you like us to go?"

I gave a quick sideways glance and saw that Rosemary's head was bent; she was filling out a customer request form.

"Can you repeat the address?" I said.

I hoped Rosemary couldn't hear him laughing. My eyes widened with delight as I watched her leave the office and head for reception.

"The Goldsmith's Arms. The food isn't great, but it's quiet," I said, hurriedly.

"Two o'clock."

"No, make it one, I always take my lunch at one," I said in a half-whisper Rosemary was on her way back. She glided into the office. I wanted to open a window and let some

41

fresh air in to rid the place of her strong-smelling perfume, but I wouldn't dare.

"Your own top – is it new?" she asked.

This morning, I had made an extra effort, hoping that Damien would phone.

"It is," I said. Then I went on to explain that I had bought it in a boutique in town where there was a twenty-per-cent discount. I thought we were back on track. There was a time I didn't mind coming to work. We used to spend our days having a laugh and trying to help customers when they became aggressive and threatened to speak to our supervisor. Now, Rosemary spent her days laughing with the customers and reporting me to Eleanor.

"It's nice," she said.

I felt uncomfortable. Rosemary could sniff out a rumour before it even became one. Gossip was the only highlight in our monotonous day.

The last thing I needed was for Gary to find out I was meeting Damien for lunch. Gary knew about Damien. Hadn't Gary held me in his arms while I sobbed my heart out and told him about the terrible thing Damien had done to me?

"How is Vincent getting on?" Rosemary asked out of the blue.

"Why do you ask?" I realised how paranoid I sounded and backtracked. "I mean he's getting on fine – you know Vincent." I attempted to laugh, but it sounded more like a wail coming from the pit of my stomach. "He hasn't got any work yet. I tried to ring him at the weekend, but all I got was his answering machine."

She ran her fingers through her shiny hair. This week

her hair was more golden than peroxide. I felt this was a good omen. She fixed it with expert fingers.

"Why don't you ring him from here?"

"You know we're not supposed to," I said in an alarmed voice.

My eyes grew tired watching her as she applied some lipstick onto her thick lips with a tiny brush.

"Don't tell me you've bought another lipstick!" I pretended to be shocked.

"I have as a matter of fact." She pouted her lips. "Cherry Red, it's called. What do you think?"

"I preferred the pink one you had on last week." I hoped I sounded convincing. I was ever hopeful that we would get back to the way we were. I hated this strained relationship.

"Frosted Pink? You liked that one? It's horrible. I thought it did nothing for me." She opened her bag and took it out. "Here, you can have it."

"Rosemary, you paid twenty euros for that! You can't give it to me! And I can't afford to buy it from you."

She waved her elegant hand in the air. "I don't want it and I can afford to give it away."

I didn't detect any sarcasm in her voice. I took the lipstick. I was confused. I wasn't sure why she was being so nice to me.

I applied the frosted pink lipstick and turned for her to inspect it.

"Put on another coat," she said.

"All ready for the big meeting." I applied another coat.

Rosemary smiled and then her phone rang. She sang off her greeting to the caller.

Carefully, I applied a third coat of lipstick. I couldn't see my whole face in the mirror, but I hoped it made me look attractive. My stomach rumbled nervously. It was probably hungry, but I couldn't eat.

"Thank you for calling, Mrs White, I'll get onto it straight away and get back to you." Rosemary hung up, turned to me and made a face. "Stupid woman. I definitely like that lipstick on you."

"Thanks," I muttered, feeling unsure. This was the second compliment Rosemary had paid me on the same day. I was beginning to feel she had inside information on me.

She opened her purse and started to pick through her change. "Have you got the loan of ten cents?"

I opened my bag and took out my purse. I knew there was no point looking in there. All my change was at the bottom of my bag. I pulled out some baby wipes and some change.

"Thanks, I'll pay you back later," she said. "Do you want something from the snack-machine?"

I told her I wasn't hungry. This seemed to annoy her and she walked off in a huff.

"How is Jack?" she asked, when she returned with a bag of crisps and a can of diet coke.

"Fine."

"Time you started working on a brother or sister for him."

I found myself blushing. I wanted to tell her to mind her own business and stop being such a bitch, but I hadn't the nerve.

She snapped her can of coke open and guzzled some down.

I took some papers out of my in-tray. Queries for Accounts that I should have passed on to them a week ago, but never bothered to. Now, I would take a trip down to Accounts and spend some time talking to Tina about the joys of motherhood. She had two children and loved to talk about them when she got the chance.

Rosemary smirked and turned to face her computer. She munched at the crisps, stopped once to take a slug of coke and then continued to munch until the entire packet was empty. There was definitely something wrong with her. She never offered me one.

I wanted to ask her what was wrong, but I didn't. I felt if she wanted to talk to me, she would. Of course I knew it was me that was at fault. Rosemary was a perfectionist. Everything in her life was planned. Her beautiful house, her professional husband, her holding off having children until the time was right.

My cream top was the only decent piece of clothing I had in my wardrobe. Rosemary would never consider a top with a twenty-per-cent discount to be her best one.

After a while she surprised me by asking, "Which lunch do you want to take?"

"I always take the one o'clock!"

"Of course, you do," she smiled, the cherry lipstick making her mouth look bigger than usual.

"Is that all right with you?"

"Have you got a lunch appointment?"

Rosemary had excellent hearing.

"Sort of. I have to meet someone for Gary."

She raised an eyebrow. "I presume it's a man you're going to meet."

I didn't reply.

"Well, the best of luck, not that you'll need it," she said and swivelled her chair back into her desk.

Gladly, I answered my phone when it rang.

"Hi, sis."

I felt tears sting my eyes. I was angry with myself for taking so much crap from Rosemary.

"Hi," I said, as I tried to regain control.

"I was away for the weekend. I went to see some friends in Boston."

"Vincent, how are you?" I said, in a quick rush while Rosemary was busy talking to a customer.

"I'm better, still pissed off that I can't get any work, but the few days away were great. I'm doing an audition tomorrow for a part in a play. So, fingers crossed."

"I'm so pleased for you. I'll call you tomorrow evening."

"Don't do that, sis. It's only my first audition. If I get through that, there will probably be another and another – it's early days for getting your hopes up."

"I see," I said, feeling deflated.

I was hoping to talk to Damien about my brother. That was how we started going out together, us going to see Vincent in a play.

"How are Gary and Jack?"

"They're fine and so is Mother. You should ring her – she's worried about you."

"Michelle, please don't hassle me now. I don't need it. Just tell her I'm okay."

Selfish bastard. I always had to do his dirty work. "Fine." I smiled into the phone.

"I've gotta go," he said. "See ya," he added, like he always did and then he hung up.

"I presume that was Vincent," said Rosemary.

I'd forgotten about her. She was sitting filing her nails and listening.

"Yes," I replied.

"Nice of him to call you," she said as she examined her nails. "Is he working?"

"No." My voice was almost a whisper. I hated admitting it, but my brother might never work again.

"Michelle," Rosemary said, alarmed.

"What?"

"It's almost one o'clock – time for your lunch!"

I picked up my bag, grabbed my car keys and left the room. The last thing I wanted to do was waste a single second of my lunch-hour talking to her.

"Bye, Michelle," I heard her say as I made my way down the corridor towards the front door.

Chapter 5

Damien was standing in the reception area, the daily newspaper folded in his hand. He smiled his welcome. "Michelle," he said, placing a quick kiss on my cheek.

"Hi," I said.

"Shall we go in to lunch?"

He ushered me into the formal dining-room. We sat down and a waitress handed us the menu.

"I've already ordered a bottle of wine."

We smiled at each other, like we were ridding the air around us of any tension.

"You're looking really great," he said.

"You too." I knew how inadequate my words were.

Again we smiled.

He shook his head. "I mean it, Michelle, you look –" He paused and then said, "stunning." He reached out and touched my hand. "Marriage suits you."

In my head I was trying to analyse this statement. Does

that mean I look well because I'm married to someone else and not him? Or does it mean I looked dreadful when I was single?

"Shall we order?" He read down the menu. "I'll have the garlic mushrooms for starters and the roast beef."

"Ah," I said, looking down through the selection, "I'll have the chicken."

The waitress arrived with the wine. Damien looked at the bottle, nodded his approval and then she poured. The dining-room was old-fashioned with red carpet, pink tablecloths and matching napkins.

"So how are you?" he said, when the waitress had left.

"Fine," I replied and I wondered how often I'd said that word and not meant it.

Across the dining-room were clients that Gary was currently doing some work for. I nodded and smiled in recognition and they did likewise.

"Colleagues?" he asked.

"No, just some men Gary works for."

"I don't want to cause you any trouble."

I sipped some wine.

Damien looked at me. "Did you tell him about me?"

"No, Damien, you don't come up in conversation in our household. In fact, I haven't thought of you at all since I left Sydney."

He seemed to flinch. "I was so stupid. I should never have done what I did to you, but I'm here now to make it up to you."

The waitress arrived with Damien's garlic mushrooms.

He prodded them with his fork.

"They look dead," I said.

"They sure do," he said, picking one up. "My father always had a soft spot for you."

I sipped some more wine. My head was spinning as I wondered where this was all leading to.

At this stage, I wanted to fast-forward this meeting. Damien refilled my glass.

"He's very ill – he's dying," he said.

"I'm sorry to hear that," I said, and meant it.

"Would you come with me to see him?"

Our eyes met and held for longer than was necessary. I stiffened despite myself. The sense of excitement and incipient danger filled me with a new energy. At that moment I felt that anything was possible. In the background I heard the clatter of plates and cups. People were talking, having ordinary conversation, but I was stepping out of myself. I was misbehaving. The wine had gone to my head.

"I haven't seen you in five years, Damien," I said. Feelings of both love and hate rose inside me. I sipped some wine. "You just stopped by to ask me to go with you to see your father?"

"Yes, he hasn't much time left." Sadness settled on his face.

"I can't. I'm married and I've got responsibilities here."

"I know." He placed the fork back on his plate. "He wants to see you before he dies," he said slowly in a tone that made my feelings see-saw in the sympathy direction. "He asked me to find you. He wants to talk to you."

"Why does he want to talk to me? I only met him a few times."

Damien shrugged. "He wouldn't tell me. When I found you I told him that you were married and you had a son; but he still insisted."

"I like your father. He's a nice man, but I can't go. I'd have to explain to Gary and I don't want to."

Damien leaned across the table, his hand touching mine. I pulled it away and shot a look around me to see if anyone had noticed.

"Sorry," he said, moving his hand away. "I just need your help here."

Listening to him in grovel mode was something I'd never dreamed of. Inside, I was smiling.

"Please, Michelle."

"I can't."

"It's the only thing my father has ever asked me to do for him."

Our eyes met across the table. His face was strained and solemn. The parameters of my world were shifting.

"Please, Michelle, help me. I can't bear the thought of going back to my father and telling him you don't want to see him." His voice was almost a whisper.

We sat in strained silence. People walked past. A waitress rushed by with a tray full of starters.

"Michelle, I really need your help here." He paused. "He has only weeks," he looked at me with big pleading eyes, "maybe only days to live." His voice broke.

"Damien, I can't," I muttered, my eyes fixed on his chest. I couldn't bear to make eye contact. I stood up as gracefully as I could. "I have to go."

"Michelle, please!"

I knew I shouldn't listen. Damien always laughed at me when I cried at movies that were sad. Tears were welling up inside me, ready to be spilled.

"It's important. My father knows you're married, he

knows you have a son – he wouldn't want to see you only it's really important to him." Now, he was standing beside me. I moved a little away, I didn't want people to notice me. "In fact, I should be with him now."

I could feel his urgency. Yet, I was determined not to give in. No amount of pleading was going to sway me.

My legs felt like they wouldn't support me for much longer. I inched myself towards the door. A waitress caught up with us.

"Do you want the bill?"

Damien nodded.

"I'd better go, I have to get back to work," I explained, my legs taking me towards the exit.

Outside, I blinked tears away as I crossed at the pedestrian crossing and made my way towards Tesco to buy a sandwich. Soft rain had fallen all morning from a grey sky.

Chapter 6

I tried not to think about Damien. I drove back to work on autopilot. I had driven this route a thousand times and I found myself going though the motions, stopping at the traffic-lights, indicating left, then taking a right, driving on, then taking a right into the industrial estate. My eyes searched the carpark for a free space near the building so I wouldn't have too far to run.

My heart thumped furiously against my ribs. I attempted to take a few deep breaths to calm me. I ran up the steps and in the glass doors. Glancing at the clock in reception, I saw I had just made it with seconds to spare.

On my desk I had a picture of Jack and Gary, the two of them grinning at me, while I said cheese. Last year I took the picture at the Christmas tree. I had better photographs of Jack and Gary together, but this one was special. Christmas had never been a happy time in my own family; the air in our house always smelled of stale beer and despair.

Vincent and I always retreated to our bedrooms, our sense of self-preservation dulling our curiosity.

Rosemary applied some more foundation to her already well-coated face, then put on some lipstick and sprayed herself and half the office with Organza perfume.

"See you later," she said in her sing-song telephone voice.

"Enjoy lunch," I said. I was glad to have the office to myself. I needed time to regain my equilibrium. I got a can of coke and a bar of chocolate from the snack-machine. Then, I rang Gary's mobile number.

"Gary," I said as I swallowed some chocolate, "I was just thinking it's ages since we've been out together."

"I know," he said.

"Why don't I get my mother to have Jack for a night and we could go out?"

"Sounds lovely," he said and then added, "It will have to be at the weekend as I'm up to my eyes at the moment."

"Gary, you work so hard, too damn hard!" I felt a great surge of guilt rise inside me.

"I know, love. But it won't be forever. In the meantime, you know those plans we have? We could start working on some of them."

I smiled to myself. I could picture a cheeky grin on his honest face. "Which ones?"

"The easy ones, the ones I like doing best."

"Mmm, can I get back to you?"

"Any time, see you later."

"Bye, Gary." I felt like crying. How could I be such a fool as to meet with Damien? What could he possibly offer me that I'd want?

My phone rang and I answered it, glad of the distraction.

After I finished the call I scrawled on a post-it. *Why does his father want to see me?* I had tried so hard to forget about Damien. I now realised how successful I had been. I couldn't remember his father's name. Furiously I tore up the post-it and threw it into the bin.

Eleanor strolled into the office and sat down on Rosemary's chair.

"You're looking nice today," she said. Eleanor was always demure and professional.

"Thanks," I replied.

"How was your weekend?"

"Quiet. We didn't do anything, just the usual chores that I don't get to do all week."

Her dark eyes looked larger than usual in her pale face.

"So how was your weekend?" I asked.

"Bob rang and asked me out," she said, her voice suddenly losing its briskness.

"Great," I said, hoping my voice portrayed the right degree of girlie interest.

Eleanor flicked back her shoulder-length brown hair. "He's very busy, he's a doctor."

"Has he got to examine you yet?" My mind was drifting back to Damien. Eleanor giggled. "Michelle – we're going away together next weekend!"

Eleanor is very private. As my mother would say, that one wouldn't let her right hand know what her left hand was doing.

"That's really great," I said, and I stretched my face into a bigger smile.

"I really like him, he's nice." She giggled again.

Serious Eleanor had finally been reduced to giggling because she had fallen for a man.

"Don't do anything I wouldn't do," I said because it was expected of me to say something like that.

"Michelle, I'm not like you."

"What's that supposed to mean?" I realised my mouth had dropped open and I shut it.

"You know," she said and shifted awkwardly in the chair.

"No, I don't know."

"Well, there was Damien and then there was Gary and before them there was –"

"Why did you have to bring him up?" I said, cutting across her.

"Damien?" she looked at me blankly.

"Yes."

"Well, you lived with him."

"That was years ago," I said a little too sharply. After all, she was my boss and it was in my interest to humour her.

"Steady on, Michelle. I was about to say you have more experience with men than me and I just wanted to talk to you about it, that's all."

"What the hell would I know about men?"

"Damien was mad about you and so is Gary and I'm just wondering how you keep them interested."

I shrugged. "I have no idea."

"I see," Eleanor said tonelessly.

Now we were back on track again. She was up there high and mighty playing the boss and looking down her long nose at me. Usually, I would smile at her and win back some goodwill. Today I couldn't be bothered.

"You haven't forgotten about our meeting this afternoon," she said, a new steeliness in her voice.

"Of course I haven't." Did she think my life was so

boring that all I had to do was think about her stupid meeting? If she only knew!

She waited for me to suggest her dropping around some evening so we could talk. Or rather so she could talk about Bob and I would listen.

I continued to fill out my customer form, thanking the gods that this was what I was doing and not scribbling on a post-it about Damien when she came into the office.

"See you later," she said and paused briefly at the door.

"Fine," I said without raising my head. I didn't want her to see that I was smiling.

Eleanor would probably remember Damien's father's name. She was good with names, but I couldn't ask her. Damien and his father looked alike. He was a nice man. I met him when Damien and I moved in together in London. Occasionally, he came to London on business and he always invited us out to dinner. I never wanted to go, but Damien always insisted. His father was a serious man, who enjoyed talking about politics and economics, things that I knew nothing about. He never ignored me – he was too much of a gentleman for that – but we never had any meaningful conversations.

I'm not flattered that Damien has come back into my life, I thought. I'm alarmed and worried. He's trouble.

I closed my eyes. I was tired after having another sleepless night with Jack.

I wanted to rest my head on my desk and sleep for just a few minutes to block everything out.

"I'm back," Rosemary announced as she breezed into the office. I could have smelt her coming.

"Did you have a nice lunch?"

"I met my Danny."

"That was nice." I found myself doodling on a post-it.

"Are you ready for our meeting?"

"I can't wait."

"Me neither. I love a meeting to break the monotony of the day." Rosemary sprayed on more perfume. I sneezed.

"Is my perfume getting to you?"

"Ah, no, not at all."

We forwarded our phones to reception and, armed with our diaries, went into Eleanor's office. She was waiting for us.

One hour later we emerged, both of us having had a very "positive" meeting with Eleanor, where she politely but firmly told us that we had to pull up our socks and do some work. Privately I was glad that Rosemary got as much stick as I did. It was a nice change.

Back at our desks, I saw Rosemary typing, then my screen flashed a message that I had e-mail.

Bitch, Rosemary had typed.

I looked across at Rosemary and smiled. Now we were both on the same side again.

Agreed, I typed back.

Chapter 7

Jack was sleeping beside me in our big double bed. He had kept us awake all night. He was teething. I got Gary to ring in to work for me. My eyes took in every detail of my baby's beautiful face. He looked so angelic. I needed to do some ironing; the laundry-basket was full. I knew I should go downstairs, take something out of the freezer and cook a nice meal for us that evening. Busy was what I needed to be. It was better than thinking, but I couldn't move myself. I wanted to lie here and look at Jack and marvel at the wonder of this child.

* * *

Eleanor had thought it was a really bad idea me moving in with Damien. I didn't. I wanted to spend as much time with him as possible. I was addicted to him and I couldn't get enough of him. Eleanor was worried that I'd forget about her. I wanted to forget about her. She was so boring, always studying. We met up at least twice a week and I'd quietly pine for Damien every minute that I was away from him.

We were going out together for over a year when he asked me to go to Australia with him. I was delighted. Now I'd have him all to myself – I wouldn't have to share him with anyone. First we came back to Ireland, Damien to visit his father in Dublin and me to visit my mother. He collected me from my mother's house.

I was so excited; finally I was shedding my past. My mother cried her crocodile tears while Damien put my cases in the boot. Vincent came home from New York just to say goodbye to me. For once I felt the world was revolving around me.

We spent the night in his father's house in Dublin. It was a beautiful old Georgian house, furnished with solid dark furniture. By comparison, my home looked so impoverished. We had a delicious candlelight dinner with his father and he said he was sorry to see us going, but acknowledged that we were young and we should see the world. We nodded in agreement, while we quietly itched to get away from him.

Early next morning we woke to get the seven thirty flight to Heathrow. From there we'd take the first stage of our journey to Bangkok and from there to Darwin and then Sydney. This was a real adventure, it wasn't a dream. I was actually travelling to the other side of the world with the man I loved and it was wonderful.

In Sydney, we spent our first night in a hotel. Then, I got the task of looking for an apartment while Damien started looking for a job.

For the first time in my life I could be a Michelle who didn't have to answer to my mother or Eleanor or anyone. I could be me. Whatever that meant. I didn't know, but at least I could find out without censorship. There was no one to remind me of the Michelle I had been, only Damien who was constantly telling me he loved me just the way I was.

* * *

I looked up at the ceiling and remembered crossing Sydney Harbour bridge, The Eagles blaring – *"Take it easy, take it easy, don't let the sound of your own wheels drive you crazy . . . "*

Finally I was free and I had Damien to thank for it. He took me away, sort of reinvented me and I loved the new me so much.

My eyes were still fixed on the ceiling; a single tear slid down the side of my face. We spent two wonderful years there. I couldn't work because I didn't have a work visa.

Then Damien met Alison. I knew before it happened it was going to happen. I could see it in the determined tilt of her chin. She wanted him and she was going to get him. I didn't stand a chance. She was brainy, beautiful and ambitious.

Downstairs, I heard the phone ringing. Something told me it was my mother. I usually rang her every morning from work. The phone stopped ringing. Jack was still sleeping. I touched his cheek and wondered what my other baby would have been like if it had lived.

I dismissed the thought quickly. I got out of bed and went downstairs. I was just in the kitchen when the phone rang again.

"Hello," I said.

"Michelle, did I wake you?"

I felt disappointed it was only my mother.

"No," I replied dully.

"Is little Jack sick?"

"He was last night – he's asleep now."

"Ah, poor baby!"

An irrational surge of jealousy rose inside, almost stopping me from breathing. I took a breath to calm me. My mother had never called me her poor baby.

"Eleanor isn't going to like all the time off you're taking."

"I know," I said and yawned.

"Did you ring Vincent?"

"He rang me at work. Vincent was away for the weekend – he's got an audition today."

"Did he ask for me?"

"Of course he did," I said a little too quickly and then I added, "He's busy preparing for the audition."

"Busy!" she echoed and snorted. "Why can't he get himself a real job?"

I couldn't find it in me to reply to this, so I didn't. I looked around my kitchen. It was like someone had started to raid the place, got fed up because they knew there was nothing valuable and left in a hurry.

"Bye, Mother." I hung up before she got the chance to start another conversation. It was twelve o'clock. I could picture Rosemary at work, playing the martyr and letting everyone know just how valuable she was to the company. I didn't know where to begin, but I felt I had to start somewhere. All I wanted to do was scream and curse, but I knew all that would do was waste my energy and I'd still have to attack the kitchen.

Calmly, I put the breakfast dishes into the sink, then I started to wash them, feeling that if I didn't build up my speed Jack would be awake and I'd have nothing done.

The phone rang. I dried my hands and answered it.

"Gary, I was just thinking about you," I said, surprised at my ability to lie to him on the spur of the moment.

"How's Jack?"

I found myself smiling: our son, our bond. A feeling of warmth crept over me and I thought, I love this man.

"He's asleep. I'm trying to clean up before he wakes."

"Eleanor wasn't too impressed when I rang and told her you wouldn't be in today."

"Oh dear, I'm not looking forward to going in to work tomorrow. Hopefully this new man in her life will take her mind off me."

A gurgle of laughter rose in Gary's throat. "It would take more than that for her to forget anything. It would take a good poke in the –" He coughed and didn't finish the sentence.

"Well, let's hope Bob gives her one," I said. I stretched out my hand and looked at my simple wedding band. "You'll be home around six?"

"I'm afraid not. I'm meeting the architect – we've run into some difficulties."

"Gary!" I said, my voice pleading.

"I know, Michelle. I'll be home as soon as I can."

Suddenly I was filled with panic. "Where are you going to meet him?"

"On the site. Maybe we'll go for a few drinks after."

I said nothing, but hoped my silence conveyed my feelings. Then he added, "Michelle, my love, there's no reason for you to be suspicious of me. I love you and Jack more than anything else. Everything I do is for us."

"I know," I said and felt my face burn with shame. "I was going to do a chicken casserole."

"Is that all that's on offer?"

"There could be more. You'll just have to come home and see."

"I'll be home as soon as I can. Bye, Michelle."

"Bye," I said and hung up.

The cluttered kitchen was eerily quiet. Gary's radio was hidden under some newspapers and magazines. I plugged it in. Another five minutes was wasted while I tried to tune in to our local station. The music was lively and uplifting. I had to turn down the volume in case I woke Jack.

Guilt made me attack the cooker and fridge. I was just about to wash the kitchen floor when I heard the doorbell.

I looked down at myself, horror-stricken. I was wearing an old T-shirt and leggings. The doorbell went again and then Jack started to cry. Frantically I ran my fingers through my tossed hair.

I took the stairs two steps at a time. Peering out the bedroom window, I saw Rosemary's car. Relief swept through me. I had been sure it was Damien.

"The place is a mess," were the first words out of my mouth when I opened the door to Rosemary.

"I don't mind," she said.

She followed me into the kitchen.

"Lunch," she said, waving a carrier bag in front of my face. "I'll make the coffee while you do whatever." Instantly I knew there was something wrong. She wasn't wearing any make-up. The seductive line of her mouth was lipstick-free.

"I'm a mess," I said.

She smiled at Jack and put out her hands to take him. He started to cry.

"He's just after waking," I said hurriedly. "He's a little grumpy."

Rosemary smirked. "I'll make the coffee."

Holding Jack, with one hand I tried to mop the floor while she filled the kettle and switched it on. To my surprise, she then put on my rubber gloves and in a flash she had the floor mopped up. I sat at the table with Jack on my knee drinking his bottle and we watched her as she tidied my kitchen.

"You're amazing," I said.

"I'm glad someone appreciates me. Danny says I get on his nerves."

She opened the shopping bag and took out two salad rolls. Jack reached across to grab one.

"Stop, Jack," I said.

"I know what we'll do! We'll give you some," Rosemary said. She cut a quarter off each and put them on a plate for Jack. "Now," she said to him.

He grinned at her. He pulled at the salad roll. Most of the coleslaw and tomato fell on the floor. Then, he started to whinge.

I got a bag of crisps from the cupboard and opened them for him. He crunched them with his hand. "Stop," I said. He looked at me, and smiled. "Jack, you be a good boy and eat your crisps," I said in the sweetest of tones. I glanced at the clock. "Sorry about this."

Rosemary was tucking into her salad roll.

I bit into mine. "These are really great," I said with my mouth full.

Rosemary nodded. "It's hard to talk and eat at the same time."

Jack continued to eat his crisps and crunch them up. Some bits fell on the floor. I ignored him.

"He's adorable," she said.

"You wouldn't say that at four o'clock this morning – he was screaming his head off."

"We've been trying for ages to have a baby," she said. She stopped eating and looked at Jack. Her eyes filled with tears. "Danny said if it doesn't happen naturally then we're not meant to have children but –" She bit her lip, her face settling into composed lines. "I don't agree, I think we should get a test done, find out which of us has the problem, but he . . ." The words faded. She sipped some coffee, took a breath and started again. "Where was I?" She looked down at Jack. "Danny doesn't want to – he's such a coward. I love him, but I hate him for treating me so unfairly. Don't you think it's unfair?"

"Give him time. Sometimes it takes men longer to get used to an idea."

"He won't talk about it – he's just such a pain in the arse." She put her hand over her mouth. "Sorry, Jack, sorry, Michelle, for using such bad language."

"Jack is used to hearing bad language from me."

Her eyes filled up again. "I'm sorry, Michelle, for coming here today like this. Usually I meet Danny for lunch, but we had such a row this morning I just couldn't bear to meet him. I just had to talk to someone – I –" She paused, took a breath and started again, "I knew you'd understand. I tried ringing earlier, but there was no answer. I just decided to come and see you." Now tears were running freely down her face. Silence fell on us, except for Jack's crunching and then she said, "I hope you don't mind me coming here like this. I know you have your own problems with Jack not sleeping at night, and Gary with his own business and everything else."

"I'm glad you came today – it's ages since we've talked."

"I've been such a bitch to you. I was just so jealous of you." She looked at me with big pleading eyes.

"Jealous of me?" I laughed at the idea. "Rosemary, it will happen for you, I just know it will."

Rosemary nodded. "I wish it was that simple. Please don't tell Eleanor – I know you and her are good friends."

"We're not that close. We're sort of friends, but she's still my boss."

"And mine – I just couldn't bear for her to know."

"I'm sorry about all the sick days I've had lately."

"I've been horrible to you lately. I can be such a bitch," Her eyes were fixed on her coffee mug. "I'm truly sorry, Michelle."

"Let's forget about it."

The salad rolls were left unfinished on the table. I knew Rosemary would attack the snack-machine when she got back to work.

"Why don't you bring your roll back with you?"

"I'm not hungry."

"Thanks for lunch and I hope things work out for you," I said at the front door. "I'll see you tomorrow."

My kitchen smelled of Flash and Organza and to me it looked wonderful and I had Rosemary to thank for it. I treasured what I had. The old cupboards were crying out to be torn down and replaced. The worktop was covered with things that should be in the cupboards. Invoices and letters concerning Gary's business made an unsightly pile on top of the microwave. I was not looking forward to helping him sort them out. Our own household bills were pushed into a drawer along with tea towels and every other piece of junk.

Every morning I got up and came down to this kitchen. I made coffee for myself and never got a chance to drink it. It was always a mad rush on weekdays to beat the clock and get Jack to the baby-sitter's and myself to work on time. It was just habit that made me boil the kettle. Gary was usually gone to work. The weekends were less hectic, even though Jack was up with the birds. At least I knew I didn't have to rush. I'd forgotten how pleasurable this domestic routine was.

We might live in this house for the rest of our lives. Gary and I might always be struggling, our dream house might always be that. But this, this was real and wonderful. Gary was right. We should start planning our second child. What were we waiting for? Inside I was growing excited.

I picked Jack up and hugged him as he wriggled to get down on the floor.

"Off you go then," I said.

As I cleared the table I thought of my mother. She was probably sitting at her kitchen table having a solitary cup of tea. It was always an effort for me to ring her. I only rang her from work because it broke the monotony of my working day. Today, I felt more gracious towards her and decided to ring. I invited her to join us for dinner that evening.

Jack threw his train across the kitchen floor as I put down the phone.

"To hell with tidying up," I said to him.

He picked a piece of tomato up off the floor and put it in his mouth.

"Dirty," I said.

He cried in protest when I took it from him. I exchanged it for a biscuit and peace was restored.

The sun had burst through the moody clouds and I felt like taking Jack for a walk on this bright May day. If I got pregnant soon, I could be having a baby next spring. This feeling excited me. Then, I thought of poor Rosemary and felt bad for her.

At six thirty my mother arrived. The chicken casserole had scented the kitchen with its appetising smell. She smiled her approval; it was her favourite.

I answered the question before she asked it. "Gary isn't coming home."

"He works too hard," she commented.

"I know," I said.

We sat down to eat. I felt our evening was going well. I poured us two large glasses of wine and felt this could only help.

"I'll be drunk if I drink all that," she said.

"Just sip it," I suggested.

Jack insisted on feeding himself and had more dinner on his T-shirt and the floor than actually landed in his mouth.

"You're a good boy," she said to him.

"Do you like the casserole?"

My mother nodded. "It's nice." Then she paused and said, "It's wonderful – isn't that the expression Vincent uses?"

I nodded, feeling disappointed.

"Are you going to work tomorrow?" she asked.

"I'd better or Eleanor will kill me."

"She'll get over it."

We finished our casserole in silence. When I had taken Jack for a walk I had gone into the supermarket and bought a tub of her favourite ice cream. In the supermarket I kept looking around to see if Damien was there. He wasn't and I felt stupid.

"I'm not sure I have room for this," she said when I placed the bowl of ice cream in front of her.

I sat down and started on mine. "We'll leave the washing up – I'll do it later."

"No, you've more than enough to do. I'll do it when I'm finished this."

Chapter 8

"Welcome back," Rosemary said when I walked into the office next morning.

I smiled warmly at her. To my surprise I was glad to be in the office. Gary hadn't come home until three o'clock and he was drunk. It brought back disturbing memories of my father. I was furious; I'd been at home doing his damn accounts while he was out getting pissed. We hadn't spoken that morning. He tried to say he was sorry. I hate that word; it means nothing to me.

"Good morning, Agent Clarke," I said in my best phone voice.

Rosemary laughed and said, "You're like a tonic."

Inside, I was battling not to cry.

I wanted to type an e-mail to Rosemary about Gary, telling her the late hour he'd staggered in at and how I couldn't sleep worrying about him. How I'd tried his mobile a few times and it had been switched off. This was so unlike him – last night was a first. I felt I needed to talk about it, to let off steam.

A letter with *Private and Confidential* written across it was on my desk.

I knew it was from Damien. Part of me was curious and wanted to open it, while fear made me want to throw it in the bin. Rosemary didn't seem to notice my confusion.

Her phone rang.

"Good morning, Rosemary speaking, how can I help you?" She giggled into the phone and then said, "Hello, darling."

I knew she was talking to her husband.

I ran my finger across the white envelope and took out the letter. It was from Damien. My stomach was in knots. I pushed it into my trousers pocket. I'd read it later in the toilet. I looked around my desk seeking reassurance: my eyes fell on my favourite picture. I smiled at Jack and ignored Gary.

Two minutes later, I was in the toilet reading Damien's letter.

Dear Michelle,

I wish I could explain myself better to you. I mean you no harm. I've not come back into your life to cause trouble. I've seen you with your husband and child and you make a lovely family. I'm envious. If there was any way I could change the past I would.

After you left Sydney, Alison moved in with me. Sometime later she moved out, to move in with another bloke. I was just a stepping-stone for her. It's then I started to realise how much I'd put you through. I should have tried to find you, but I was afraid of you turning me away.

A year ago my father got cancer and I left Australia and came back to London to be closer to him. He's living in Westport now – his family was from there and it's where he wants to die. At the moment he's in good spirits. Unfortunately it's only a matter of time until his life is over.

He wants to see you, Michelle, because he wants to give you some jewellery belonging to my mother. I've no idea how valuable it is, but he always liked you and he'd like to give you these things. Please do it for him. I know it's a lot to ask, but it would make a dying man happy.

Regards, Damien.

I re-read it. Damien had left his mobile number after his name. I wanted to ring him. I folded the letter up and put it back in my pocket. I had to think. I just couldn't rush into this. My face was flushed and I splashed some water on it to cool me down.

"Are you all right?" Rosemary asked when I returned to the office.

My phone rang. "I'm fine," I said, as I picked up my phone. "Good morning, Michelle speaking; how can I help?"

At home I could picture my kitchen, the sink full of last night's dishes, the casserole dish soaking on the draining-board. I should have let my mother do the dishes when she suggested it. Instead, she played with Jack while I attempted to put some order on Gary's accounts – and for what? Now the only words that came to mind when I thought of Gary was bastard and selfish. How dare he stay out all night! Did he think I was going to forgive him? My head was heavy with ammunition. I was ready to gun Gary down.

Names started to come into my head: James, Eddie, Hugh. I was trying to remember Damien's father's name. I couldn't. I wanted to phone Damien and ask him. His father hadn't the same twinkle in his eye that Damien had; maybe he'd lost it after the death of Damien's mother. I couldn't imagine loving someone so much that when they died a piece of me went with them.

I shared my bed with Gary. We made love as often as little Jack let us and I couldn't say if I really loved him or if I married him because I was battered and bruised after leaving Damien and he was a safe harbour.

The hands on the clock hadn't moved in ages; it was only a quarter to ten. *Roll on, Day*, I scrawled on a piece of paper.

An angry customer was looking for his package. It should have arrived yesterday – he needed it to do a presentation. I endeavoured to calm him. The morning was frantic, one call after another. Every customer was looking for miracles and we didn't do them. We just delivered packages; if you were lucky you just might get it on time. Rosemary left a message on my desk that Gary had rung.

Before I knew it, it was lunch-time and I thanked the gods. Only four more hours to go. After I popped out to get a sandwich I rang Gary.

"Hi, love," he said, his voice soft and soothing.

I wondered how I could ever doubt this man, how I could think I could live without him?

"How are you?" I said, my voice full of sympathy for his sore head.

"My head is thumping and my stomach isn't too good – apart from that I'm fine," he said and laughed. "Sorry about last night."

I said nothing and then he continued.

"I tried to explain this morning, but you were in no mood to listen."

"Let's forget it," I said.

"I met with some developers last night. I was hoping to go into business with them, but I'm afraid I can't come up with the type of cash they're looking for."

I could hear the disappointment in his voice. Gary was ambitious; he wanted to go forward, shape out his own life.

I took Damien's letter out of my pocket, tore it up and threw it into the bin.

"Never mind, love; there will be other opportunities," I said.

"I'd have loved to have been in on this, to see how a big job gets done."

"I know." After a slight pause I asked, "Will you be home late?"

"About eight."

"See you then," I said. "Gary, I love you."

I finished my sandwich. I was glad I had the office to myself. I looked into the bin at the torn letter. I knew I had done the right thing.

Days passed uneventfully. Gary was still pissed off that he hadn't enough money to join the other developers. The bank would only loan him half of what he was looking for. Jack had grown so much. Rosemary said that things hadn't changed between her and Danny.

Eleanor was still seeing Bob. This was good news for us – when Eleanor was happy, so were we.

Vincent got the part. It was only a small part, but nevertheless it was work. My mother seemed contented which was an improvement on being discontented. Me, I was in limbo. I was living my life, going through the motions without the feelings.

Gary suggested that we should go away for a weekend, but I knew we couldn't afford it. Yet I longed to escape the dreariness of my routine.

There were tiny moments in my days, especially when I was at work, that I found myself wondering about Damien. So many conversations were going on in my head. So many things I longed to say but couldn't. I knew they were better left unsaid.

In Tesco's I seldom ran around; I just drifted. Sometimes I came back to work having forgotten what I went into town for. No more casserole dinners: it was pizza or burgers, something that required minimum effort. Gary made no comment on the drastic changes in our evening meal; perhaps like me his taste buds had numbed.

Chapter 9

"Are you pregnant?"

I looked into Eleanor's sharp eyes.

"Are you?" I retorted.

She laughed. "Nice one."

I threw my pen down on my desk. Rosemary had just gone out to join Danny for lunch.

"It's just that myself and Rosemary were wondering. You look awful." She smiled sweetly at me to take the sting out of what she had just said.

"For the moment that is none of your business," I replied and returned her smile with a bigger brighter one.

She laughed. "Michelle, you're a howl!"

"Am I?" I said in amazement. I was trying to insult her and she thought I was being funny.

"So how is Rosemary?"

"Fine. Is there something wrong with her?"

Eleanor lazed back in the chair. "She's putting on weight or haven't you noticed?"

"She could do with gaining a few pounds."

"You're joking."

My phone rang. Gladly I picked it up. "Good afternoon, Michelle speaking, how can I help?"

"Michelle, it's me, Damien."

"Hello."

"Can you talk?"

"I'm glad your package arrived safely." I was hoping this would put Eleanor off the scent.

Eleanor stood up. I could hear her move across the office floor. She stood behind me.

"Thank you for calling," I said and hung up.

"It's nice when customers take the time to phone us and thank us for a job well done."

"Yes, it's very rewarding."

My hand shook a little as I drank some mineral water. Thankfully, Eleanor didn't notice.

"Would you mind taking the phone for a minute? I've got to go to the loo," I said and made a quick exit before she got a chance to respond.

To my relief there was no one in the toilets. I went into a cubicle and closed the door behind me. I felt weak. Gingerly I sat down on the toilet. I covered my face with my hands.

I'd better get back to my desk. Damien would ring again; he wasn't going to give up. I hadn't felt this afraid since I left Australia pregnant with his child.

I took a few deep breaths to compose myself.

Back in the office, I saw Eleanor sitting at my desk scribbling a phone number on my pad.

"Acron computers would like us to pick up a package for them and have it delivered to an address in London tomorrow," she said. "I took a phone number and told them you'd ring back."

"Thanks."

She vacated my seat and I sat down.

He didn't phone again. Part of me was relieved; part disappointed. Over and back my feelings swayed.

After I picked Jack up from the baby-sitter's, I stopped off to see my mother.

I hated my mother's house. The minute I walked in her front door I felt my past starting to creep up on me and I felt I had to get out before I let the memories invade my head.

"How's Gary?" my mother asked.

Today I was glad of the distraction. My thoughts were winding down another avenue. "Not good. He was hoping to expand, but he hasn't got enough money."

My mother was contented to hear this; people that follow the yellow-brick road to success, wealth and happiness made my mother very uneasy.

"Maybe the next time," she said, not meaning a word of it.

My mother has long resigned herself to the status quo; never ever try to break out of the rut.

"But we're happy," I said with sarcasm.

"Good," she said and smiled at Jack.

She broke the silence between us by saying. "I got a phone call from Vincent at some ungodly hour." She shook her head. Yet I could tell she was pleased to have some news to tell me. "He's not coming home for Christmas. He's going to LA if you don't mind."

"Christmas! This is only May and you're talking about Christmas already!"

My mother grunted, then she got up and switched on the kettle. "Will you have a cup before you go?"

"Yes, thanks," I said and felt all the energy had been sapped out of me.

In an attempt to brighten up the place I had bought a yellow and blue tablecloth to cover up the old table that we once all sat around. I had got matching cushions for the chairs.

Jack had started to get restless. This was good news for me as it meant I could leave my mother without feeling guilty. I left my mug of unfinished tea on the table. My mother retreated to her sitting-room to watch TV.

Back home, I left Jack watching a Postman Pat video while I started to hoover the stairs. I switched off the hoover – there was something blocked in the tube. Then the phone rang.

"Michelle," Damien said.

I found myself sitting down on the bottom step of the stairs. "Damien, you shouldn't ring me at home!"

"I know, I was going to hang up if your husband answered," he said.

"What do you want?"

"To see you."

"I don't want to see you," I said coldly. A thousand lines that I had rehearsed in my head were lost to me now that I wanted them.

"Michelle, I've been a shit to my father. Ever since my mother died, I blamed him. I should have grown out of it, but I didn't. This is the only thing he has ever asked me to do: to get you to visit him."

I gripped the phone even tighter and remained silent. I

was sitting on the stairs. Postman Pat's tune was playing on the video. Jack was very quiet – a little too quiet; I knew he was up to something.

"I'm sorry for all the hurt I've caused you," said Damien. "I'm sorry that I didn't follow you when you left Sydney."

"Damien, I have to go."

"No, please don't go," he said, his voice slipping into a humbler tone.

"I'd better check on Jack."

I was surprised to see Jack was still sitting on the floor watching the video.

"I'm back," I said to Damien in a normal voice, as if I was talking to Vincent or one of the girls from work.

After we got married, Gary and I painted the walls terracotta. We couldn't make up our mind if we wanted a dado rail or not but eventually we decided that we did and we painted it white. Gary's mother gave us some pictures that she picked up on holidays in Italy. He varnished the floorboards. We had every intention of buying a rug but we never saw one that we liked. When we did, Jack was born and we couldn't afford to buy it.

I had a past in this house, in this hall, happy times. Memories that I could treasure. I saw myself sitting on the bottom step of the stairs, listening to Damien talk, apologise, grovel even and I knew I shouldn't be listening to him. He was slowly but surely reeling me in.

"Damien," I said, my whole body tensed. "I'm really sorry, but I can't meet you or your father. I don't want you to phone me here again or at work. I want you to leave me alone."

"Michelle, I need your help here," Damien said.

These were words I never thought I would hear. It was like I had just been told I won the Lotto.

"Damien, I can't –" The rest of the words formed in my head, but I couldn't speak them. "Oh, Damien!"

Jack came running. *"Mammy, Mammy!"*

I slammed down the phone as Gary walked in.

"What's the matter?" he asked.

"Nothing, I'm just tired," I said and surreptitiously wiped my tears away with my sleeve.

"Hello, Jack," he said and kissed his son.

I looked at my family and waited for the reassuring warmth to run though me. It didn't.

"What's for dinner?"

"Ah, I thought you were working late so I didn't bother cooking," I said, standing up.

Gary grinned. "That's good because I'm going to order us our usual take-away." He scooped Jack into his arms. "How about us two going for a spin and giving Mum a break?"

Jack wriggled to get down. He loved going for drives in the van.

"Bring back milk and bread! I forgot to get them at lunch-time," I shouted after them.

I sat back down on the stairs and waited for the phone to ring again, but it didn't.

Chapter 10

A watched phone never rings, unless at work, when I don't want it to. Every time the phone rang I thought it was Damien. The never-ending oscillation of my feelings . . . By the time Friday evening came around I was exhausted. I left Jack with my mother while I did my so-called weekly shop. I was planning on having a lie-in Saturday morning. I knew it wouldn't happen, but I wanted a change in my routine and that seemed like a good place to start.

I was unpacking the groceries when the phone rang. It was Vincent.

"Hi, what's up?" I said.

"Nothing is up. How are you?"

"It's Friday," I said. "I'm trying to encourage myself to get happy for the weekend."

"I can't see why you stay in that place when you hate it so much."

"That's easy for you to say! You don't have a baby to support and a mortgage to pay."

"Agreed, but you can't waste your life there," he said.

"I'm not going to."

"I know Damien has been in contact," he said levelly.

The shock rippled through me. "How do you know?"

"Because he came to see me in New York. He got my address from my old agent in London." He paused. "Have you seen him?"

I hoped my silence would make him think I had not.

"I take it you haven't?" He paused, waited for my response, then went on. "It could be worth your while meeting with him. Did he tell you? Apparently his father wants to meet you. There are a few things belonging to his wife that he'd like to give to you."

I remained silent.

"Michelle," he said, impatience creeping into his voice, "what harm can it do for you to meet his father, take the few bits of jewellery that he has for you? They might be valuable and you'd let an old man die in peace."

"I'm afraid to meet him," I said calmly, while I felt my heart thumping against my ribs.

"Why?"

"Because I am and I don't want to explain it."

"Michelle, he only wants to meet you, nothing more."

"Vincent, I can't."

"Michelle, stop being so afraid! Damien isn't asking you to leave Gary or anything. He's just asking you to visit his father, that's all!"

"So that's all you called for, to tell me what to do," I said acidly.

"That's it, sis," he said.

"So how are the rehearsals going?"

"Don't ask."

I smiled to myself, pleased that I had annoyed him.

"Phone him," he said.

"I haven't got his number."

Vincent had and he gave it to me. I scribbled it down and hung up as Gary walked in the door.

"Chicken curry and chips," he announced.

I pushed the piece of paper with Damien's phone number under the fruit basket. He set the table and took the last can of beer from the fridge, poured half into a glass for me and took a long slug from the can.

"Great," he said.

"You're drinking too much."

"Michelle, for god's sake, I haven't eaten all day – don't spoil my dinner."

"You're out every night."

"Working, Michelle."

I could tell he was holding back on his temper. "Working and then the pub," I said.

I saw the confused expression on Gary's face. We shot dagger-looks at each other. Jack was sitting on the floor and he started to whimper.

"Now look what you've done," I said, my voice laced with rage.

We both reached for Jack. I let Gary pick him up. We ate our food in silence.

"Coffee," he said as he switched on the kettle.

"Yes, please," I said, and then added casually, "Sorry."

I wasn't sure what I was sorry for, but it was Friday and suddenly I was in a generous mood.

He rubbed my back affectionately. I knew we'd feel like

heading up the stairs in minutes – but we couldn't, because of Jack. I would have loved just some simple straightforward sex, just a good shag, with no complications. I knew it would make me feel good, if only for a few minutes. At least I could lose myself for those few minutes and fantasise about Tom Cruise, or Damien or anyone and I wouldn't have to feel guilty because I'd be doing it with my husband.

"I had to let two of the lads go – call it cash-flow problems, call it bad management," Gary said.

My anger faded. Gary was holding Jack close to him. I thanked the gods that he couldn't read my thoughts.

I hugged Gary. "Oh pet," I said, my voice soothing, "I'm so sorry."

He nodded as he acknowledged what I had just said. "I feel such a failure."

"Gary, you're not!" I replied.

"I'm not due a payment for another two weeks. How the hell am I going to keep going until then?"

"What about the bank?"

"Those bastards won't lend me another penny."

"I'd better get Jack ready for bed." I want to be distracted. I didn't want to hear his problems. I had enough of my own.

"I thought we might go out tonight. I feel like getting pissed."

"Gary, we've no bloody money," I snapped. Instantly I was sorry for saying the obvious.

He rubbed his eyes with his hands. "Do you mind if I borrow some from you? I'll pay you back at the end of the week."

I opened my purse and looked into it. I had sixty euros.

I was hoping to buy Jack some new shoes. I handed him twenty euros. "Is that enough?"

Gary's mother was a teacher. She always had money to give to her little darlings when they found the going tough. Vincent and I knew better than to trouble our mother looking for money.

He took the twenty-euro note and shoved it into his pocket. "It will have to do."

I snapped my purse closed. He passed Jack to me, then he gave me a quick peck on the cheek and walked out the back door.

I found myself dialling Damien's number. Jack was busy pulling a box of cornflakes out of the cupboard.

"Hello, it's me – Michelle."

"Michelle."

I closed my eyes and conjured up a picture of his handsome face.

"What's your father's name?"

"Tom."

"I was trying to remember it and I couldn't."

"You were never very good at remembering people's names."

"No."

"I'm here in Westport with my father. It's only a matter of time until –" His words faded.

"I'll come tomorrow," I said hurriedly. Immediately I regretted not giving it more thought. Who was going to mind Jack for me? Could I afford to go? Had I anything decent to wear?

"Thank you, Michelle. I'll give you directions."

"Hold on a minute while I get a pen." The decision had

been made. A combination of things had set the course for me. Now all I had to do was go. I pulled almost half the contents of the drawer out before I found a pen that actually worked. I scribbled the directions down on the back of an envelope.

"See you tomorrow," were his parting words as I hung up.

The floor was covered in cornflakes. "Come on, young man, you've done enough damage," I said as I pulled the box from Jack.

To my surprise he gave in.

Upstairs I opened my wardrobe door and looked inside. I had nothing new to wear – my clothes were so out of fashion they were almost antique.

From the bottom of my wardrobe I pulled out my best pair of jeans. They were dirty. Jack had spilled a drink on them a week ago. Instead of putting them in the laundry-basket, I had thrown them into the wardrobe and forgotten about them. All my shirts and tops were faded. I couldn't afford to buy something new.

I put my jeans into the washing machine and switched it on. I looked through my old tops in the vain hope that some Fairy Godmother might have left a nice new one in the pile for me. There was nothing there. Eventually I picked up a white shirt that I didn't like which meant it looked quite new. I ironed out the creases.

I rang the baby-sitter, but she couldn't take Jack tomorrow. Then I phoned my mother, but there was no answer. I couldn't believe it – she was never out.

"Hi, Rosemary," I said and smiled down the phone. I was hoping she wouldn't ask too many questions, just agree to take Jack tomorrow.

"Michelle, is everything all right?"

"Yes, why?"

Rosemary made an attempt to laugh, but it got lost somewhere down the line. "You never ring me," she said.

"Oh, don't I?" I made a face and said, "I was just wondering what you're up to tonight?"

"It's Friday and I should be looking forward to the weekend, but I'm not. Danny has just gone out and left me here on my own."

"Join the club," I said.

"You mean Gary has gone out without you? What's wrong? He never does that!" I could see her ears pricking up. Rosemary loved drama.

"Everything," I said.

"Oh Michelle," she said her voice high-pitched and full of emotion.

"We've no bloody money and Gary has gone to the pub. I'm pissed off."

"Why don't you come over?"

"I can't. I've got to put Jack to bed."

"Michelle, I don't mind you bringing Jack. I know !" She paused to giggle. "You and Jack can stay the night."

"I've just put my jeans in the washing machine. I need them for tomorrow."

"You must have another pair you can wear tomorrow."

"I have, but they're old."

"Michelle, I have about six pair of jeans. We're about the same size – you can have your pick."

My mind was racing as I tried to think of another excuse. I didn't want to spend the evening with Rosemary.

"Pretty please," she said in her best Miss Piggy voice.

I laughed. I couldn't say no.

"You get ready, I'll be over in five minutes to collect you."

"There's no need – we'll drive over to you."

I raced around the house collecting a few changes of clothes for Jack, some pyjamas, his blanket that he goes to bed with every night and his favourite teddy.

I grabbed a big T-shirt of Gary's to sleep in, two pairs of clean knickers and some make-up. By the time I arrived at Rosemary's, I was already regretting my actions.

I didn't want to share my thoughts with her. I didn't want to share them with myself.

Rosemary led me into her sitting-room. She poured a large glass of white wine and told me she was on her second glass of red.

"I thought today would never end," she said.

She was sitting on her cream oversized sofa, her legs curled up under her. My son was crawling around on the floor, delighted at this new ultra-clean room that he had been let loose in.

"Relax," she said. It came across more as an order than a request.

Rosemary was already getting on my nerves. I gulped down my glass of wine. I needed to lighten up if I was going to spend the evening with her.

"What's wrong?" she asked.

I gripped my wine glass tightly. "I can't relax here, with Jack."

Jack had made his way towards her coffee table. Any minute now his finger prints would be all over the glass.

Rosemary lazed back and laughed. She was tipsy. "He's fine, you worry too much."

"Rosemary, this room is not child friendly."

Rosemary looked around her like she was seeing the room for the first time. She sighed deeply and said, "You're right. Come on, Jack, let's go into the kitchen." She picked up her glass of wine.

I followed with Jack, his teddy, blanket and my glass of wine.

"Happy now?" she asked me.

"Sorry, Rosemary, I'm just pissed off." The wine had loosened my tongue.

"Join the club," she said and poured more wine into her glass. "Did you eat?"

"We had a takeaway."

"Let me guess: chicken curry and chips."

I nodded.

"You're still hungry."

"No, I'm fine," I said.

"You're never bloody hungry," Rosemary said. She got up and walked over to the fridge and opened the door. Jack followed her, his tubby finger pointing at something he saw.

"Let me see, what shall I cook?" She slammed the fridge door closed and Jack started to whinge. She opened it again, took out a yoghurt, opened it and gave it to him with a spoon. He sat down on the floor and started to eat it. She opened the freezer door, pulled out something and stuck it into the microwave. "Dinner will be ready in a few minutes, young man," she said and tickled him under the chin. He laughed and looked at her with pleading eyes, so she had to do it again and again, until he eventually he got tired of it.

He started to open the cupboard doors. He took out all the saucepans, covering the floor with them.

"Leave him! Hubby can put them back," she said when I attempted to put them away.

Later, I noticed how quiet Jack had got. I tiptoed over to discover that he had fallen asleep on the floor.

"He's gorgeous," Rosemary whispered. "Would you like to put him up to bed?"

"No thanks – if you don't mind I'll keep him here with me. If he wakes up in a strange bed he might get upset," I whispered as I gently cleaned his yoghurt-stained face.

"I wish I could have a baby."

"It's early days," I said.

"Have you been talking to my doctor?"

"No, I read it in a magazine."

We started to laugh and poured ourselves more wine.

Back in the sitting-room we settled down to do some serious talking. I left Jack down on the sofa beside me and covered him with his blanket.

"What will Gary say in the morning when he finds you're not at home?"

I shrugged.

"Won't he be worried?"

"Probably," I said.

I knew I was drinking too much. My tongue would take over and babble out all the things that I'd never say if I was sober.

"Rosemary, I was wondering if I could get you to look after Jack for me tomorrow? There's something I've got to do and I can't bring Jack along."

She eyed me suspiciously as she sipped her wine. "What are you up to?"

I finished my wine in two quick gulps and threw caution

to the wind. I tried to measure my words carefully and not let her imagination run away with her as it usually does.

"I'm going to visit friends in Westport."

"Oh," she said.

"Their father is very ill," I said.

Rosemary's eyes glinted. She was making more of this than was necessary.

"Of course I'll look after Jack for you," she said.

We smiled at each other.

"Is he really very ill?" she asked before I got a chance to thank her.

I nodded.

She poured more wine into my empty glass. She sat down beside me and continued her interrogation. "Do I know them?" Her eyes were fixed on my face.

I composed myself as best I could before I replied. "No, you don't."

"You've probably talked about them in the office, but I've been so caught up with myself lately that I mustn't have heard you."

"No, I've never talked about him."

"Oh," she said.

"I've never talked about him," I repeated as I searched for the right words, "because I didn't know he was sick."

A heavy silence fell on us. I felt the need to talk. We'd worked together for five years and there was very little she didn't know about me. It was her speciality to draw people out and find out all there was to know about them.

"It's Damien's father," I said and then wondered why I had said that.

Rosemary smiled triumphantly.

Inside I was cringing. "It's not what you think," I found myself saying. "Damien, the guy you went to Australia with?"

"Yes, please don't tell anyone," I said hurriedly. I found myself looking over my shoulder; it felt like we were in the office and Eleanor was going to walk in at any time.

"Your secret is safe with me," she said and smiled to seal it.

I sipped some wine, unsure of what to say next.

"So you'll be wanting an early night. It's a good drive to Westport."

"Rosemary, I've told no one that I'm going to Westport. I have to go, I feel I've no choice. His father wants to see me."

Her eyes grew bigger with curiosity when she asked, "How did he find you after all these years?"

"He got my address from Vincent."

"I see," she said.

"I don't feel right about this."

Rosemary tutted. "I wonder, what's bloody right?" She had finished the bottle of wine and was drinking brandy now. "Danny is never here. Lately I'm beginning to wonder if he's got another woman." She felt I'd given her licence to open up and talk about herself.

I yawned. I couldn't help myself.

"He tells me he's going to this meeting or else he's off playing bloody golf. He'll do anything but face facts." She rubbed Jack's head. "Men, they're impossible!" Then she announced that it was time for bed. "I'll show you your room." She glided out like she was walking on air. I waded behind her with Jack in my arms.

"Maybe it's best if I leave Jack with my mother," I said.

She shook her head vigorously. "Not at all! My sister is coming with her two children tomorrow. He'll have a wonderful time."

At the bedroom door, she hugged me. I stood there, feeling detached.

"Thanks, Rosemary," I whispered.

"Don't worry about Jack, he'll be fine," she said, her words slurring into each other.

Chapter 11

My first glimpse of the sea lifted my spirits. My little son had never seen the sea. I was missing him.

I had memorised the directions in my head. Once I had reached the Octagon in Westport, I was to drive out of town until I reached the top of the hill. Quay Hill, Damien had called it. On my right I would see a high stone wall. Follow the wall to The Quay, he told me, take a left and drive on for half a mile until I came to black wrought-iron gates.

I had promised Rosemary to phone her when I arrived.

"I'm here," I said.

"Oh, this is exciting!"

"Rosemary, please!"

"Sorry," she said and giggled. "Jack is fine. By the way, did you phone Gary?"

"No, I can't. I feel bad enough doing this behind his back without phoning him."

"What's the house like?"

"I don't know, I'm just at the gates."

"You *are* coming home tonight?" she said and started to giggle again.

"Of course I am. Bye." I attempted to hang up.

"This is exciting," she said again. "You have to tell me everything when you get back."

I agreed. I hadn't a notion of telling her anything. "Kiss Jack for me."

* * *

"Hello, is that you, Michelle?" Damien said after I dialled his number.

The sun was trying to break through the clouds. Seagulls glided across the sky with enviable ease.

"Don't tell me you've spent all morning beside the phone?"

He laughed. "That's the good thing about mobiles – they are mobile."

I ventured to look through the gates, but all I could see was graceful trees swaying gently in the breeze.

"Where are you?" he asked.

"Outside your front gates."

"Just give me a minute and I'll be down."

Then, the line went dead. I got out of the car and waited. The sea glinted like jewels in the bright sunlight. The smell of the sea air was refreshing after the long drive.

I turned back to look when I heard footsteps on the gravel. He walked towards me, smiling. My heart missed a beat. I felt like I had come home.

"Michelle," he said, "Welcome to Westport." He took my hands and held them in his.

"Hi," I said. I turned again to look at the sea. "This is really nice."

"Yes, it's lovely here. A little quiet, but I like that."

"It can't be as quiet as home."

"In winter it's worse," he said.

Thanks to Rosemary, I was wearing the latest cream trousers with a matching jacket. I had listened with bogus interest while she waffled on about why she didn't like the outfit, but when she brought it back to the shop they wouldn't change it because she'd kept it for too long. Eleanor was right: Rosemary had put on weight and it wouldn't fit her.

"I'm so glad you came. Thank you," he said. Those simple words seemed to be weighted down by something more.

I said nothing. We stood for what seemed an eternity, looking out at the slow rhythmic movement of the sea.

Damien shook his head and said, "You look great."

"Thanks for the compliment, but I don't feel great," I replied.

He reached out and touched my hair. I moved slightly away and smiled my apologies. I didn't want him touching me. It was enough to be here, to see his face, to let my eyes take in every detail, to get used to this man again.

"Michelle, I can't thank you enough for coming."

I shivered. The wind had picked up and was blowing through my fashionable clothes.

"You're cold," he said.

"A little."

"Would you like to drive up to the house? We could have a coffee in the kitchen. The doctor is with my father at the moment. Or would you rather we went into town and got a coffee?"

Our eyes met.

I shrugged and said, "I don't mind."

"The same old Michelle," he said with a lopsided grin.

"Let's go up to the house." Suddenly I had become very decisive.

We got into my car and drove up the winding avenue. The house, Damien told me, used to be a rectory. It was Georgian, he added. Two steps led up to the blue front door. He told me the flagged floor in the hall was made of sandstone, as he led me down the hall and into the kitchen where a solid fuel stove was emitting heat.

The spacious kitchen had fitted cupboards and a large table in the centre of the terracotta floor. My eyes took in every detail.

I was about to go overboard and say how beautiful the house was. I edited my words and said, "This is nice."

We always used to make real coffee – I loved the smell of it. The only time I hated the smell was when I was pregnant.

"Do you still drink yours black?"

"I do, do you?"

He smirked. "Yes, I do." He placed two mugs of coffee on the table and a plate with some scones.

"Nancy comes in every morning to help with my father. She's brilliant. I don't know what we'd do without her."

Damien sounded so mature, I thought to myself as I buttered my scone.

After we finished the coffee he went off to see his father. I strolled around the kitchen. I was amazed to find the back door didn't lead outside. Instead there was a pantry and a utility room. I walked through them and outside. Across the cobbled yard stood some old stone houses with faded red doors. The only thing that was missing was a dog. I turned around when I heard footsteps.

"My father would like to see you now," Damien said, walking towards me.

"Do you have a dog?"

"He died a year ago and my father couldn't bear to get another."

We walked back into the house and Damien led the way upstairs. Rosemary would love this house. Ornate ceiling work and cornicings that looked as old as the house.

Damien gently tapped on his father's door and then opened it.

"Dad, Michelle is here."

Even though the room was big it smelt stuffy. The curtains were drawn on the two large windows, blocking out the light. I smiled at the frail body that was lying propped up in the bed.

When he'd come to visit us in Sydney, I'd taken him around to see the sights. Armed with a dozen guidebooks we had set off. When Tom suggested we should dump them and just go around and look at things I was delighted. I thought he would want to know the facts: when, what, where. Our favourite way to pass a morning was to go down to Sydney Opera house. If we were lucky some musicians might be playing. We would sit outside and watch all the tourists go by.

"Michelle, my dear, thank you for coming," he said now as he gasped for breath. "I hope you won't be insulted when I give you these bits of jewellery that my wife had."

"Of course I won't," I said.

Damien handed me a small jewellery box. I rubbed my sticky hands on my trousers before I opened the box. It smelt musty when I opened it.

"Susan loved her jewellery. That's why I want you to have them. She'd have liked you." Then he started to cough.

"Thank you, that's very kind of you," I said, feeling that I was using the lines out of some script.

A pearl necklace, some earrings and what looked like a diamond ring were neatly arranged on the old red velvet.

"I have a lot of time to think." He coughed into a tissue. Damien gave him a drink of water and then he continued. "I couldn't get you out of my mind. It was I who insisted on Damien finding you. I just had to know that you were alright before I died."

Damien eyes were studying my face intently when I looked at him.

"Damien should have married you," said Tom.

"Dad," Damien said gently.

"These may be my last bloody words so let me say them," he said and then he started to cough. Damien put the glass of water in front of him. Tom pointed with a long bony finger towards the curtains. "Open them bloody things!"

I opened the curtains. After the murky light of the bedroom, I was assaulted by shades of blue, from the mountains, sky and sea.

I was horrified when I looked back at Tom. This was not the man I once knew. He was worn down to his skeleton. I found it hard to look at him.

"Michelle, when I was in Australia – were you pregnant?"

It felt like someone had just boxed me in the stomach. I wanted to bend over and protect myself. I leaned against the wall for support.

"Dad!" Damien said. "That is none of your business."

"If I have a grandchild I'd like to know about it before I die," he said.

I was unable to look at Tom or Damien. I turned to look at the sea. The smell of the room was nauseating. I was physically retching. I clamped my hand firmly over my mouth.

"Are you okay?" I heard Damien ask as I ran from the room. In the hall all I could see was big white doors. Damien was at my side. He grabbed my hand and pulled me into a bedroom. We ran, like we were in some action-packed movie and the bad guys were after us. He opened another door. I saw the toilet and with relief I bent down and threw up the scone.

A few minutes later Damien arrived back with a glass of water. I sat on the bathroom floor, my hand across my stomach. Tears fell uncontrollably down my face. He took me in his arms and hugged me.

"Michelle, Michelle," he said. He rubbed my back in a soft caressing motion. I felt myself relax, wallowing in the comfort of his loving touch.

I lay in his arms, limp, like a rag-doll, unable to move.

He picked me up and brought me into the bedroom. We sat on the bed together.

"Would you like to lie down?"

I shook my head. I was unable to speak. I knew if I spoke the words would be gibberish, a flow of chatter with no meaning, no direction, nothing, just me waffling.

After a while, Damien disturbed the silence by suggesting we go for a walk. We used to walk on the beaches in Sydney, the waves lapping at our bare feet while we walked hand in hand, heady with the feelings of love, lust and passion.

Those feelings were gone and no matter how we back-tracked I knew we would never find them again. I wanted to say this to Damien, but I couldn't.

Tears pricked my eyes and I blinked them away, determined not to break, not to crumble. I sat very still, holding myself in, composing myself, waiting for the pain to pass. It would go, eventually. Gently, he pushed strands of hair off my face.

I needed to get out of the house. I needed some fresh air, but I didn't think my legs would carry me.

"I'd like to go for a walk," I said and then added, "Can I borrow a jacket or something? I forgot to bring one."

He opened a wardrobe door and took out a navy fleece. "Will this do?"

I nodded and took it from him. I was always wearing his shirts and jumpers when we were together. Slowly our past was unfolding in front of us.

My hand grazed his, our eyes met and held. Suddenly and quite unexpectedly we were in each other's arms.

"I'm so sorry, Michelle, I'm so sorry," he said and started to cry.

I hugged him closer and found myself telling him it was alright. He wiped his eyes while I put on his fleece.

As we came out of the house I could smell the sea. The sunlight was blinding, my head ached. We walked in silence down the gravel drive, across the road and towards the beach.

On Monday when I was sitting at my grey desk, with all my familiar things, I would think of this walk to the beach; of this time together. No doubt Rosemary would have a few probing questions and I knew I would end up lying to her.

The tide gently swayed in and wet my boots.

"How are you feeling?"

"A lot better," I said.

We stopped walking.

"What happened after you left me in Sydney?"

I stared out to sea and felt the question run over me. So much happened. I turned to look at him, my eyes on his face. He looked down at me, his eyes full of compassion.

"Why did your father think I was pregnant?"

Damien looked down at the sand. He bent down, picked up a stone and threw it out to sea. "He guessed. He noticed you'd stopped drinking coffee and he thought he heard you getting sick in the bathroom."

"I was pregnant," I said, my eyes fixed on his face. "I tried to tell you, but you didn't want to listen to me and I had my suspicions that you were seeing Alison, so I just decided it was time for me to move on."

"You should have spelled it out to me. I thought you were just looking for attention, I didn't realise –"

I butted in. "Damien, I tried, I really tried. Your father was staying with us and you were out all the time, pretending to be working while you were fucking Alison, you –" I stopped myself, knowing words couldn't change things. "I knew I didn't stand a chance against Alison. She was very pretty and to make matters worse she was also your boss, so I just knew . . ." Tears filled my throat and prevented me from continuing. I took a breath and then said, "I asked your father to take me to the airport. I had this idea that once he told you that I was gone you'd follow me, but you didn't. I had stomach cramps on the plane. I started to bleed. I bled all the way to London. When I arrived in London I went to the hospital. They told me I'd lost the baby. I was never more relieved in my life and then the guilt kicked in. I was hoping my knight in shining armour would come to save me, but he didn't. I just fell apart. Eleanor was going back to Ireland – she had done really well for herself. She gave me, a job in customer support. Then, I met Gary. I've know him all my life. We started going out together, next thing we're planning to get married, then we had Jack and that's it."

"Michelle, I'm so sorry. My father wanted me to go after you. He said I'd always regret it, but I was too fucking stupid to listen." He ran his hands through his hair, a habit of old that I once loved. We turned and started to walk back towards the house.

"I'll say goodbye to your father and then I'll go," I said as we reached the house.

"I'd like to take you out to lunch. It's the least I can do."

"I'm not very hungry."

His father waved to us from the old Victorian-style conservatory, I waved back. We walked inside. Damien led the way through the drawing-room into the conservatory.

"Sorry about that," I said. I was surprised to find Tom's bloodless hand was warm when I touched it. His frail body was wrapped in a quilt.

"I lost the baby," I said while I held his hand.

"I'm sorry to hear that," he said.

"I know. Thanks, Tom, for the jewellery. I'll always treasure them."

He waved a frail hand. "I wish," he started to say before he was overcome by a fit of coughing.

A small woman wearing a green and white stripped apron came in, a tray in her hands. "Are you alright?"

Tom nodded.

"This is Nancy," Damien said.

She was small and chubby with dark hair swept back from her round face.

"I've made your favourite soup," she announced to Tom.

"Would you like some?" Damien asked me.

"Why not?" I didn't want to go. I wanted to stay for just another while.

"It's the best soup you'll ever drink, isn't that right, Nancy?" Damien said.

I looked into Tom's faded eyes and saw his disappointment that he had got no grandchild. He pointed a bony finger towards the jewellery box on the table.

"Don't forget that," he said, his tone lifeless.

Damien picked up the jewellery box.

When we were in the kitchen he said, "My father hates goodbyes, always has. It's his way of saying goodbye to you."

Coward that I was, I felt relieved that I didn't have to say goodbye. Damien filled two bowls with soup, sliced some home-made brown bread and left it on the bread board. He took the butter out of the fridge and placed it on the table. I watched him do all these ordinary things. He walked over to a drawer and took out two soup-spoons. He gave me one and then sat down. The soup looked wholesome and nutritious. My stomach rumbled.

In quiet moments, I knew I was going to find myself thinking about this kitchen, wondering who was he sharing his meals with. Would he get a new dog when his father passed away, or would he sell up and leave? Was I going to be tormented for the rest of my life? As I lived one life, would I always wonder what my life would have been like with Damien, now that he'd nudged dormant feelings awake?

I tasted the soup. It was delicious. When we'd finished it, Damien made coffee. We sat facing each other, mugs placed on the pine table in front of us.

"Didn't you offer her anything with the coffee?" Nancy said as she burst through the door.

"What is there?"

"Apple-pie," she said, her arms akimbo.

"Would you like some apple-pie?"

"Of course she'd like some! She needs more than a bowl of soup to take her home!"

She waded across the floor and opened the fridge door. She took out some whipped cream in a glass bowl, heated some apple-pie in the microwave and put it in front of me.

"You can get your own," she said to Damien.

"Thanks, Nancy," he said. "You're too kind."

"I'm going into town to do some shopping."

"No problem," he said. "I'll just go and check on Dad." Then he left the kitchen.

The apple-pie looked appetising, golden brown. I spooned some cream on it and tasted a forkful.

"This is delicious," I said.

Nancy smiled her thanks. "The apples come from the orchard."

I wondered if I was supposed to be impressed by this. I took another forkful and ate it slowly. My stomach still felt sore.

"Damien is capable of eating the whole pie in one sitting. As for his poor father, he hasn't much of an appetite." Her voice was thick with tears when she said, "You know he hasn't much time left?"

The kitchen clock seemed to tick louder. I wanted to say some comforting words, but I couldn't think of any. When Damien walked into the kitchen I felt relieved.

"He's dozing," he said.

"All those pills would knock anyone out," Nancy said. She took her raincoat from the door where it was hanging and put it on. "I won't be too long." Her gentle face broke into a weak smile. "Thanks for coming, Michelle."

Damien was lost in his own thoughts. When we lived together, I used to try to get his attention, but would fail miserably because he was always more interested in the TV, or the book he was reading, than in me. At the top of the table, the newspapers were folded. I could picture him sitting reading them all morning while he waited for my phone call.

"She's nice," I said.

"Yes, she's very fond of my father."

"I hope she doesn't mind your father giving me the jewellery."

"Believe me, my father has looked after her. She certainly can't complain even though she likes to complain about everything."

I sipped some coffee and then I said the words I had rehearsed in my head for the last few minutes. "I'd better go."

"So soon?" Damien stood up, his chair scraping against the floor.

"I have things to do," I said and felt the words wobble out of my mouth.

"I wish you could stay." He was looking out the kitchen window, his hands shoved into the pockets of his jeans.

"I can't," I muttered and hoped he heard me because I couldn't speak any louder.

He turned to face me. "Michelle, Michelle, what have I done?"

Suddenly we were in each other's arms again, holding onto each other, clinging, knowing that we must separate, but feeling unable to.

"Damien," I whispered his name into his chest. It was such a relief to be able to say his name, to admit to myself that I once loved this man.

"Please stay," he said.

I shook my head, tendrils of my hair falling around my face. He pushed them back.

"I have to go, it's Saturday, I have to spend some time with my son," I managed to say without the words breaking.

"I wish –" he started to say and then stopped.

I pulled away from him.

"Thanks for lunch," I mumbled.

We walked together into the hall. Then Damien followed me as I walked towards the front door.

Outside he said, "I'd like to ring you, to see you again."

"Please don't."

I took the jewellery box and thanked him. The warm sunlight had taken the chill out of air. I placed the jewellery box under the seat of my old Toyota Starlet.

"Your jumper," I said, handing it back to him.

"Keep it."

"I'd better not."

My eyes looked past him, at the beautiful landscaped

gardens. A tapestry of summer flowers was starting to appear. There was a timeless aura about the place. Tom's white head was resting back against his pillows in the conservatory. I inched myself away from Damien, hating the moment when I would finally get into my old car and drive away from him.

"Michelle, there's something I should tell you before you go."

Our eyes met.

"I love you. I have from the first time we met, but I was too stupid to realise it."

I turned away from him and got into my car. Tears filled my eyes as I turned the car keys in the ignition. I felt the god of old bangers was looking down on me when it started on my first attempt.

Damien backed away from me. I could see him in the mirror, his face solemn as he watched me drive away. Before I knew it I had reached the road. Glancing quickly at the sea I saw the waves rolling in and sliding back out again. I turned and headed for home.

Chapter 12

In the newsagent's I picked a card with a single lily floating on a pond. Inside I wrote:

Dear Tom,

Thank you for the lovely jewellery. You are in my thoughts and prayers.

Love Michelle.

I closed the card and posted it. It was Monday lunch-time. I was on a go-slow. Damien was in my head all the time.

When I returned from Westport, I picked Jack up from Rosemary's. She wanted to hear about Damien and his father. I told her I would fill her in on Monday. When I got home on Saturday evening, Gary was mowing the lawns.

I switched on the kettle, knowing Gary would come in for a coffee when he had finished.

"Where did you go? I was worried about you," he said. There was no reproach or anger in his voice.

"I spent last night and today with Rosemary." I wondered

if my nose would grow bigger with the lie, yet it felt the same size on my hot face.

"Rosemary," he said, amazed at my fickleness. Only a week ago I was giving out about her; now we were best buddies.

"We went shopping in Mullingar."

"Did you buy anything?"

"No, I couldn't afford to."

He took the mug of coffee from me. We walked outside. Jack was playing with his tractor.

"I'm sorry," he said, pulling me towards him. We hugged.

"That's alright." I couldn't bear to look into his honest eyes.

I didn't want to be here, sitting in this garden, the smell of newly mown grass filling my nostrils with the promise of summer.

Gary talked about his disappointment at not being able to join the other developers. I listened with bogus interest. I longed for him to go and play with Jack, to let me be.

Inside I felt shattered. I walked back in time, forward again. And now I was back again in my life, filling out the place where I was supposed to be, where I belonged.

Jack fell and Gary ran to pick him up. He kissed Jack's wounded knee.

"Hush, hush," he said lovingly to his son.

They walked back to me.

"You look tired," said Gary, scrutinising my face. "Would you like to lie down? Jack and I could go and visit my folks."

"If you like," I said, my spirits lifting at the thought of getting some time on my own.

When they were gone, I pottered around and felt severed from the things that once were familiar to me. An echo of pain was playing in my head, a quiet throbbing reminding me of Damien, of another life that I could be living.

Sunday morning, we made love. I closed my eyes and dreamed of Damien. It was he who caressed me, who kissed me, who held me. I knew it was wrong, I knew I should stop, but I couldn't.

The thing I discovered about routine was you could sink into the groove and go on doing the same things you've done every day in a zombie state and no one knew, not even you.

By Tuesday, Rosemary was fit to be tied.

"Go on! Tell me everything!" She wagged a finger. "Leave nothing out!"

"There's nothing to tell. His father just wanted me to have his wife's jewellery."

"You're a dark horse – I bet there is more!"

"Rosemary," I said, my face set in earnest lines. "Five years ago, I got on a plane in Sydney and left Damien. He was seeing someone else while we were living together. He could have followed me, but he didn't. He's left it too late. I'm married now and I have Jack."

"Are you saying if you weren't married that you might get back together?"

I shrugged, trying to sound casual when I said, "Who knows?"

Rosemary smirked. "What does he look like? Is he as handsome as Gary?"

"Rosemary, can we change the subject?"

"Of course we can." She turned to her desk and hit a few keys on her keyboard. I knew by the tilt of her chin that she had drawn her own conclusions.

We busied ourselves trying to empathise with customers

who were looking for information about packages that should have been delivered yesterday. We couldn't tell them that the truck driver went on the piss for the weekend and had only just sobered up. Instead we rhymed off about technical faults in our computer system that had led to some packages not arriving on time and we were doing everything we could to get them delivered as soon as possible. My throat was dry from lying. I hated my job and I wanted to tell every one that the truck driver was dead, because he would be if I could get my hands on him.

"Men," Rosemary said, more to herself than to me. Then she transferred a call to me.

"It's for you," she said. I knew it was personal by her tone.

"Hello," I said expecting to hear Damien's voice.

"It's Nancy," she sniffed. "Tom died last night." She sniffed again. "In his sleep."

"Nancy, I'm so sorry." I could hear her sobbing.

"Damien asked me to ring you."

"Nancy, I feel so helpless – is there anything I can do?"

"Damien would like you to come. He wanted to ring you himself, but there are the funeral arrangements and to tell you the truth he's exhausted – we've been up with his father every night. It was Tom's wish to die here and not in the hospital."

I listened to her as she wept. I looked across at Rosemary. She stretched her face into an obliging smile.

"Nancy, I'm so sorry!" I knew my words were inadequate and of little comfort to her.

She continued to cry, then blew her nose loudly. "The funeral arrangements will be in the daily paper." She hung up.

I turned to look at Rosemary. "Damien's father is dead. He's expecting me to go to the funeral."

"What are you going to do?"

"I – I –" I started to say and then stopped myself. I was lost for words. "I don't know." I looked at the photograph of Gary and Jack. A strange feeling of sadness enveloped me. I felt its weight dragging me down. "I don't know what to do."

"You'll have to go to the funeral," she said, her voice lifting into the same sing-song voice she used with customers.

"How can I? What will I tell Gary?"

"We'll think of something," she said, in a conspiratorial whisper.

"Rosemary, I can't just go to the funeral – I mean, I can't say to Gary I'm going to my –" I paused and then continued, "my ex's father's funeral. I mean if he did that to me, I'd go crazy, I just couldn't take it, I wouldn't take it. I mean to say Gary would never do that, he's never done anything shitty to me – if he did, I could go off so damn easily, but he hasn't so I can't, can I? Would you like it if –"

The phone rang and stopped me in mid-flow.

"Bloody phone," Rosemary said and then picked it up, "Rosemary speaking, how can I help?"

I sat listening to myself breathe. Tom was dead, his pain was over. I could see Damien walking down the gravel path, across the road and towards the sea. I wished I could be there with him, just to walk with him, to reassure him that he was not alone, but I couldn't. I was here, bound to Jack and Gary, my precious family. When I didn't value me, Gary did. I owed him my life, my love, my loyalty.

Rosemary put down the phone and said, "It's that prat Alex from Celtic Fibres. He said we didn't get back to him about a package he sent to the US. Apparently it hasn't arrived."

I picked up my customer request forms. "Ooops, I forgot to phone them."

"Would you like me to do it?"

"Would you?"

"Consider it done." She took the page from me. She opened her drawer and took her glasses back out. A tough call called for some serious conversation. She tapped in the number. Under normal circumstances, I would be worried. This was an important customer and he was anything but satisfied at the moment.

I smiled my thanks, she smiled her "you're welcome".

I stared at my PC, then my eyes turned to the grey wall. I looked at all the pieces of paper I had stuck up there; once upon a time I had considered them important.

"Michelle, what are you going to do?"

I turned to look at Rosemary. "Do?" I asked.

"Yes, about the funeral," she said with exasperation.

"What can I do?"

"Well, that's up to you!"

"I don't know what to do."

Damien always teased me about never being able to make up my mind. It wasn't that simple. No matter what I decided to do I felt I was going to hurt someone. It was two-sided. Go or stay. Decision time. If I went to the funeral I'd have to explain it to Gary. If I didn't go then I wouldn't have any explaining to do. On the other hand I could go to the funeral and not tell Gary, but then I'd be lying. I couldn't do that. I couldn't lie to Gary.

"I can't go," I said.

Rosemary frowned.

"Suppose you brought me with you? Suppose we told

Gary that I asked you to come? That it was a friend of mine who died and I didn't want to make the trip on my own."

"I would be lying. I can't do that, I feel bad enough as it is. I just want to leave things. I don't think I can handle seeing him again – it's too confusing."

"Fair enough," she said and turned in to her desk.

"I'll send some flowers." I tried to concentrate on filling in my timesheet; it was the one task at work that I enjoyed doing.

"I wish we could go to lunch together. We can never talk properly here," Rosemary said.

"Why don't you come around after work tomorrow and I'll cook dinner for us?" I suggested.

"Are you up to it?"

"Of course I am," I said, wondering to myself was I up to it.

"What would you like me to bring?"

"Wine," I said, "so we can get pissed."

* * *

I sent flowers to the funeral.

Days passed, an endless stream of sameness. In my head, I often rang Damien. "Hi," I would say. "How are you?" Mostly I would start by saying, "Nancy rang me and told me about your father passing away. I'm so sorry. I wanted to go to the funeral, but I couldn't."

Then, Damien would reply, "Michelle, thanks for the flowers." Then, he would go on to say, "I wish I had done things differently, I wish you weren't married . . ."

At this point I would stop my mind games. They were too scary.

Sometimes I would write to him, just little notes.

Dear Damien, I'm thinking about you at this painful time. Or *Dearest Damien, I wish I could be with you.* On and on I would go, developing the plot instead of trying to forget about him. Like I did when I came home from Australia.

Once I came to realise that Damien wasn't coming to London to get me, I put him out of my mind, with a steely determination that I didn't know I had. I came back to Longford and reinvented myself, sort of.

I knew Eleanor didn't believe me when I told her that homesickness was the reason I left Australia. I looked terrible and everyone kept telling me so. Except for Gary. He thought I looked wonderful and we started to go out just as soon as I had unpacked in my mother's house. I stayed with her for a month, then I moved in with Gary. A year later, on the anniversary of our first date, we got married.

I fooled myself into believing I loved Gary. Maybe I did. I'm not really sure. I was one hundred per cent confused. It was like I had unfinished business with Damien and I had to sort it out. Like the Hollywood story where the heroine has got that glint in her eye; she's carrying a torch for some man or cause and she can't content herself until she gets it out of her system.

On Saturday, I spent the afternoon in a bridal boutique fitting on dresses. Gary's sister had asked me to be her bridesmaid – her best friend couldn't do it because she was pregnant. Rachel picked out a mint-green dress, fitted with shoe-string-straps and an organza wrap for me. They agreed that I should wear my hair up.

I stood there staring at the mirror while Rachel and the shop assistant looked at me critically to see what improvements they could make to me.

"There is something missing." Rachel said.

"What?" I asked.

"You just seem lost. Is it the dress? Don't you like it?"

"The dress is fine, I love the dress," I said. "It's the shoes."

All heads turned to look down at my feet.

"Could I try a different pair?"

I knew it wasn't the shoes. It was me inside. I was miserable. I was longing to see Damien again, but I knew I couldn't. My head told me that I should forget about him, my heart told me I would never forget him. I had to think about my son, of my wonderful family life. The shop assistant arrived with another pair of shoes.

"Try these," she said.

I slipped into them and walked around, trying my best to look the part.

"How are they?" Rachel asked cautiously.

"They're fine," I said, doing a twirl. We all giggled girlishly. "Isn't this exciting?" I said, a smile plastered on my face.

The shop assistant looked at Rachel. She was patiently waiting for her to make up her mind.

"We'll take this dress and the shoes," Rachel said.

"Great," the girl said with the minimum of interest. I caught her making a face behind Rachel's back. I smiled at her to let her know I didn't care. Rachel deserved it. I had fitted on every dress in the shop.

"You look beautiful. Wait until Gary sees you," said Rachel.

"Thanks," I said. And in my heart I wished Damien could see me.

* * *

"You look dead sexy in that dress," Gary said. He was

holding Jack in one arm and pulled me into his other one. We were at the wedding reception. The last time I was this dressed up was on our own wedding day. "I'm the luckiest man in the world."

"And I'm the luckiest woman," I said, inwardly cringing at my capacity to lie.

"Michelle, I love you," he said. His hands were hard from labouring. I took his hand in mine and we headed for the bar. People shuffled to make space for us. Everyone was wearing smiles and greeting each other. I had forgotten just how attractive Gary was. My eyes had become accustomed to seeing him in faded jeans and T-shirts.

I hugged him. "And I love you," I said. The words flowed easily, too easily. I wasn't sure if I meant them.

I couldn't help but run my hand through Jack's hair. He grinned at me; he had the same warm smile as his father. In the distance I could see my mother sitting at a table with some neighbours. She was listening intently. Her head was nodding like one of those dogs you see in car rear windows. I knew they were gossiping. They were probably talking about Gary's family. I waved over at her and her thin lips formed a mean smile. I knew she didn't want me over – they were on a roll, it wouldn't do if I interrupted.

"You look lovely, Michelle," Gary's mother said.

"Lovely is not the word. She looks beautiful," Gary said, his arm placed possessively around my waist.

"Thanks," I said.

"It's about time Jack had a little brother or sister," said Gary's mother. Her pleasant face was flushed with excitement.

I said nothing. I wanted to tell her to mind her own business, but I knew how much that would hurt Gary.

Gary hugged his mother.

"Gary, you're a treasure," she said. She took a tissue out of her sleeve and started to wipe her eyes.

"What's going on here," Gary's father asked. His face always reminded me of a friendly gargoyle.

"Dad," Gary said and gave his father an affectionate pat on the back.

"Doesn't she look lovely, son?"

"She looks great," Gary said, looking at me.

Gary's father shook his head. "Your sister – Rachel!" he said. "Doesn't she look beautiful?"

Rachel had lived on lettuce leaves and fat-free food for the past three months. She had gone from a size fourteen to a size twelve. The figure-hugging cream dress with its daring scooped neckline made her look glamorous and less like the Rachel we all knew.

"She does and so does my wife."

Gary's father chuckled. "Your wife always looks beautiful."

"You're so lucky, Gary! I can't recall my parents ever cuddling me or saying nice things to me," I said as I watched Gary's parents walk hand in hand towards the dance floor.

Gary took me in his arms. "I know, Michelle, but I'm here now." He said the words with conviction.

I could see Eleanor at the bar. She wore a simple pink dress that did wonders for her dark complexion. Rosemary had gone shopping with her and insisted that she buy it. Her face was transformed with a bright smile when she saw me. I waved at her to come over and join us.

"Michelle, what will you have to drink?" she asked.

"That dress was worth every penny," I said.

Eleanor raised an eyebrow. "Pink is not my colour."

"Well, Rosemary said it looked divine on you and I have to agree."

"To Rosemary!" Eleanor said and we clinked glasses.

We danced together, Gary and I, with Jack running around us. The best part of the wedding for me was when it was over. Everyone was too damn happy for my liking.

* * *

The weekend passed in a haze; next thing I knew, it was Monday and I was back at my desk again.

"Tell me all about the wedding," Rosemary said.

"We had a wonderful day and Sunday we went out for lunch and brought Jack to the cinema."

"I see," she said, her tone sceptical.

The evening Rosemary came to my house for dinner, I handed her a glass of wine and asked her never to mention Damien's name again. I told her not to take any messages from him for me. I answered the phone to him once and hung up straight away. The next time I thought it was Damien, I hung up, only to find out later it was a customer.

I did all these things and yet here I was on Monday morning, wishing she'd mention his name. Just to hear his name out loud would conjure up a picture of him.

"How about I make us two coffees?"

"It's my turn," I said, jumping up.

I couldn't trust myself to be left in the office alone with the phones.

Eleanor was in the canteen. Her eyes looked glazed.

"I really enjoyed the wedding and you looked great," she said, as she spooned two sugars into her coffee. "I can't remember if I told you on Saturday or not."

"Thanks," I said. "Bob seems nice." He had joined her for the evening part of the wedding.

"Mmm," she said. She was about to pour boiling water into her cup. She paused and said, "Yes, Michelle, he's a nice man." Her face fell into composed lines.

I spooned coffee into two mugs.

"I'm afraid I've had some customer complaints," she said.

"Who from?"

"Baxter and he's a good customer."

"It's not my fault that stupid driver lost his package."

"Michelle, calm down! We can discuss this in a civilised manner."

I poured boiling water into the two mugs.

"I'd like for us to meet, say eleven. I have the new schedule and I'd like to go over a few things."

"Great," I said and I longed to add, 'I can't wait'.

I got two Twix bars out of the snack-machine. We would need some comfort food before our meeting.

At five to eleven, just as I was about to forward the phone to reception, I took a call. Listening to a customer complaint was better than being bored stiff by Eleanor going on and on about customer service and how we could improve.

"Hi," Damien said.

"Hi," I responded.

My heart was drumming against my chest.

"Sorry about your father," I said. Rosemary was standing in the corridor waiting for me. She waved at me to hurry up.

"Thanks," he said.

"How are you?"

"I'm okay. I suppose. I'm in a kind of limbo. I don't know how I am. I suppose I'm numb."

"Damien, I wish I could be with you but I can't," I blurted out.

"I know," he said. He paused and then added, "My father made a will and he's left something to you. I'm going to see the solicitor tomorrow. You have to come along too."

"Michelle," Rosemary said, stepping back into the office. She looked at me knowingly.

"I have to go – a meeting," I said.

"Will you ring me?" His voice was low. He sounded unsure, almost nervous.

"Of course."

"What was that all about?" Rosemary asked.

I stabbed at the phone, punching in the keys to forward to reception.

"We're late," I said ignoring her.

"I know we're bloody late! Tell me!"

"Not now."

We trotted down the corridor to Eleanor's office. I could see by the clock on her desk that we were seriously late.

"Sorry, I was dealing with a customer and I couldn't get away from him," I said.

We all exchanged smiles, then Eleanor opened her little notebook.

"I've just jotted down a few things which I'd like to discuss with you," she said.

"Great," said Rosemary.

I smiled indifferently.

Eleanor looked down at her list. I felt like Mr Bean. I was bored rigid and any minute now I was going to fall off the chair.

My head was filled with thoughts of Damien. When I was

about twelve, my mother's uncle left her money in his will. We were so excited. We thought we were going to be rich. Fifty miserable pounds was all he left. We were so disappointed.

"So Michelle, have you any suggestions?" Eleanor asked.

I stared at her blankly.

Then Rosemary said, "Well, we need more staff. It's impossible for us to do everything. Sometimes we can't even go to the loo because the phones never stop ringing."

"I'm well aware of how many calls you take," was Eleanor's crisp reply.

She looked at me levelly, waiting for my contribution. I had none to make.

"Eleanor," I said. "You've already made up your mind on what you're going to do. You're just humouring us asking for our contribution."

I could see she was a little taken back by what I had said. I knew it was a wrong career move to speak my mind. What you say and what you think are never the same in office politics. But how can the lines of communications ever run free if you can't speak your mind? I knew I should have kept my mouth shut, but I just couldn't. I was tired pretending.

Her phone rang. Rosemary and I exchanged quick glances. We could tell it was the MD. I stood up, dismissing myself.

Outside the office, Rosemary said, "I guess it's back to work for us."

"I hate my job," I confessed.

"Then you should look for something else. You shouldn't waste your life away here."

"Agreed," I said.

Chapter 13

"I presume that was Damien on the phone," Rosemary said.

"Yes," I replied. I picked up my nail file. It was ages since I had filed my nails. "He wants me to go to the solicitor's tomorrow. His father has left me something in his will."

"Michelle, that's great news!"

"How could that be great news?"

Rosemary's raised her eyes towards the ceiling. "Michelle, he could have left you money or property!"

"That sounds too good to be true."

The phone rang. Rosemary swore under her breath and then answered it.

"Can I call you back? My computer has just crashed," she said and hung up.

"Rosemary, you're asking for trouble doing that." I continued to file my nails.

"What time is your appointment with the solicitor?"

"I didn't ask."

"Michelle, ring him back!"

"I can't, it's too risky."

"Michelle, you're going to regret this." Her phone rang again. She put the caller on hold. "Ring him, go see the solicitor! Are you not dying with curiosity?"

"Rosemary, forward that call to me; I'll take it."

She put on her glasses. "How can you not want to know what he's left you?"

"Rosemary, take the bloody call and mind your own business," I said. The words were almost a snarl.

She flicked back her blonde bob, picked up the phone as elegantly as she could and spent the next ten minutes listening to a customer complaint.

"Sorry," I said when she eventually hung up. She took off her glasses, wiped them in a tissue and put them back on again.

Then my phone rang before we could warm up to another conversation.

"That was Mrs White, again," I said with disgust.

"What did she want?"

"For us to collect a consignment and drop one in Dublin and another in Dubai or some place like that."

"Couldn't you tell her to post it?" Rosemary said, then we laughed.

"It would probably get there before us."

The last thing I wanted to do was fall out with Rosemary. She was becoming so assertive. She had read numerous books and articles on how to have a baby and she was determined to have one. The only problem was that Danny was not co-operating. Things had to be assessed and monitored. Men had less sperm nowadays due to the fact that they sat in cars driving for too long, or they wore their underpants too tight. If the temperature went up by one degree sperm couldn't live. Of course, modern living didn't help. Danny drank too much, took too little exercise and all these factors killed off sperm. For herself she had taken to the new regime like a fish to water. She cut out the junk food, well almost, and reduced her intake of alcohol. She gave up wearing a thong and constantly monitored her temperature and charted her cycle on a daily basis. Still, nothing was happening.

She was growing more determined with each passing month and Danny was less and less interested in having intercourse, as she called it now. She never went out to have lunch with Danny. She had become aggressive. Some days I was actually afraid of her.

"This could be your one lucky break in life, like winning the Lotto. It's not every day something like this happens and you're just going to throw it away. Tell Gary – I'm sure he won't look a gift horse in the mouth even if you can." Again the glasses came off.

At that moment I wished every sperm in Danny's trousers was a dud. She just never gave up.

Eleanor was passing and stopped when she saw Rosemary wiping her eye with a tissue – she thought Rosemary was crying.

"What's wrong with her?" she mouthed to me.

"Nothing," I mouthed back.

I was in the canteen making coffee for Rosemary and myself, when she forwarded a call to me.

"I think you should take this call," she said.

"Is it Damien?"

"No, it's his solicitor's secretary."

"What does she want?"

"I don't know," she said.

"Would you ask her?"

"Of course I will," she said in a concerned tone, "but she mightn't want to tell me. They can be quite sticky about these things."

"Please ask her! I'll treat you to a Twix!"

"Make it a Kit Kat and you're on."

"You have an appointment to see the solicitor at twelve o'clock tomorrow morning," Rosemary announced the minute I walked back into our office. She picked up her pad and read out the address to me. "The office is on South Frederick Street – it's off Nassau Street."

"In Dublin," I said. I sat down because my legs were shaking. "I have no idea where South Frederick Street is – or Nassau Street."

"You can get a taxi from the station," Rosemary suggested.

"I'm not going," I said in a no-nonsense voice.

I picked up the phone the minute it rang. I took down the details for a delivery, I checked them twice with the customer. The last thing I wanted to do was get the address wrong or some other detail. I could tell he was losing patience with me. I was not in a caring mood, so I thanked him for his call and hung up.

"Aren't you dying to know what he's left you?" she asked for the twentieth time, breaking into my thoughts.

"Please, Rosemary, let it go!" I was still filling in the customer's details.

"Sorry," she said. She patted my hand with her long elegant one. "I'm just trying to help."

"I know."

Rosemary never mentioned Damien or the will for the rest of the afternoon. But she put the piece of paper on my desk, with the address of the solicitor and train times to Dublin.

Next morning I left Jack at the baby-sitter's and, instead of heading to work, I went to the train station. I had to wait half an hour for the train. I phoned work and told Eleanor that I had to take the day off. The line went quiet, as she waited for my explanation. I didn't have one.

Eventually, the train trudged into the station. I found a vacant window seat and sat down. In my pocket, I had the address of the solicitor's. I was steeling myself to be distant with Damien. I wanted to get this over with as quickly as possible, so I could get back to my life. My insides had turned to jelly and they wobbled all around.

I knew I was going to regret this, but I kept going. Fields unfurled in front of my eyes. I couldn't remember if I had kissed Jack goodbye that morning. I was too busy applying make-up, trying to fool myself that I didn't care.

Finally, the train arrived at Connolly station. I got out with all the other passengers.

Twenty minutes later I was standing outside the blue door that led into the solicitor's office. Inside, the place was ultra modern and it made me nervous.

When I told the secretary my name, she asked me for my full address. I gave it, then she wiggled off to make me a coffee and I sat back in the soft leather armchair.

Damien arrived in and sat down beside me. He refused coffee when she offered it.

We traded greetings.

Then, with that over he asked, "Did you drive or take the train?"

"I took the train."

He crossed his legs and uncrossed them again. I could tell he was nervous and a part of me was flattered.

"How are you?" I asked.

He rubbed his hands together, something I often saw my mother do.

"I'm fine," he said and forced a laugh. "I can't get used to this weather, all the rain. I'd forgotten that it rains all the time here."

I was dreaming of Sydney, wondering why the hell I had been so hasty. Why didn't I stay and see what would happen? Why did I have to run?

"Damien, good to see you," a loud voice said, making us both jump.

"I'm John Keating," he said, shaking my hand. "Tom's solicitor." Eventually he let go of my hand. "And you're Michelle." He was a tall man with a confident air about him.

Before I got a chance to say anything, he ushered us into his office and sat us both down. Damien and I exchanged nervous looks. He put on his glasses and then he started to read the will.

When my name was mentioned, automatically I turned to look at Damien. I wasn't sure if I heard the solicitor right. His father had left me his house in Westport?

"Gosh, that can't be," I said.

They both looked at me suddenly. I felt like I had grown a third head. "Sorry," I muttered. I sensed the atmosphere in the room had changed.

To his only son he left his house in Dublin. At this point John stopped and took a drink of water before he started to read down though the various investments that he had left to Damien.

Afterwards, John took us to a very fashionable restaurant. The place was full of executive types talking to themselves or into mobile phones.

"I can't take the house," were the first words out of my mouth when John went to the bar to get us a drink.

"My father wanted you to have it if you had his grandchild, and when he found out you hadn't he still wanted you to have it."

"How do I explain that I've inherited a house?"

Damien's face was shadowed. I knew that expression of old: he was sulking and this was something I didn't mind not having to endure regularly.

"Are you upset that he's given me the house?"

"No, no, I'm not. I just wish . . ." and the words trailed off. Then he laughed and said, "I'm shocked. I knew my father was going to die, but when it happens you realise how short life is. You see things differently."

After lunch John went back to his office.

"What now?" I said to Damien.

We were still sitting at the table. The restaurant was almost empty.

"We could stroll around town or go back to my father's house."

"I didn't mean that," I said. My heart was pounding against my ribs. "I meant what are you going to do?"

He shrugged. "I'm going to stay in Dublin," he said with calculated ease.

I glanced at my watch. "I have to go." I picked up my jacket.

"Go?" he said.

"Yes."

"I thought you were going to stay –"

I butted in and said, "Damien, I only came because you wanted me to."

"I thought you'd stay. I'd love some company – it's not much fun walking around the city on your own."

"I can't," I said. Strings of tension had started to snap inside me. At any minute now I was going to break. "Bye," I muttered and moved away.

"I'll call you!"

Round and round the words went. Crashing off the corners of my head and back again. *I'll call you!* I wanted to forget those words. I couldn't afford to hang onto them. They'd cost me too much.

For the first time in my life, I owned something. The most valuable thing I had before was my leather jacket and that was a present from Gary.

I started to invent a story. A distant cousin belonging to my mother has left me a house. The train trudged out of Connolly station. I rested my head back on the seat and wished I knew a way out of this. A safe easy route, that wouldn't hurt any one.

When I arrived at Longford station. Rosemary was there with Jack.

"Michelle, I just collected Jack for you. I'll see you tomorrow."

"Choo-choo!" Jack was saying, his tubby little finger pointing.

"Slow down, Rosemary, don't go," I said, holding her arm.

"I brought Jack to feed the ducks and then we went for a burger and chips," she said hurriedly.

"Thanks," I said. "I need to talk to you."

"No, Michelle, it's Gary you need to be talking to – I'll see you tomorrow."

"You're right," I said.

"I'll see you tomorrow."

Jack and I waved at Rosemary as she drove off in her red saloon car.

"Hello, darling, did you have a good time?" I asked.

Jack hit my face with his hand. "Stop that," I said. He hit me again. "Stop," I said more firmly.

I wrestled with him and strapped him into his car seat. He fought me every step of the way.

The kitchen smelled stale; I opened the window and the back door. The rain had stopped so I could let Jack out to play. I switched on the kettle and made a cup of coffee. Jack was busy unloading sand off his tractor, while it was my job to shovel it on. We played this game in relative silence. I was waiting, listening to hear Gary's key in the front door. I had nothing planned to say to him.

I knew I should be preparing dinner, or at least washing up the dishes; these chores that always seemed to be left for me to do. Seeing Jack playing, looking so contented, soothed me.

When the phone rang I was expecting it to be Damien or my mother. I was surprised when it was Gary.

"Gary, what time will you be home?"

"I don't know," he said.

"Do you have to work late every evening?" I asked.

"Yes," he replied sourly.

"Gary, it's a lovely evening. Jack is outside playing with his tractor." I was hoping to tempt him.

"See you later," he said.

* * *

Days passed. I sat at my desk, staring at the grey wall and wondering what I was going to do. It was the only thought in my head. I asked myself this question, attempted to answer it, then my insides would quiver with fear at the thought of doing anything.

Eventually, Damien rang, setting the wheels in motion. He invited me to Westport. He wanted to give me the keys and a tour of the place. Could I wait until Saturday? I had to. I didn't want to, but I had to.

I wanted to tell everyone I owned a house, that I was rich, but I couldn't get the words out of my mouth. The only person I confided in was Rosemary. I had her told before I could stop myself.

It was Tuesday. The week stretched out in front of me, endless hours of monotony and boredom. Outside, it was raining.

Gary was working on Saturday. I told him that I was going to spend the day with Rosemary. He was hardly listening to me when I said it. My mother was delighted to have Jack for the day. I was free to go to Westport on my own. I had everything organised.

I was busy in my lunch-hour dashing into boutiques looking at clothes. I ignored the price tags and just fitted on what I liked.

Chapter 14

I felt like a child again. It was Friday night and I couldn't sleep I was so excited. In fact I couldn't believe that I had waited for the weekend. Whenever I looked forward to something it never happened.

My foot was pushed hard against the accelerator all the way to Westport. I had never treated my car so badly. I drove up the drive, my eyes taking in every detail as I looked around at the magnificent place that was now mine.

Damien came out the front door.

We hugged. I pulled back from him, my eyes turning towards the house.

"Gosh, this is really posh," I said.

He pulled me towards the front door, swept me up in his arms and carried me over the threshold.

"Welcome home," he said and kissed me.

"Put me down before I break your arms," I said in protest.

We both laughed as he put me down in the hall. His arms were around me and before I knew what was happening, he was kissing me and I was responding. Logic was abandoned. All reason was gone. The pleasure of kissing his lips was sending shivers of excitement up my spine. I couldn't wait for more. He took off my jacket.

In a corner of my mind, something was saying that this was wrong, but I didn't want to listen. I was having too much fun. The best fun I had in a long time. My new jacket was thrown on the floor. I tugged at his shirt, pulling it out from his jeans and running my hand up towards his nipple. I knew this always excited him.

He groaned with pleasure. Damien kissed my neck in just the right place. I felt myself relax. My whole body was limp and liquid and eager. We were mounting the stairs, taking two steps at a time, laughing and touching each other as we went. At the top of the stairs, I tripped. We fell together. We stopped there, both of us yanking down our jeans. I guided him into me.

"Oh Damien," I said.

Five years was a long time, yet my body responded to him like it always had. An exquisite feeling ran through me again. We were holding on; I knew he wanted to make it last for me and at the same time I knew we were reaching a climax. I knew us so well.

He shouted my name and then went quiet.

We lay for a few minutes at the top of the stairs, just holding each other.

"Where is Nancy?"

"Making scones in the kitchen"

I looked at him in astonishment.

"Joking," he said.

I punched him playfully in the ribs and he pretended to be hurt.

"Sorry," I said, kissing him on the nose, on the cheek, on the forehead, on the chin, like I did with baby Jack.

"Nice," he said, his voice thick with emotion.

"Does Nancy know that your father has given me this house?"

Damien nodded. "I told her. She's worried about her job – she doesn't think you'll be keeping her on."

I laughed at the thought.

He stood and helped me up. He ran his hands through my tossed hair and helped me fix my jeans. I had forgotten this part of the ceremony.

"You look great," he said.

I wrinkled up my nose like I used to and he kissed it.

He took my hand in his and we walked down the stairs.

"Let me show you around," he said.

The guided tour came with a lot of kisses and hugs. I couldn't take it all in. I was left speechless by the grandeur of the whole place. Reception rooms that Jack would delight in cycling his tricycle through, antique furniture covered in chintz fabric. I didn't feel this house was mine; I didn't deserve it. When I tried to say this to Damien, he refused to let me speak about it. In fact, we didn't do much heart-to-heart talking.

We sat in the kitchen and had coffee, then we strolled into the garden and down the gravel path towards the sea. We were hungry and started to walk towards town.

Did I dare to enjoy this, to forget everything? I dared to,

but I couldn't. As we walked into the pub I saw a little girl in a buggy. I looked at the woman who was pushing the buggy; I could see a resemblance. They looked like mother and daughter. My stomach muscles took on a life of their own and made weird noises.

"I'm starving," I said.

A man was standing at the bar and for a minute I thought he was Gary.

The pub was almost empty so we got the window-seat. In the distance I could see the blue line of the sea. It felt like I was on holiday.

Damien took my hand in his. "Would you like something to drink first?" He seemed so relaxed, oblivious to all that was going on in my head.

"I'm not sure – I'm driving," I said. I felt relieved he knew my plans.

"Michelle," he said, "you can't go back today! I thought you were going to spend the weekend with me!"

"I can't do that."

Our eyes met and held.

"Shall I order us a drink?"

I nodded and he walked up to the bar.

"They'll bring our drinks down," he said when he came back. He took my hand in his. "Why can't you stay at least tonight?"

In the distance I could see that the little girl had got out of her buggy. She started to push the buggy. Her mother frowned, took the buggy from her and put it in the corner. She said something to the little girl who, I could tell, was ignoring her.

"It's not that simple."

"Michelle, it is that simple."

A glass of white wine and a pint of Guinness were put on our table.

I sipped some wine, for something to do, to divert myself. "I have a son called Jack – I need to spend time with him too."

He ran his fingers through his hair. He took a long drink out of his pint, then picked up the menu and started to read it. I looked at the blackboard with today's specials, my eyes then returning to the little girl and her mother. My heart felt heavy in my chest.

"I'll have the catch of the day with chips," I said.

"Me too," Damien said and closed the menu.

We sat, an uncomfortable silence growing between us.

"What's your son like?" Damien asked.

"He's wonderful," I said. "I feel guilty for leaving him behind. He has never been to the sea."

"Why don't you take a few days off work and bring him down?"

"Gosh," I said. Stunned by this. "Are you going to stay in Westport?" My heart was thumping so hard against my ribs I could hardly hear his answer.

"Weekends, if you let me. After all, it's your house now, not mine."

"Great," I said.

Our food arrived. I missed my son's chubby little hands, pulling at my plate, stealing my chips while he ignored his own lunch.

"Sarah, come back!"

I turned to look. The little girl had run out of the door, her mother running after her. A few seconds later they returned.

The little girl was screaming and kicking to get out of her mother's arms.

"What a racket!" Damien said.

I knew I had to go home this evening regardless of how wonderful a time I was having. Then it dawned on me: I was miserable without my son.

"What's wrong?" Damien asked, the words soft and coaxing.

"I'm missing Jack," I said.

"How about a walk on the beach?"

"Great," I said.

"We can finish up with coffee at home and then . . ." He didn't finish the sentence.

I opened my wallet.

"Please let me," he said.

I protested.

"No, I insist," he said.

"I'd like to."

Damien paid. We walked out hand in hand. I made a point of not looking for the little girl and her mother. I didn't want to see them.

We strolled at a leisurely pace towards the sea.

"Do you ever wonder what our child would have looked like?" Damien asked.

I stopped, turned my back to the sea and looked at him.

"Damien," I said, my voice almost a whisper, "I'm not sure I can find the words to answer that."

He looked from me to the sea.

"I wish Jack was my son," he said.

"I know," I said, rubbing his arm softly.

We walked on in silence.

The sea was almost still, but not quite. I heard its timeless motion as it rolled in and retreated out again. In the distance, the sky dipped into the sea and they both merged into one. I tried to take in every detail. I wanted to remember this day for the rest of my life. This was the day that we walked together and mourned the death of our child. I could hear our footsteps on the wet sand.

Damien squeezed my hand as we walked on. We seemed to be walking in a vacuum; it was like the wind was holding its breath. I looked at the sullen sky and wondered if Tom was up there with our lost baby. I squeezed Damien's hand and turned to look at him. I could read nothing in his passive face.

When I'm lying in my bed staring at the ceiling I want to recall this memory, I thought, and yet I felt I would not be able to. It felt like I was standing in a picture postcard. Nothing was familiar about this beautiful scene. I didn't know this place, I was a stranger here. I was used to a different landscape. A familiar boring landscape that's easy on the eye.

Damien was lost in a world of his own. I squeezed his hand again. He responded by squeezing mine.

"I love it here," he said.

"It's beautiful," I replied. We stopped and turned towards the sea. A seagull was riding the wind; at last this tranquil picture had got some life in it.

"I don't want this day to end," I said.

"Neither do I," he said and kissed my hand. "I want you to come back to my house and stay the night."

I watched the gull, effortlessly hovering.

"I was glad I lost the baby. I couldn't face having it on my own," I said. At last I had spoken the words that I had held in for an eternity.

Damien kissed my hand again. "I'm sorry, darling, that I wasn't there for you."

The seagull was joined by others.

"Let's go back," Damien said as he turned around.

I wanted to stay longer.

He tugged my arm a little. I smiled to myself – he reminded me of Jack.

"I have to go," I said. I hated saying the words, but they had to be said. I needed to convince Damien and myself at this stage.

"Please stay!" He turned to me and kissed me on the lips.

"Damien," I said, my voice a plea, "I can't."

He let go my hand. We walked on, the only sound our feet crunching the gravel.

Tears welled up in my eyes. I wiped them away.

My car keys were in my pocket. I squeezed them hard. When we arrived back at the house I walked towards my car. Damien ignored me.

"Bye," I muttered.

I sat into my car and turned the key in the ignition.

I could hear his quick footsteps on the gravel. He opened my car door.

"Please don't go," he said.

"I have to. I have to spend some time with Jack, he needs me," I said as softy as I could.

"I know you have to go, but I want you to stay."

"Damien, I have to go and I think it's best if I go now." I wrapped my arms around his neck. "I love you, Damien, I always have and I always will, but right now I have to go. I

143

don't want to go. I want to stay here with you, but I have to go."

He nodded. "Sorry. I'm just being a selfish bastard." He laughed. "I can't help myself."

I remained sitting in the car, even though every fibre of my being ached to get out and be with him.

He stood up.

"Bye, my love," he said.

"Bye," I managed before the tears started to come.

I willed myself to turn the key in the ignition. The car started. When I reached the road, I had to stop and wipe my eyes. I looked at the sea. I felt Tom was looking on at us. I wondered if the baby I never knew hated me for wishing it dead. I felt sick at the thought.

"Jack, Jack I love you," I said as I turned the car for home.

I felt I had to cry. I wasn't sure why, but a few tears slid down my face and I felt better. At least now I wasn't totally enjoying myself. I phoned my mother. She waffled on about all the things Jack had done. I promised myself that I would spend all the next day playing with Jack.

Chapter 15

I had all this guilt inside me. I didn't know where I was going to hide it. No matter how I tried to conceal it, I felt that everyone saw it. Behind every casual comment something more was lurking. I suspected that everyone knew what I was up to.

My time was spent dreaming up situations and playing them out. I had lost touch with reality, my day-to-day reality.

It was Sunday afternoon. Gary was sitting across the kitchen table reading the newspaper. Jack was upstairs having a nap. Usually, we would make love while our son slept. We had broken away from this traditional Sunday ritual and I was relieved.

The air between us was punctured with tension. I didn't have the energy to patch it up. So, we walked around each other, functioning. The kitchen looked even more neglected than usual. The floor needed to be washed. It seemed to me that I was the only person in the house that noticed; therefore I chose to ignore it.

It was when the front doorbell rang that I snapped out of my self-induced daze and looked around me in horror.

"Who the hell could that be?" I said, panic-stricken.

I braved it to the door and opened it. Gary's parents stood there.

"We haven't seen you all week, so we decided to drop by and say hello," his mother said.

They were dressed up in their Sunday best. I smiled weakly and stood frozen to the spot. I didn't want her to see the mess that we were currently living in.

"Can we come in?" Joe said and clapped his hands together, his aged face bright with a friendly smile.

I opened the door and allowed them to enter. "Of course you can." I shouted down the hall to Gary, *"It's your parents!"*

He came out to the hall to greet them, a smile plastered on his face as he gave his mother a big hug.

"Hello," he said.

I wished I was anywhere but there.

"Gary, we told you we might drop by today," his mother said. Her long nose had sniffed out my distress.

"Come on in," Gary said and led them into the sitting-room. "Jack is in bed."

I walked into the kitchen and switched on the kettle. In the sitting-room, Gary switched on the TV. They laughed at some joke that he made.

"Gary, can you come here, please?" I shouted from the kitchen.

"What?" he said as he sauntered in.

"You knew your parents might drop by today and you never bothered to mention it," I said in a loud whisper.

"You're never bloody here to tell you anything," he replied, his voice slightly raised.

"They're your bloody parents – you entertain them! I'm going for a walk."

"You can't do that," Gary said. He opened the cupboard door to look for some clean mugs. There were none. They were in the sink, dirty.

"Your mother gave us some Denby mugs. They're packed in a box in the spare room upstairs. Why don't you get them? It'll be easier on you than washing up."

He gave me a dirty look and then turned his back on me. I heard the sink filling with water as I put my coat on in the hall.

"Gary never told me you were coming. I have to pop out, see you later," I said, hoping my voice had the right degree of sincerity. They smiled at me. I felt his mother's beady eyes zoom in on my face – she was trying to read my thoughts. "Bye," I added and left before they got a chance to delay me with some small talk.

I drove into town and parked the car.

Rain trickled down the windscreen. I sat and stared and wondered what was I doing on a Sunday afternoon here on my own.

A man in a worn coat passed the car. Two children ran on ahead of their parents towards the newsagent's. They almost crashed into the woman that was coming out armed with a bundle of newspapers. It was Eleanor. I could tell she was annoyed by the children's behaviour.

I got out of my car and walked over to her. "Hi," I said.

She fixed her papers under her arm. "Hi, Michelle."

"What are you up to?"

"What do you mean?"

"Only out buying the papers now," I said.

"Oh, yes," she said. She blushed. "I slept in this morning." She was dressed in faded jeans and an old sweatshirt. Her face was make-up free; she looked younger.

"I see."

"And what are you up to?"

I looked at her and shrugged. "Nothing." I was thinking about Damien. I wanted to phone him, but felt it was better to leave it until tomorrow. I reasoned that today was my family day.

I was here in this space, acting out the part of Michelle who I once was.

"I don't suppose you'd like to come back and have a coffee with me?" she asked.

I really wanted to go to the pub and have a drink, but it was the best offer I was going to get, so I accepted. "I'd love to."

Eleanor looked at me, surprised. Normally I would make up an excuse. Spending time with her always reminded me of work.

"You've done loads since I was here last," I said, looking around.

Eleanor had bought her own house last year. The place had a minimalist feel about it. Me, I liked a bit of clutter – it's what I was used to.

"Michelle, it must be over a year since you were here," she said in that formal air that she always used at work.

"Time flies," I replied.

She led the way into her spacious kitchen, which was equipped with every cooking utensil you could possibly

148

want. I wondered why she bothered with all this as she
hated to cook.

"Coffee?"

I nodded. She took out two pottery mugs and started to
makes us coffee.

"How's Bob?"

"He's fine."

I noticed the way she smiled at the mention of his name.

"Is he Mr Right?"

The vase of lilies looked lush and extravagant in this
otherwise minimalist kitchen.

Eleanor placed a plate of biscuits on the table along with
our coffee mugs before she sat down. Then she surprised me
by saying, "Yes, I think he is Mr Right."

"That's great," I said.

"I'm not so sure."

"Oh Eleanor," I butted in. "Why are you always so cautious?
Give it a chance – just fall in love and stop thinking about all
the other things."

She sipped her coffee, her eyes glazed, immersed in her
own thoughts.

"But I can't help thinking about all the other things as
you put it. He's separated, he's got three children."

She looked across her coffee mug at me. I felt sympathy
for this professional woman. She had invested her life in her
career and now wanted someone to share it with.

"He'll go back to his wife, they always do."

"Eleanor, you can't know that for sure."

"He's with them now," she said. She unfolded her
newspaper on the spotless table. "And look at me, here on
my own."

I noticed the tiny lines around her eyes. She opened her Sunday paper. She was steeling herself not to cry. Tomorrow, she would be fine. Eleanor would be back on her stage performing her role and giving it everything.

"Thanks for the coffee," I said.

"You're welcome." Her voice quivered a little. She folded her paper. "Sorry, Michelle, I'm not much company today." She stood up and stretched her arms over her head. Something about the gesture reminded me of the young Eleanor. "Fancy a drink?"

"Yes, just a small one, I'm driving."

She poured us two generous glasses of wine.

She sat with her eyes closed, composing herself. This was a side of Eleanor I had never seen before. Her solitary life had suddenly become tinged with other people's domestic concerns and she didn't like it.

"Give it time," I said softly. The universal slogan, give it bloody time. I wondered if that was what I was attempting to do. Was I going too fast? Or too slow?

"It must be hard for him. He probably feels guilty leaving his children."

"He bores me to death when he starts talking about them."

"He loves them, they're a part of him. He can't just forget about them."

Eleanor was drinking her wine too fast. "I wish he was single. I hate all these complications." She poured herself another glass of wine.

"Life is complicated."

"It sure as hell is."

I knew this was my chance to slip in about Gary needing

help with his accounts. It was a good idea. Eleanor would have him so busy doing everything by the book he wouldn't notice what I was up to.

Eleanor looked at me, a glimmer of interest in her eye.

"Gary's not doing very well. I know everyone says there is a building boom on, but it hasn't benefited us."

"Gary," she said and shook her head as if she was reminiscing about something. "I never thought you'd end up marrying Gary." The wine had loosened her tongue.

"Why?"

She gulped some wine and said, "Because he's Gary."

I raised an eyebrow.

Eleanor giggled into her hand. "Sorry, the wine!" She poured some more into our glasses. "Gary is just so," she shrugged, "nice and ordinary and uncomplicated."

I drank some wine down. "His accounts are very complicated. They're stacked high in my kitchen."

Eleanor gulped down some more wine. "Accounts, probably the only thing I'm good at. I could take a look at them if you like. I'm not promising anything, but at the moment I have a lot of time on my hands."

"Eleanor, that would be great! We could do with all the help we can get."

"I'll give Gary a ring."

I finished my wine and said, "I'd better go."

She tilted her head sideways. "Okay."

I hugged her. "Thanks. Are you going to be all right?"

She nodded and whispered a throaty, "Of course I'll be fine – you know me."

Chapter 16

I stared at the ceiling, my eyes following the cracks down from the centre. Jack was asleep beside me. He always fell off quickly when he was in bed with me. Gary had gone into town, to see his friend Donal. The minute I walked into the house Gary walked out. He was annoyed with me for leaving him to entertain his parents on his own.

I wanted to talk to Gary. I wanted him to anchor me down, to put an end to the craziness that was going on in my head. I wanted to show him the jewellery and the solicitor's letter hidden under my car seat.

I lay on our double bed in the muted light, staring at the ceiling. I tried phoning Damien, but his mobile was switched off. I tried phoning his house in Westport, but it was ex-directory. I couldn't remember the Dublin address, so I couldn't try him there.

In my head, I was actually packing my suitcase. I could see myself folding up Jack's buggy and putting it in the car.

I would wrap Jack in his blanket and put him in his seat in the car. I wanted to leave. I wanted to walk away from Gary, just go. But something kept stopping me, something kept holding me back.

I closed my eyes and thought of Westport. Fragments of the picture came together. The Atlantic, magnificent as it moved in light and shade under a canopy of blue sky.

Damien hadn't given me the keys for the house in Westport. I turned on my side. I was fed up of looking at the ceiling.

A single tear slid down my cheek as I thought about the baby we lost. I turned to look at Jack. His beautiful face always made me smile with maternal pride. I heard Gary's key in the door, his quiet footsteps as he climbed the stairs. He gently turned the handle of the bedroom door.

"Hi," he said.

He looked down at our sleeping son, then he bent down and kissed him.

"I should have told you my parents were coming today – it just slipped my mind," he said.

I looked at this honest man who I had known since childhood and I couldn't understand how I could cheat him. All men are not bastards. I thought they were until I fell into Gary's waiting arms when I returned from Sydney. It didn't make sense. How could I be unfaithful to Gary? How could I cheat on him? He was the father of my son. My lover and my best friend. But I had only to hear Damien's voice and I went weak.

"Let's forget about it," I whispered.

"What's happening to us?"

"What do you mean?" I said, my eyes steady on his face even though I couldn't see it with the growing dark.

"I mean, you've changed, maybe I've changed." He sat down on the bed.

"We're stressed," I said and reached out and touched his arm.

He nodded his agreement, but I wasn't sure he believed me. He ran his fingers though Jack's hair. I knew the time was right to say something, to be honest with Gary.

"He's gorgeous," he said.

"He is, isn't he?"

I knew he wanted to get into our double bed, but he was waiting for me to say something. I yawned.

"Will I put Jack in his cot?" he asked.

"You'll waken him."

"I mightn't," he said.

"I'm not prepared to risk it."

After a pause he said, "Goodnight." His shoulders drooped as he left the bedroom.

I lay awake. The darkness turned to a grey light. Soon it would be morning and I would have to get up and go to work. Another bloody Monday morning awaited me. I closed my eyes and thought about Damien.

* * *

"You look great," Rosemary said and smirked at my dishevelled appearance.

"Thanks," I said, aware that I was very late.

"How was your weekend?" she asked, oblivious to my sensitive mood this morning.

"Rosemary, I'll make the coffees and then ask me how I feel."

She beamed me a bright smile. My phone rang and she picked it up. "It's for you."

I took the phone, gripping the receiver like it was my lifeline.

"Damien," I said. "It's so good to hear from you."

Rosemary picked up our two coffee mugs and left the office.

"I missed you," he said.

Rosemary's phone rang.

"Can you hold on? I have to take a call – I won't be a moment."

I cut the caller off, then returned to my seat.

"I'm in Dublin today. I'm meeting with David, remember him? He's got his own company here now."

"I see," I said, pretending to be interested. "When will I see you again?" I hadn't meant to ask that question, yet it slipped out before I could stop it.

There was a pause and then he said, "I'm not sure."

"Damien," I said, feeling unsure of myself. I was lost and I couldn't read the directions. My heart almost sprang out of my mouth. Surely he wasn't phoning to say goodbye?

"We could meet next weekend?"

I swallowed, relieved that at least he was still interested. "I – I –" I stuttered and then said, "I'd love to, Damien."

"Then I'll meet you in Westport next Friday night."

"Damien, I can't just –"

"Michelle, I've got to go, I'll ring you later. We'll talk."

The line went dead.

Then, I got an irritated caller who claimed he had spent the last ten minutes trying to get through. Every customer that we had ever done a delivery for was ringing, making stupid enquiries that were on the brochure if they'd care to read it.

I wanted to talk to Rosemary, but the phones just kept on ringing. I hadn't time to clock-watch, but I eyed it occasionally.

Eventually, the day ended. I was tired of talking. All I wanted to do was collect Jack and go home. My evening would be filled by monotonous, never-ending housework. I knew this wasn't the frame of mind I needed to get things done. If I got really engrossed in my chores perhaps it would help me forget about Damien. Then I could sink back into my marriage, to that place where I was before Damien came back into my life.

I opened the front door. My shoes felt like lead boots weighing me down. I felt unable to walk down the hall with my groceries.

"Jack, come on, hurry up," I shouted urgently at him.

He was standing outside, a ball in his hand.

"I haven't time to play ball!" I heard myself yell.

Jack started to cry. I dropped the groceries and ran to him. "Sorry, pet, sorry, Mammy is tired." I soothed back his curly hair. "Come on, let's play ball."

Chapter 17

Time stood still. Every minute dragged by, making the hours feel longer than they actually were. I watched the clock with an intensity that was disturbing to Rosemary. She kept telling me to stop looking at the clock.

I just couldn't wait for Friday evening. We'd drive separately to Westport. A key for the back door was under a stone beside the big old flower pot. When I asked him to be more specific, he told me to just stand back and look at the back door, then turn my head slightly to the right and I'd see the flower pot and to the left of the pot was a big stone. Already I was exhausted. "It's been there for years," he said, "and no one has ever thought to look there for it. It's one of the family's best-kept secrets!" What family, I wanted to ask him? A father and a son living on opposite sides of the planet didn't add up to a family.

I wanted to bring Jack with me. Was it too soon to introduce them? I didn't know. I had nothing organised.

Rosemary had taken a new approach with Danny. She was in her surrendered phase. She rang him constantly. She actually started to agree with him and say things like "Yes, Danny" and "If you say so, Danny". Rosemary, the resident fashion expert, had started to ask Danny for his opinion on what clothes she should wear. I couldn't see it lasting – somewhere along the way the real Rosemary was going to erupt.

She wanted me to surrender too. Then she asked me the awkward question: Which man did I want to surrender to?

The two of them, of course. I didn't want to hurt Gary and I certainly wasn't going to hurt Damien – he was after losing his father, he needed me.

Rosemary made the stupid suggestion that I should tell Gary the truth. Gary was going to find out eventually, so why didn't I come clean?

On Wednesday night, we sat watching *Coronation Street*. I had gone to the trouble of cooking a chicken with roast potatoes and vegetables. I had even attempted to make gravy. It was one of Gary's favourite meals.

Baby Jack was sleeping on his father's chest. I looked at the two of them and felt nothing but hatred for myself. It rose in my gut and swelled in my chest, making it hard for me to breathe.

I thought of Damien and me walking on the beach, our hands entwined, the never-ending music of sea in my ears. I wanted to live by the sea, to wake up every morning to the sound of it, to feel the spray against my face, to feel myself living instead of existing here with Gary.

I had my lines rehearsed for Gary.

He kissed his son on the head. "I'll put him to bed," he

whispered, then took him in his arms and went upstairs with him.

When Gary came downstairs I had two coffees made.

"Thanks," he said.

"Are you busy this weekend?"

I felt his eyes on my face. I looked into my coffee mug, I couldn't look him in the eye.

"Fairly," he said.

I opened my mouth and said, "Rosemary has invited myself and Jack to Westport for the weekend." Rosemary and Danny were off to Pairs for the weekend.

We didn't travel in the same social circles so the chances of Gary finding out were slim.

"Oh," he said. I heard the hurt in the word. I felt him aching to say; what about me? Like I would say if he had suggested going off to Westport without me.

"It will do you and Jack good," he said.

My hair fell down on my face. I peered at him through a curtain of hair. He smiled at me. I pushed my hair off my face and smiled back.

"This place is going to be quiet without you."

"Eleanor said she'd look at your accounts for you if you want," I said.

Gary made a face. I ignored him. We turned and stared at the TV.

Later that night, we made love. With my eyes closed I felt every touch, every caress was Damien's and not Gary's.

* * *

"Michelle, you're mad," Rosemary said next morning when

I informed her of my plans. "I don't like you using me to lie to Gary."

"Rosemary, you were the one who told me I should go to the funeral!"

"Don't look at me like that!" She put on her glasses. All this surrendering was making her into a right bore. "I can't believe you're doing this."

"Rosemary, promise me you'll tell no one."

"Of course I bloody won't tell anyone, not when you're using me," she said. She took off her glasses and added, "I'm as bad as you, bloody swearing all the time."

I raised an eyebrow at all this high drama. "Rosemary, I have to do this," I said, my voice steady. "I don't enjoy lying to Gary, but I feel I've got to do this."

"I know, I'm just worried for you."

"No need to be. Think of it – I have a box of jewellery and the deeds to a house in Westport under the seat of my car."

"You're a mad bastard," Rosemary said and picked up her phone to answer a call. After the call she swung around in her chair and said, "You haven't thought this out very well."

"What have I missed?"

"Eleanor knows I'm going to Paris. What if she bumps into Gary and they start talking?"

"Well," I said, my head spinning as I tried to think of something, "I'll say I went to Westport on my own, that I just needed some time . . . and some space."

"Your plan is not fool proof."

"Any suggestions?"

She was in thinking mode; the glasses came off again.

"Please don't make them complicated," I added.

"Tell him the truth."

"I can't do that."

"What's the alternative?"

My phone rang and then Rosemary's. I had a thousand things to do, all work-related. I looked at my desk and wondered where I should start. The backlog had increased due to my lack of enthusiasm. The office door was always open. I looked down the corridor towards the front doors.

I wanted to pick up my bag and jacket and walk out, leaving all this behind. I felt if I did, I might take the next step and leave Longford behind me and go to Westport to live with Damien. I knew that's what he wanted even though we hadn't discussed it.

My eyes fell on my photograph of Gary and baby Jack. I knew he loved his son and would be devastated if I left him. I felt like I had been sedated for a long time and I had just woken up.

I took a pen and started to write my resignation.

Dear Eleanor,

I've enjoyed working here for the past number of years. I feel it's time that I moved on. Sorry to leave at such short notice, but I can't stand this place any longer. Bye Michelle.

I looked down at what I had scribbled on my post-it. Rosemary was busy typing. Was she sending me an e-mail? I waited, nothing happened. Damn, she was working. I tore up the note into tiny pieces and threw them into the bin.

* * *

"It's well for some," was how my mother responded when I told her on Thursday evening that I was going to Westport for the weekend. "And you're leaving Gary behind?"

161

I ignored what she had just said and turned my attention towards Jack who was sitting on the kitchen floor playing with a ball.

"Catch!" I said as I gently threw the ball. "Good boy!" I clapped when he managed to grasp it.

My mother grunted. She switched on the kettle.

We sat opposite each other at her kitchen table and drank tea. She told me the same gossip she told me yesterday. I listened, pretending to be interested. I was already packing. The countdown had begun. It was only a matter of hours until we were together. I couldn't believe everything had worked out so well for me.

I couldn't wait to see Damien and Jack together.

Gary suspected nothing. I was going to wake up on Saturday morning and hear the sea. I would look out my bedroom window and see the Atlantic. My insides quivered with excitement.

"You look happy with yourself," my mother remarked.

"I am happy."

She nodded. "Enjoy it while it lasts," she said.

Chapter 18

Eventually, Friday evening arrived. We drove to Westport. Jack slept most of the way which was good as I could drive in peace, but I knew he was going to be up all night.

Some things are hard to admit. It's easier to fool yourself and pretend that things are going well, when they are really not. The weekend was a disaster – there I have admitted it. Isn't it supposed to get easier when you admit, when you stop denying, when you take your head out of the clouds and see what's really going on. I know I'm spending to much time with Rosemary; she's into self-therapy now. We're trying to discover our real selves.

It was like Jack was programmed to do everything to upset my weekend. It was like going away with Gary. There was no long-drawn-out love-making because Jack was being his usual demanding self. And we had hardly any time to ourselves.

We were determined to make the most of it. Damien

drove us Achill Island. The place was deserted. He gave us a guided tour. He pointed at a mountain and told Jack and myself it was called Slievemore. He drove around the island and showed us Kildownet Castle where Grace O'Malley had a tower. He wanted to show us the beach at Keel. "It's one of my favourite places," he said.

Jack got sick in the car. When we arrived at the beach it started to rain and we couldn't go for a walk. We had to sit in the car and watch sheets of rain fall softly onto a metal ocean.

The car smelled of vomit. Damien went for a walk; he said he needed some fresh air. I wanted to go with him, but I couldn't leave Jack.

The next time would be better. It had to be.

* * *

Sitting down at my desk on Monday morning, exhausted was the only word that came to mind. I yawned and looked at the heap of paperwork that needed my attention. Rosemary had the day off.

It was a relief to have the office to myself. I switched on my PC and listened to the familiar hum. I picked up the phone to see if it was working. I was surprised at how quiet it was. Usually, Monday mornings were hectic.

Eleanor walked into the office.

"Hi," I said, putting a real effort into the greeting.

"You look exhausted. Motherhood doesn't suit you," she said and folded her arms across her flat chest.

"Thanks," I mumbled.

"Michelle," she said and sat down on Rosemary's seat, "I've split up with Bob."

I looked at her and felt nothing for her loss. Listening to her talk was like listening to my kitchen tap drip.

Eleanor tapped her hand impatiently on the desk. "He was the first man that I've really fallen for."

I looked at her and realised she was speaking my language now.

"When I'm with Bob, I just feel so comfortable, so relaxed. I met him at a history society evening. The minute he walked into the room, it was like my life stopped. I just couldn't take my eyes off him. I knew he was married and he had children, but I just couldn't help myself."

She pulled a tissue from the box on Rosemary's desk and blew her nose vigorously.

I was relieved when my phone rang – I was lost for words.

"Good morning," I said.

Eleanor picked up my coffee mug and waved it in front of my nose. I nodded and mouthed a thank you.

I was disappointed when it wasn't Damien. I knew he was going back to Dublin that day. I needed to hear his voice again. It would help to take me through the day, to face Gary this evening, to continue until next weekend when I was meeting Damien on Saturday in Dublin.

It was only Monday: four more days to go until I saw him again. I felt like an addict; I couldn't wait for my next fix. What was it about Damien that I couldn't say no to him? Here I was back in my life, pretending to be someone I wasn't – I was a fraud. How often had my father sat across the kitchen table from my mother and promised faithfully never to drink again. His words weren't worth the spit they were spoken with. The last person I wanted to be like was my mother and now I had ended up being a duplicate copy of my father.

We would meet this weekend and that would be the end of it.

Eleanor returned with my coffee.

Two girls were laughing in reception and it surprised me when Eleanor sat down again in Rosemary's chair. Usually, she would glide out past reception, throw a frosty look their way and everyone would pretend to get back to work.

"Had you a nice weekend?" she asked.

"It rained all weekend."

"Gary told me you'd gone to Westport with Rosemary. He rang me to have a look at his accounts."

I held my breath. I didn't know what she was going to say next.

"He told me you'd gone to Westport with Rosemary," she said.

I sipped some of the strong coffee; my body temperature was rising at an alarming rate. I felt myself blush.

"I just needed some time on my own," I said. "I told him Rosemary was coming with me because he'd only worry if he thought I was going on my own." The words came together easily.

She remained fixed in her position, her face unreadable.

Thoughts floated into my head like feathers and then they drifted away again before I got the chance to pin them down.

"Did you tell him that Rosemary was in Paris?" I found myself having to ask when she didn't volunteer the information.

She looked directly at me and said, "Michelle, I'm not stupid."

I smiled at her, relieved. "I'd appreciate if you didn't say anything to him."

"Is everything okay between you and Gary? I know it's none of my business, but he looked down when I met him on Saturday evening."

I sipped more coffee, hating the strong taste of it. I looked at my phone and silently urged it to ring.

"We're fine," I said.

My prayer was answered and my phone rang. She left my office and I watched her walk across the corridor to her safe world of numbers. I looked at her with envy: her world was controlled by figures. It was all very straightforward, laid down in black and white.

I was tempted not to take the call. It was five o'clock. Then, I decided to.

"Hi, Michelle," he said.

I had been waiting all day for this call.

"Damien." I leaned back in my chair.

"I'm shattered," he said and yawned.

"An early night for you," I said.

"Mmm," was his lazy response. I had to go home and do all the housework that hadn't got done all weekend.

"Michelle, you've got to tell Gary about us," he said, cutting short on the preamble, like he was losing patience with me. "You have to. I want you to come to Dublin."

"Damien, just give me some time."

"How much time do you need? Do you think it's fair what you're doing?"

"No."

"Well then, talk to him, tell him."

"Yes," I said.

"And, ring me when you've done it."

"Aye, aye Captain," I shot back.

"Michelle, I know you, I know you'll never do this unless I force you."

I said nothing; there was nothing I could say.

"Bye, Damien," I said, and hung up.

Eleanor looked up from her desk, surprised to see me in the building.

"Is everything all right?" she asked.

I took a breath and plunged in. "Did Gary say anything to you about me?"

Eleanor tilted her head and looked at me curiously. "No, he didn't."

"Oh, I see," I said.

"I went over some accounts with him – it's a dreadful mess, I'm surprised he's lasted this long. Then he treated me to a Chinese and he told me that you have been acting strangely lately."

I laughed. "Have I?"

Eleanor thought for a minute before she said, "Yes, you seem listless, like you're in another world."

"Things have been getting to me," I said. "That's why I thought the weekend away would do me good."

"It can't have been much fun with Jack."

"See you tomorrow," I said.

"Bye, Michelle," she said and turned her attention to her computer.

* * *

The evening didn't go according to plan. Gary's parents

arrived and we spent two hours making polite conversation.

"Eleanor said you're a mess," I said to Gary after his parents had left.

He laughed. "I am. But she said there's hope." He looked at me with honest eyes.

"Let's go to bed, it's late," I said, taking his hand in mine. I couldn't do it, I couldn't get the words out of my mouth. How do you say to your husband: I'm having an affair, give me some space and I'll get over it?

"I missed you and Jack," he said. He leaned his forehead against mine.

"Ah, Damien," I said.

He stopped. "What did you say?"

"This Damien guy kept ringing me today about a consignment that we charged him for that we never delivered," I said, all the words running into each other, "and, his name keeps popping into my head."

Gary chuckled. "Oh, Michelle!"

"Sorry," I mumbled and felt my world was going to come crashing in.

"First things first," he said and he took my hand and led the way upstairs.

* * *

Next morning, I walked down the corridor towards our office. Rosemary was sitting poised at her desk ready to fill me in on her exciting weekend. I was glad she was here to fill the office with her chatter. I noticed the duty-free bag on her desk. I knew there would be a dozen samples of perfumes and lipsticks in there for me to try out. A small box with gold wrapping paper was on my desk.

"Rosemary, you shouldn't have," I said.

"It's only perfume, I hope you like it."

I opened it and sprayed on the perfume. "Thank you very much!"

"You're welcome!"

My phone rang, then Rosemary's: our day had started. Today it was an air strike that had stopped packages being delivered. We attempted to explain to customers, tendered sympathy and round and round we went on the great big wheel of words, repeating over and over again why packages hadn't arrived on time.

I was glad of the hassle – we had no time for talking and more importantly no time for clock-watching.

For once, I was last to switch off my PC. We forwarded our phones to the answering machine.

Gary rang to say he was on his way home. This was a nice surprise. Since my weekend away he had become more attentive. I had just left down the phone when it rang again. It was Damien.

"Michelle, sorry about the last phone call," he paused. "I'm just scared of losing you," he said simply and clearly.

"Damien, I can't really talk," I said and yet I couldn't bear to hang up. I wanted to hold onto him. "Gary will be home soon."

"You haven't told him," he said.

"No," I said softly.

"Oh, Michelle."

"I have to go," I said. Gently I replaced the receiver in its cradle.

"I'm home," Gary shouted as he walked in the front door.

"Daddy, Daddy!" called Jack as he ran towards him.

Next morning, I rang Damien and told him I couldn't meet him that weekend. He got angry that I hadn't told Gary. I got angry that he couldn't give me some more time. He rang back and apologised, then rang later and told me he loved me. I rang him back and told him I was missing him and maybe next weekend we could meet.

Chapter 19

"Hi sis," Vincent said.

"Hi."

"You sound a little gloomy. Or were you expecting someone else to ring?"

I looked across the kitchen table at Gary. He was looking at some invoices with a confused expression on his face.

"No, I'm just trying to help Gary with his accounts. And I wish you'd stop calling me 'sis'."

"Oh dear," he said.

"Enough about me," I said quickly. "How are you?"

"Good."

"Good as in good good or good as in middle-of-the-road good?"

He pondered on this, and all the while I was wondering if he was going to mention Damien's name. Gary looked up at me, chewing on a biro.

"Good good," said Vincent. "And where are you on the scale of good?"

"It's Sunday afternoon – I'm quickly plummeting to not-so-good."

"Ah, work tomorrow."

Gary threw down the biro and started to scratch his head. "How's Jack?"

"He's fine. He's in bed having a nap."

"I see."

"And Gary is fine too," I added. Gary grinned at me.

"So you're still a happy family?"

"That's right," I replied brightly.

"And Damien?"

"No comment," I said.

"So what's it to be?"

"Did you ring Mammy lately?" I asked.

"Michelle, what are you doing?"

I put my hand on the phone. "Gary, I think Jack is awake."

"But we've only put him down!"

"Please, Vincent," I said when Gary had left the kitchen, "I don't need a lecture."

"I should never have given Damien your address. I feel I'm responsible in some way –"

I cut across him. "Don't be silly, Vincent. I need to sort this out – at the moment I'm so confused. I don't want to hurt Gary or Damien for that matter."

"Sis, you're digging a great big hole for yourself."

"I know I shouldn't see Damien again, but I can't help myself."

"Sis!"

"I know. But the last person that should be giving advice is you."

Gary was coming down the stairs. I put down the phone.

He opened the kitchen door. "He's asleep," he said, and grinned at me.

I felt myself sag. The last thing I wanted to do was go upstairs and make love to Gary.

"We've got these damn accounts to do," I said.

"We can finish them this evening."

"Okay," I said and followed him upstairs.

* * *

Damien rang me every morning at work and every evening before I went home. I lived for his phone calls. We would talk for a few minutes, then I'd have to put him on hold because I had to take other calls, or he'd get interrupted. As a last resort we e-mailed each other. Damien was working as a consultant for a Dublin company. He was thinking about setting up his own company in the computer business. He was still insisting that I tell Gary.

"Give me time," was my constant reply and I was sticking to it.

Rosemary would pretend to work while all the time her ear was tuned into everything that was said.

"What am I going to do?" I asked her.

"Who do you want to be with?" she asked. This sounded like a very simple question, but to me it was more complex.

I paused and tried to explain myself. "I'm not sure. It's all such a big shock, Damien coming back into my life. I'm confused. It's exciting being around him and at the same time I can't bear to hurt Gary. I just thought if I let things go they'd work themselves out."

Rosemary shook her head, like she was an expert on having an affair. "What if Gary finds out?"

"He won't, if I play it cool," I said.

"Gary will find out," she said with a knowledgeable tilt of her head.

"Well, then, I'll just have to be extra careful, won't I?"

Things were not going according to plan. Gary wanted to spend Saturday with us. He said we might go swimming in the Leisure Centre.

I had started to dress differently. Where once I never bought clothes, now I bought clothes with sex in mind. Tight tops with plunging necklines, skirts with daring slits up them, lacy bras and dozen of pairs of knickers. These were my little thrills as I waited for another rendezvous with Damien.

"I need to see you," Damien said, when I rang and told him I couldn't see him on Saturday.

"Damien, there's nothing I can do," I pleaded. "Next weekend."

"Tell him, for christsake," he said and hung up on me.

Rosemary picked up my coffee mug. It was Friday evening. "One last coffee for the weekend?"

"Whatever."

As soon as she left the office I dialled Damien's number. "Please, Damien, be patient with me. I'm missing you too."

"I know. Can I ring you tomorrow?"

"No, don't. I'll ring you Monday morning first thing."

"Tell him."

"Bye," I said and then added, "I love you."

The weekend was a disaster, which was to be expected. Every time Gary asked me what was wrong, I said nothing. I just couldn't get myself to speak, to verbalise what was going on. Gary just ignored me and spent his time playing with Jack.

This was his way of dealing with me. When I came home

from Sydney I had stopped eating. I existed on coffee and toast. My mother fussed about me and the more she did, the less I ate. Gary ignored me – he knew it was the best way for me to regain my appetite.

Wednesday evening, the doorbell rang. It was Damien. He was just after phoning a few minutes before on his mobile so he knew Gary was out for the evening and I was on my own in the house. Except for Jack who was asleep upstairs.

I asked the obvious question: what was he doing here? He replied, like it was self-evident, that he was here to see me. Of course I was flattered that he had travelled all way from Dublin to see me, but . . .

I had put a wash on and was on my way up to make my bed. Layers of dust covered every surface. Every known bacteria must have been having one hell of a party in my house. I couldn't remember the last time I had given the place a lick, never mind a real clean.

I said we couldn't go all the way. This seemed to excite him and he suggested we go a bit and take it from there.

Tiny ripples of excitement went up my spine. This was certainly a change in my evening routine. Just one kiss, I said to myself, one long delicious kiss and no more. We'll stop there. We moved into the sitting-room. We stood inches away from each other. The air felt electric.

This wasn't right, this was wrong, it was dreadful. I hated myself for being so damn weak. I should tell him to go, to leave. This was Gary's house – our son was upstairs asleep. All these facts flashed in front of me. I said no to Damien over and over again. With each slow sensuous step of our reunion I kept repeating the one word "no".

This was the most exciting thing I had ever done. Having Damien in the house was so *dangerous*. Even thinking of it made me horny. I couldn't do it again, I reasoned. It was too risky. Yet, I could see myself hopping up on the sink like Glenn Close in *Fatal Attraction*. I longed to be body-slammed against the wall and my skirt hoisted up and for Damien to plunge himself into me. His hands on my bottom, the growing excitement as we hurried in case Gary would walk in.

Rosemary said most women preferred chocolate to sex – I had to disagree.

Chapter 20

This was going to be the last time, I told myself. I was waiting for Damien to arrive. We had arranged to meet in a posh country hotel outside Dublin. I felt guilty that I had taken the day off work and should be spending it with Jack, not with Damien. This had to stop, really stop and I had to keep reminding myself of that fact.

He arrived soon after me. He went directly to reception and got the key for our room.

"We have to talk," I said.

A lot of organisation had gone into the day. Rosemary and I had gone to every boutique in town to find just the right outfit. I had spent a lot of money on my appearance and I was hoping it was paying off.

"Sure," he said, playing along with me. He sat down beside me.

"Damien," I said and took a breath. He was running his fingers up and down my bare arm. It was having the desired effect. Even though I didn't want to admit it. "Please, stop."

He looked at me earnestly.

"This has to stop," I said.

"Agreed," he said. "I'm tired of this, let's –"

I didn't want to hear what he had to say. If he was making plans for us then this was a first. It was too scary. I couldn't have him believing that we had a future. Because we didn't.

"You don't understand," I said.

He stopped stoking my arm.

"Damien, I can't be with you. I'm married and I have a child and I –"

"What are you saying?"

"That –"

"Michelle," he said taking my hand, "I love you and you love me so what's the problem?"

Part of me was curious. I wanted him to go on, tell me what the future might hold for us. "It's not that simple." Suddenly I was fearful this was getting out of hand. This was supposed to be our few last hours of fun and here we were arguing.

Damien shook his head. "It is that simple."

"It's over," I muttered.

We sat in silence, each of us waiting for the other to make the next move.

"You're all I have," he said, after an eternity.

"Damien –"

"Michelle, please, don't do this."

There was no need to talk anymore. We were gaining nothing by talking.

* * *

The worst about taking a day off is that there is hell to pay the next day. Everyone hates you. You even begin to hate yourself. Eleanor was in a foul mood – we had lost a major contract. A good customer had slipped from being dissatisfied with us to terminating our contract. Rosemary and I mourned the company's loss for about two minutes and then recovered.

As I felt I was to blame for everything else, I might as well take the blame for losing the customer.

Rosemary didn't ask me if I had enjoyed my day off. She just sighed a lot and spent the day trying to help customers who had queries, while I spent the day in a daze, trying to get my head around the idea that I was having an affair and I didn't want to stop.

When I got home I encouraged Gary to go and see his friends. He was a little surprised, but he didn't give it a second thought and off he went. Meanwhile, I rang Damien on the mobile and told him the coast was clear. He told me he would be with me in ten minutes.

This was going to be our very last time. After this evening I was going to put Damien out of my mind for good.

Once I had Jack tucked up in our double bed asleep, I had a quick shower. The minute I heard the doorbell I ran downstairs wearing a silk dressing-gown that Damien had got me with nothing underneath.

"Jesus," Gary said, when I opened the door.

"Gary."

Across the road I saw Damien's car parked.

"I forgot my key," he was looking at me funny. "I came home, I'm too tired for the pub." He pushed the front door shut with his foot and pulled me into his arms. "Is this for me?" he asked, his finger caressing the silk fabric.

My heart was beating hard against my chest. I put my arms around him and kissed him.

"Come on," he said taking my hand and leading me upstairs.

Our lovemaking was electric, I had so much nervous energy trapped inside me I had to get rid of it.

Afterwards, as we lay together, Gary confessed that he was worried about me. He admitted that he had grown suspicious of me because I had been acting so strangely lately. Tonight, when we made love he felt reassured that nothing was wrong.

"Work," I said. That one word led to a lengthy discussion about all I had to do and all the hassle I got every day from ungrateful customers, who didn't realise the amount of pressure that we were under. And Eleanor was so hard to please and we never seemed to do enough for her. This was my prayer of thanks to whoever was out there watching out for me. I had almost been caught. Thank you, thank you, I said to myself.

"Don't forget Damien," he said.

I was rendered speechless: *he knows*. I attempted to open my mouth, but I hadn't the courage to.

"Remember, the bloke you were on the phone to the other day?"

"Ah," I said and fell back on my pillow relieved.

Later, when Gary was asleep, I got up and looked out the window. Damien's car was gone.

* * *

It had started out as another ordinary day. I dropped Jack at the baby-sitter's and then went on to work. After work Damien was waiting in the carpark for me.

He said the same things he always said only this time we had our clothes on. He loved me, he wanted to be with me. He couldn't bear the idea of me being with Gary, he didn't like *sharing me*. I sat and listened and agreed that I was going to do something. I knew I had to do something – this couldn't go on. I was exhausted.

My car rattled and spluttered as I drove as fast as I could to collect Jack from the baby-sitter's. Damien and I had talked and kissed and cuddled in a secluded spot – it made me feel like a teenager again.

Damien was going to book into a hotel a few miles outside town. He'd wait in the room and I would go up to him. We'd get room service so no one would actually see us together. All the way home in the car I was visualising my wardrobe and trying to decide which sexy number I would wear.

By the time I got a quick dinner together for Gary and Jack I had no time to dress up the way I wanted to. I ended up wearing my faded jeans and a T-shirt. Damien didn't mind, but I had wanted it to be more fun. After we made love we lay in each other's arms and I made the mistake of telling him that I accidentally called Gary 'Damien'. I knew by the way his body tensed that I shouldn't have said it.

"Michelle, if you won't tell Gary, then I will."

I got up and started to get dressed as it was late and I still had to drive home.

I bargained with him to give me more time. I knew this would work out – if we just left it alone for the moment.

Every time Damien rang now, he asked the same question: had I told Gary? Each time he asked I responded with the same answer: I needed more time.

* * *

"Gary, you're home early," I said when I walked into the kitchen. Jack was in my arms.

"I know about you and Damien," he said.

I shouldn't have been surprised when this happened. Damien had warned me often enough. If I wasn't going to tell Gary, then he was.

"Gary, I can explain," I said, the words running after each other. "You see, his father left me a house in Westport . . ."

"Shut up, you bitch!"

My face still stung from the hard slap he gave me. Then he charged out, banging the front door after him. His revved his van up and drove off without a backward glance. I watched from the sitting-room window, Jack crying in my arms. I dialled Damien's number. "Damien," I said through sobs, "Gary knows."

"I know, I'm here, I'll be with you in minutes," he said.

"No," I wailed. "No, no, you can't come here! This is Gary's house!"

"Michelle, it's for the best."

"The best for who?"

"For us," he said. "I knew you were never going to tell Gary about us, so I did it for you."

"Damien, how could you?"

"Because I want us to be together."

I hung up, banging the phone against the wall. Jack was sobbing uncontrollably against my shoulder.

"Hush, hush," I said, my voice strained. Eventually, he stopped crying, yet I still walked with him across the kitchen floor, out to the hall, back into the sitting-room.

Each time I stopped at the sitting-room window and stared out. I wished Gary would come home and talk to me.

I dressed Jack in his pyjamas and put him in our bed. I poured some whiskey into a glass, drank it down and lay beside our son.

I was afraid to move. It was like someone had pushed the fast-forward button in my head. I wanted to stop. It was all happening too fast for me.

I wanted to talk to Gary, to reason with him, to plead with him, apologise, even grovel, just do whatever it took to get him to listen to me.

Deep down, I knew it was no use. I let the knowledge harden into solid facts and slip into my head.

Should I be glad that Gary knew? Wasn't I saved the unpleasant task of telling him myself?

I massaged my jaw. I swayed between wanting to see Gary and not wanting to see him.

My mother's judgmental voice was playing in my head. She would be lecturing me on what a sinful thing I had done. This mess was all mine, all mine. I owned it. I was to blame.

Tomorrow loomed as the sky grew paler. My little son looked so contented in his sleep.

I listened for the familiar noisy sound of Gary's van. I heard nothing, only a stupid cat whining and my neighbours coming home from the disco. I lay awake all night waiting for Gary to come home. He didn't.

My stomach rumbled nervously. I got up and got dressed. Outside the birds sang. They had breakfast and now they had something to sing about. I didn't want to go to work. I showered, washed my hair – I even had the time to put on make-up.

Jack woke with a smile on his face. I hugged him.

I dialled Damien's number, but all I got was his answering service. I was relieved – I had nothing to say to him. In my mind I was rehearsing my lines for Gary.

"Gary, I'm sorry, please let me try and explain . . ." I said these lines over and over again. I would tell him the truth about Damien coming to the supermarket, about his father leaving me his wife's jewellery and his house in Westport. I would tell the bits I didn't want to tell because I felt if I was totally honest with him, I might stand a chance.

The minute I heard a van, I ran into the sitting-room. My heart drummed against my chest. I couldn't believe it. Gary was back. I peered out the window. It wasn't Gary. My whole body tensed. If I had listened more carefully to the sound of the van I would have saved myself the disappointment.

"*Mama!*" Jack shouted from the kitchen.

"*Stop it!*" I shouted at him. "Stop, stop . . ." The words faded as I broke down and started to cry.

I dragged myself back into the kitchen. Any minute now I would crumble under the weight of my guilt. Jack started to cry. I picked him up and kissed his face. "Sorry, sorry," I said in a soothing voice.

Tears filled his eyes and trailed down his chubby face. I kissed him again on the nose and on the lips, like his father did.

"I'm so sorry, Jack," I said.

First I dropped Jack at the baby-sitter's and then I drove on to work. The one big difference was, I was early. I was doing what I was programmed to do.

The minute I dropped my bag the phone rang. It was a customer. I took details for a delivery and then forgot to take their telephone number.

I wasn't going slow today, I was going backwards.

Rosemary eyed me occasionally. When Damien phoned I told him I was busy and hadn't time to talk. I pretended to be occupied with the heap of papers that was on my desk. I shuffled the forms around a bit, filled in some spaces, blanked out others and filed a lot under miscellaneous.

I was stuck in no man's land – not knowing which way to go – motionless – frozen, stunned by my own inertia. I had tailored myself to fit in this office. Now, I felt too big, like I had swelled to double my size. If I got up from my desk everyone would notice, so I stayed put.

In the carpark, I turned to Rosemary. I wanted to be on my own and yet I didn't want to go home. I had a feeling Gary wouldn't come home this evening. "Rosemary," I said.

She touched my arm. "I know, it's written on your face. Danny is in Dublin – we can go back to my house if you like."

The tears that I had held back all day suddenly appeared. "Gary knows," I said, as I wiped my tears away. "Rosemary, I've made such a mess of things."

"Go and collect Jack – we'll talk later."

I loved the way Rosemary could take control of a situation.

*　*　*

"I feel terrible for Jack. He loves his daddy and I know Gary loves him."

Rosemary insisted that I eat some soup. Then I had to give her a detailed account of everything that had happened. We played with Jack until he fell asleep. "The last time Jack was sleeping here, we were still a family."

Rosemary yawned. "You have to talk to Gary – perhaps you should try and phone home."

"I'm afraid to. I know Gary, I know he's gutted, I know he won't want to talk to me."

"What about his son? Doesn't he want to see Jack?"

"I hope so, I hope . . ." The words broke in my mouth. I started to shake as tears streamed down my face. "Fuck Damien for phoning him! Why couldn't he have left it alone?"

Rosemary rushed to my side. "Don't cry! Gary is a nice man – he'll get over this given time."

"I wish I could believe that."

Rosemary yawned again.

"Let's go to bed," I suggested.

She smiled in relief. We went upstairs and she put me and Jack into the same guest-room we had stayed in before.

I woke after having a terrible dream. Damien and Gary had joined ranks against me. It was like we were in the school playground and they were standing together sniggering about me.

Chapter 21

Next morning, I had a quick shower to wake myself up and rid myself of the smell of guilty perspiration.

My first call on my mobile was from Gary.

"Where are you?"

"With Rosemary."

"I thought you'd gone to Westport."

"I . . ." I turned to look at Rosemary she crossed her fingers for me. "Gary, I want to talk to you."

"I don't want to talk to you, but I'd like to see my son."

I got up from the kitchen table and walked out to the hall.

"Gary," I attempted to say.

"I want to spend some time with my son," he said.

"I'll bring him home."

"Fine."

"We can –" I attempted to say.

"You bitch," he said, viciously.

"I'll see you later with Jack."

"I'd rather not see you."

I gripped the phone tightly and leaned against the wall. "We have to –"

"Michelle, I want to see my son, I don't want to see you, get the message? This was my fucking house before you came along, so I'm staying put. You find a place of your own."

The line went dead. It was Saturday. I wanted to ask Gary what I was supposed to do? I had nowhere to go.

Rosemary was playing with Jack when I walked back into the kitchen.

"He wants me to move out."

"You're welcome to stay with me," she said.

"No, I can't do that."

I played with the piece of toast that was on my plate. I told myself that it was not the end of the world, but it felt like it. I went upstairs and rang Damien.

"Gary is so angry," I said.

"Michelle," he said in a sleepy voice, "the worst is over now."

"Is it?" I asked.

"Of course it is. We can be together."

"I can't take all this in . . . everything is happening so fast." I sat down on the bed. I had to slow myself down or else I'd fall out of my life.

"It's better this way, trust me," Damien said.

Is it better this way? I asked myself, but I couldn't find an answer. This was like complicated maths; it was beyond my comprehension.

Familiar feelings of uncertainty filled me. I felt clumsy and kept thinking I was going to let something fall as I helped Rosemary tidy up.

Suddenly, I had nothing to do. I couldn't spend the day with Rosemary. Yet I didn't know where I could park myself for a few hours.

We drove around. Jack sang to himself in his car-seat, oblivious to all that was happening around him. I found myself driving down a narrow winding road, one that I hadn't been down since I was a little girl. Chestnut-trees flanked each side. They were weighted down with elegant flowers shaped like candelabras. Underneath bluebells and delicate primroses peeped out from the long grass. I had often spent hours here picking flowers for my mother. She would nod despondently when I showed them to her. I would fill a jamjar with water and put the flowers into it and leave them in the window.

The Skellys had a cherry-tree in their garden. I loved the delicate pink blossoms that appeared each year. I asked my mother to get us one. I stopped myself from begging when I realised how much she would have loved it herself.

I was trying to get my bearings, trying to inch myself out of this mess.

In my dazed state I took a call from Damien. He would meet me that evening in Dublin. I told him I couldn't.

He sighed impatiently. "How about tomorrow?"

"No, not tomorrow."

"You're still in shock; how about you take a few days off work, say Monday to Wednesday, and come to Dublin to me."

"I can't," I muttered.

"Michelle, we need to see each other," he said in a reasonable voice.

"I'll ring you," I said.

Gary's van was parked outside our house. I pulled in and took Jack out of his car-seat.

He was in the kitchen making coffee.

"Gary," I said.

He took Jack from me without looking at me. Lines were etched at the corners of his eyes. He hadn't shaved. He seemed to have aged overnight.

"Please go," he said and turned his back to me. "Jack is spending the weekend with me."

I didn't kiss Jack goodbye. I walked out and felt myself slip down another notch on the human scale.

Sometime later I found myself walking up the garden path to my mother's terraced house. I felt I had no choice but to ask her if we could move back in. I didn't want to. I hated this house and all the memories that came with it. I only had to walk into the hall to feel all the pain of my childhood engulf me.

A black hole of despair opened up inside me and I felt I was being swallowed up by it. My mother was surprised to see me on a Saturday without Jack.

"Where is Jack?"" she asked.

"With his father."

She knew by my tone that something was wrong.

We sat at her kitchen table. She took a cigarette out of the box and lit it.

I watched her. She never smoked when Jack was here. She just wanted me to breathe in her poison.

"Is it all right if Jack and I move in here for a while?" I said.

She inhaled deeply on her cigarette.

I was holding my breath, waiting for her reply.

"Oh no!" she said at last in a whisper. "I never thought that there was anything wrong."

I exhaled. The ear-bashing had yet to come.

"Remember Damien," I said.

She looked at me, flicks of steel in her old eyes. "I do." She sat back in her chair as if she was bracing herself for what was to come.

"He came to see me. His father left me his house in Westport. I have been seeing him."

"He left you his house. Where is he living now?"

My mother always made a point of asking stupid questions.

"His father is dead."

She took another long drag from her cigarette. "How did Gary find out?"

"Damien rang him and told him."

"I see," she said. "So Gary's upset."

I buried my face in my hands.

"Michelle, you can stay here as long as you like. I wish the circumstances were different."

"So do I." I contorted my face to stop myself from crying.

She moved around the table and placed her hand on my shoulder.

"Don't cry," she said and patted my back. Since childhood I had longed for an affectionate touch from my mother and now I had got it. I was so unaccustomed to her gentle touch it made me feel worse.

"What about the neighbours? They'll all be taking about us," I said, voicing my mother's thoughts.

"Aye, they will, but next week we'll be old news, it will be somebody different."

"Thanks." I was grateful for her support. The familiar track of my life was slipping away from me.

"You've got to get tough," she said.

I wiped my eyes.

"What's getting tough going to do for me?" I said.

"Michelle, I watch all the soaps on the TV."

I looked at her, bewildered.

"And the women are all tough," she said.

I laughed. She had said something amusing.

"Now let's get you something to eat. Then I'll get your old room made up."

I sat in the kitchen and watched her potter round in her slippers. She was taking care of me.

By ten o'clock I was itching to see my son. I knew a twenty-minute drive would take me to Gary's house. My mother was sleeping in her chair by the fire.

"I'm going to pop out for a few minutes," I said.

She opened her eyes and looked at me. "Are you going home?"

"No," I said. I avoided making eye contact. "I'm going to go for a walk."

"It's late and it's dark. Don't be long."

It was on tip of my tongue to tell her that I could look after myself, but I knew better. I was living in her house now.

I could imagine Jack and Gary lying side by side on the sofa, the TV on and they asleep.

Bright stars winked down at me when I looked up at the night sky. I was nervous. I gripped the steering wheel and turned the key in the ignition. I didn't think about what I was about to do, I just did it.

When I arrived at the house that I once called home, I noticed the light was on. I was tempted to put my key in the door and walk in. Then I thought it might be better if I rang the doorbell. But what if Jack was asleep? I might wake him up.

I walked around the house. The back door opened when I tried the handle. The house was quiet. I walked into the kitchen and saw the familiar mess. The mess reassured me that they still needed me. I stood in the kitchen, unsure what to do next. I wanted to see my baby, I wanted to kiss his face and hold him close to me. I wanted him to comfort me, to make me feel human again.

I stood in the kitchen, waiting, listening. Eventually, I built up the courage and walked into the hall. The sitting-room door was closed. I urged myself to turn the handle, open the door. I could see myself doing it. Yet I remained motionless. I squeezed my hands into tight fists at my side. A hard ball of tension pressed against the walls of my stomach. It banged harder and harder. I ran my hand across my stomach, trying to ease the pain. It was only a gesture – I knew it would do no good. I ached to climb the stairs and see my little son.

The house was sleeping. I turned and looked at the stairs. A new urgency took hold of me. I had to see my son.

I tip-toed across the wooden floor and headed for the stairs. I was on the second step when the sitting-room door opened.

"I thought I heard something," Gary said. He looked like he had just woken up.

"I came to say goodnight to Jack," I said.

Gary looked at me in disgust.

"Gary . . ." His name came out in a whisper. I couldn't remember the last time I had spoken so softly to him.

He turned his back to me. "Say goodnight to Jack. You can collect him on Monday from the baby-sitter's."

"Monday," I said, my voice raised.

"Don't wake him."

"I want to spend some time with him!"

He turned around and glared at me. "I thought you might have other plans for the weekend."

I shook my head vigorously. "No, Gary, I haven't." He stood where he was. I mustered up the courage and said, "Gary, we've got to talk for Jack's sake – we need to sort things out."

"You should have thought of that when you were whoring with Damien."

He walked into the sitting-room and slammed the door closed.

I ran upstairs and into Jack's bedroom. He was asleep in his cot. The lamp beside his cot filled the room in a soft comforting glow. Tears clouded my vision. My heart was filled with such joy when I saw him that it almost made me forget the mess I was in.

"Goodnight, darling," I whispered. The floorboards creaked under my feet when I moved. I was hoping the noise would wake Jack. I peered into his cot – his soft breathing told me that he was still asleep.

Up until now I couldn't make up my mind. I didn't know which one I wanted to be with. It was like I had tossed a coin in the air: Gary one side, Damien the other. And as the coin twirled in the air I knew who I wanted: it was Gary and I got Damien.

I left the house in silence. I kept driving. I was busy inventing new scenes of Gary and me together.

Gary would call to my mother's house tomorrow. I would answer the door to him and he'd say, "Michelle, the house is so quiet without you."

I would hug him. "Oh Gary," I would say, tears falling freely, "I'm so sorry."

He would kiss me. We would walk into my mother's hall, Jack in his arms.

Then, I realised I was driving on a road that I didn't recognise. The petrol gauge told me I was almost out of petrol. I slowed down, turned at the first gate and headed back for my mother's house. Eleanor's car was parked outside her mother's house. I didn't feel like having a heart-to-heart with her.

My mother had left the lights on. A note rested beside the kettle in the kitchen.

I picked it up and read my mother's scrawl: *He rang.* I knew she meant Damien. And, I knew by the flow of her pen that she was a reluctant messenger.

In the sitting-room I sat down in her armchair and dialled his number.

"I'm missing my baby," I said as he picked up.

"I'm missing you," he said softly.

I closed my eyes and dreamt that I was lying in his arms.

"Oh Damien, I feel so awful, I've . . ." My words faded. I didn't know if I could explain to Damien how badly I felt about what I had done to Gary and Jack.

"Michelle, darling," he said.

I leaned back in my mother's chair and let the words flow over me, feeling their comforting timbre soothe me.

"Come to Dublin," he said.

"I can't."

"You can," he said, his voice soft and seductive. "Please."

"Mmm," I said.

"So you'll come," he said.

I thought of all those people, queues everywhere. I hated crowds: they always made me feel small and insignificant, like I was a miniature person in the great cog of the world.

I squeezed my eyes tight and said, "I have a son, I have responsibilities."

"What are you trying to say?"

"I'm not sure."

I heard him sigh. "Do you want some time to sort things out."

"Sort of."

"Do you want to get back with Gary?"

"I've hurt him so much, he wouldn't have me."

"So how about we meet next weekend?" said Damien.

"I'm not sure."

"Think about it," he suggested.

I gripped the receiver tightly. I was trying to find the right words. "I'm just exhausted and confused, and I hate myself for all the hurt that I've caused."

"I know, love."

"Damien, I wish I was lying there beside you!" I urgently needed someone to cuddle me.

"Me too. Michelle, I love you. Thank God my father made me find you again."

I heard the conviction in his voice. I was unable to reply. Right now I felt like I was the worst person on earth.

I was too restless to sleep. I had no body to snuggle up to, to lull me into sleep. I switched the TV on with the remote control. I flicked through the channels and then switched it off.

Chapter 22

I climbed the stairs and walked into my old bedroom. Everything was exactly the same except for the wallpaper: she had changed it two years before. The bed sagged when I sat down on it. My mother had left a new nightdress on my bed and a dressing-gown. The room smelled nice. I lay down in my old bed, hugging the towelling dressing-gown for comfort.

I waited on the threshold of sleep, but I never stepped inside. Sometimes I felt myself drift off and then I would wake again.

All I could see was the hatred in Gary's eyes when he looked at me. I could see Jack sleeping in his cot, his arms thrown out each side of him, his pursed lips and those adorable curls that formed a halo around his head.

I twisted and turned and still nothing happened. I watched the dark fade to light. I heard the milk van drop off milk at the houses. I was glad my vigil was over. I gave up on sleeping and got up.

The kettle had just switched off when my mother came into the kitchen.

"You didn't sleep," she said.

"No," I said, sourly.

She sat down at her kitchen table. "What are you going to do today?"

I shrugged my shoulders. I didn't feel like talking. My mind was elsewhere. I was wondering if Jack was awake yet. It was five in the morning. I was tempted to get into my car and drive down to the house. Then I realised I had no petrol.

"I'll make the tea if you like," she said.

"No, it's alright, I can do it."

I took two mugs out of the cupboard. I stared out the kitchen window, towards the distant line of the horizon. I wanted my son, I needed my son, I loved him so much. Outside the birds sang at full volume. I wished I could tell them to shut up. The sky was light blue with cartoon clouds puffing across it.

I wiped my eyes with my mother's dressing-gown.

My mother broke the silence by saying, "You should take today easy."

"That's a great idea," I said with sarcasm.

"I've a few hundred euros in the post office – you're welcome to it."

"Thanks, but I couldn't take your money – you need it," I muttered.

"What would I need it for?" she said, her eyes directly on me.

It's all you have, I wanted to say, but didn't.

I placed her cup of tea in front of her.

"Thanks," I said, my voice a whisper.

"It's cold sitting here," she said, taking her cup. "I think I'll go back to bed."

She left and closed the kitchen door quietly after her. I switched off the kitchen light and stared out the window. I watched a jet plane leave a trail of white smoke after it as it traced its way across the sky.

I had no clean clothes. After nine I decided to phone Gary and ask him if I could go down to the house and get some.

"You certainly can," he said.

I felt my spirits lift.

"We're going to my mother's for the day. Come and take all your stuff." Then the phone went dead.

* * *

My mother's washing machine was full of dirty baby clothes. Gary never bothered to put on a wash – he just took them from the hot press. It never occurred to him that a chain of events brought them to that warm destination.

Jack was sitting on the floor crying. He was looking for his teddy bear. My mother and I exchanged baffled looks.

"It must be a new teddy that Gary bought him," I said. "I didn't notice it when I was packing up his stuff."

The phone rang. It was Damien. I pretended to be cheerful. It was Monday evening, I was just in the door from work – didn't he realise I hadn't time to talk to him? Jack had a new routine to get used to and we both needed time to adapt to it.

Jack stuck a toy tractor in front of my face. I ignored him, then he screamed. Damien wanted to know if he was always like that? I tried to explain to him that this was not a good time. Jack pulled the phone out of the wall: this was his way of telling me to shut up, that he was tired of being ignored. I yelled at him. He ran into the kitchen to his granny, leaving me feeling like shite for my bad behaviour.

I hardly lifted my feet off the floor as I shuffled down the hall and into the kitchen.

"I'll go and look for his teddy," I mouthed to my mother. She nodded.

I opened the back door to Gary's house with my key and walked into the kitchen. The sun was shining in through the back window. I was tempted to open it and let in some fresh air. This task required more energy than was in my reserve. I walked into the sitting-room and looked around. The place was a mess. Jack's teddy was under a blanket on the sofa.

I was in the hall on my way out when I heard Gary's key in the front door.

"I came to get this – Jack has been crying for it," I said.

"How is he?" Gary asked.

"He's okay." I hugged the teddy closer to me. "Gary . . ."

He held up his hands. "You'd better go, I'll only lose my temper."

"We have to talk."

"No, we fucking don't have to talk. Get yourself a solicitor. I'm looking for a divorce."

"Gary!" I shouted above him. "Let me talk! At least give me five minutes!"

"Talk," he said.

"I love Jack and you love him. For his sake, can't we try and put this behind us?" Silently I vowed never to see Damien again if he would give us a second chance.

"I can't," he said.

He opened the front door and let me walk out.

Tears pricked and stung my eyes. "Bastard," I muttered over and over until I reached my mother's house.

I could hear Postman Pat on the video. Jack was lying fast asleep on my mother's lap. She was running her fingers though his hair.

"Thanks," I said.

She bent down and kissed his head. "I'd love to take care of him while you're at work. You could save your baby-sitting money – you'll need it. We could go to feed the ducks and do the shopping."

"That would be great, if you feel you're up to it."

"I am," she said with a new determination that I had never seen in her before.

Chapter 23

There are always arguments for and against. I didn't know what to do. On the one hand I wanted us to be a family: Jack, Gary and myself. On the other, Gary didn't want me, he refused to speak to me, so I wasn't going to make much progress there. Damien, on the other hand, wanted me and maybe I wanted him, only I was afraid to admit it. Maybe I was afraid of him letting me down again. The once-bitten twice-shy syndrome. There I was, stuck in the middle.

Rosemary said I should think myself lucky. There were plenty of women who would like to have one man in their lives, never mind two. But that was it: I wasn't lucky – this wasn't me being blessed with good fortune. I wouldn't know good fortune. We'd never had it. It was alien to us. It would make us uncomfortable, uneasy. We wouldn't know what to do with it. We'd run away in the opposite direction. I didn't realise that my family were my fortune until it was too late.

I could tell by the way Eleanor looked at me that she was outraged at what I'd done. Of course, she didn't say anything, but her silence spoke volumes.

So what should I do? Do what I usually did, nothing. I'd just wait and let things happen. As I'm scared shitless to make my own decisions because I've always made the wrong one, I let other people suggest things, or take the lead and I end up there, without really having to make a decision about it myself.

Rosemary said it's all related to my childhood. Suddenly she has become an expert on human behaviour. That was how I came to be sitting in the Royal Dublin Hotel on a Friday evening waiting for Damien.

Gary was picking Jack up that evening from the baby-sitter's and having him for the weekend.

The hotel was littered with well-groomed people. My eyes trailed from group to group. I was early or else Damien was late.

* * *

My heart missed a beat when I saw Damien walk into the place. I saw another woman stare at him. Her eyes followed him until he reached me.

"Darling," he said.

We hugged.

"Oh, Damien," I said. I let myself fall into him, to be cradled by his arms for a few minutes.

"I've booked dinner for us, in a nice restaurant not far from here."

"That's nice," I replied.

We sat down on the sofa, and looked at each other.

"Michelle, you look wonderful."

I smiled, trying to conceal how uncomfortable I felt being complimented, when I had caused so much misery.

He took my hand in his and kissed it. "We're going to have a great weekend – I've got it all planned."

My heart filled with the lead that had been coursing through my body all day.

"What is it?" he asked, his eyes trying to read my face.

"Nothing. Everything."

"I need a drink, it's been a long day."

"I'll have a brandy," I said, a new crankiness slipping into my voice.

He returned with two brandies. We sat close to each other, trying to feel our way back to middle ground.

Damien talked at length about his plans to set up his own company. My life was very simple by comparison: work and motherhood.

"How was your week?" he asked. He was sitting close to me, our bodies brushing against each other.

"Horrible, I hate living with my mother," I said.

After we finished our drinks I got another round.

He peered at his gold wrist-watch. "Are you hungry?"

"I'm starving," I said.

"Good," he said.

"I hope this restaurant you've booked isn't too posh – I don't want shavings of food served on a massive plate." I looked at him directly. I was trying to tell him that I wasn't the old Michelle – there was a new one evolving. "At least not tonight."

He grinned at me and kissed my lips. "I've missed you so much."

"Why don't we get a takeaway and go home?" The minute I said it, I regretted it: it was what Gary and I did on Friday nights. I didn't want relics from my past, I wanted to erase them. "On second thoughts, I'd like to eat out."

He glared at me. "Make up your mind. I don't want to be sitting in a restaurant and for you to say, oh no, I want a takeaway."

I was standing beside him, breathing in his mixture of perspiration and expensive cologne.

"Damien, this is the easy bit, deciding where we eat!"

I turned and headed for the door. He followed. We stood on O'Connell Street. The place was pulsating with people out having fun.

He took my hand in his and kissed my lips tenderly. "I know, love," he said.

We walked across the Liffey, around by Trinity College and up Dawson Street. He stopped outside a restaurant.

"Here we are," he said.

Damien was busy reading the wine list after we had ordered. The couple at the table next to us spoke in hushed voices. A group at another table listened attentively to what a middle-aged woman was saying. I tried to listen in, but I couldn't hear with the background music.

I looked around at the polished brass, the elegant table settings. Gary and I could never afford to eat here. Every morsel of food that I put into my mouth got stuck in my throat. I wanted to relax, to fit in, to feel I belonged here, but I couldn't. I sipped wine, hoping that it would relax me.

It was tempting to look at my watch and see what time it was. I wanted to ring Gary and say goodnight to my son.

"Michelle," Damien said, stroking my hand, "why don't we take a holiday? Go somewhere really nice and romantic?"

"That's a lovely idea." I paused, trying to find the right words, trying to ease the blow. "I just don't think it's a good idea." His soft manicured hand was so unlike Gary's.

"Why not?"

"What about Jack?" I gulped down some wine. I was trying to lighten up. I hoped bubbles of joy would burst inside me. I had to laugh or else I would start crying.

Our eyes met and I realised that he had no intention of including Jack. I felt a little deflated and drank some more wine, wishing for the bubbles to start bursting.

It stuck with me: Damien didn't want to include Jack. Didn't he realise that Jack had to be included?

We took a taxi back to his father's house. Summer was here, yet it hadn't stopped raining. I followed Damien into the kitchen. We were both tipsy. He put all his efforts into making us coffee. I watched him spoon the coffee into the mugs.

"You fraud," I said.

He looked at me, puzzled.

"I thought you always made real coffee."

"Well, sometimes there isn't time for real coffee and instant just has to do . . ." He leaned across the worktop and kissed me. It was just what I needed to get the bubbles going. I could feel them dancing in my stomach, hopping into my arteries, the new oxygen making me light-headed.

"Oh Damien," I purred, taking off my leather jacket and letting it fall to the floor.

"Do you want coffee now or later?"

"I want music!" I floated into the sitting-room and switched on the light. Damien was beside me, opening a dark cabinet and switching on a CD. It was the Beatles. *"Here comes the sun . . ."* was blaring out. I started to sing with them.

"I didn't know you liked the Beatles," he said.

"I used to love them," I shouted. "Vincent and I used to play them all the time when we were young."

I pulled at his tie – he helped me open it.

I took off my sandals and wriggled out of my jeans. Damien was moving beside me, his hips swaying to the beat. We were dancing together now, singing the words together. The bubbles had started to burst inside me and for the first time that night I felt high and loved and desired. Things were going to be okay, I felt it in my bones. I unbuttoned my blouse, one button after another, while the music played. Damien started to open his shirt buttons. I stopped him.

"Wait," I purred. I was acting like the whore Gary said I was.

More bubbles started to burst. I could feel them, my insides were lusting for this man. I was undoing my bra, wriggling my bum, touching my breast, making him lust for me, like I was for him. He was standing there – I could tell he wanted me. He pulled me to him. I laughed and felt his hardness through his well-tailored pants. I moved away, every movement a deliberate attempt to seduce him.

Slowly I pulled off my knickers and only then did I walk over to him and let him feel my naked body against his clothed one. I felt his excitement – his heart was racing, his eyes bright with desire. Slowly I undid his zip.

Later, when we lay in his bed, I felt my body ache all over. We had made love on the rug by the fire. We sipped coffee afterwards and drank more brandy and made love again in his bed. We lay together staring at the ceiling. A feeling of contentment swept over me.

"Michelle, I'm scared of losing you," he said.

I didn't turn to look at him. My eyes were fixed on a point on the ceiling. "I'm scared too." I could see the bubbles floating away, leaving me now, warning me that the good time was over. "All I know is I love my son. He will always come first."

Damien sat up and looked down at me. "Where do I fit in?"

"I've always loved you," I said.

He kissed my forehead. "Good. Now what would you like for breakfast?"

"Breakfast? It's almost lunch-time."

We went into town and had lunch. I bought an outfit for Jack. It looked so cute in the window, I just had to have it. It was like stepping back in time. We went into music shops and bought some CDs. Then we went to the cinema, did some shopping in M&S so we could have a quick dinner when we got back to his house.

* * *

Next morning when I woke I could hear the rain hitting off

the window-pane. I felt contented lying there with Damien beside me. I glanced at the digital clock: it was almost ten o'clock. I couldn't remember the last time I had slept in.

We were sitting in the kitchen, reading the Sunday papers like we used to, when my mobile rang. It was Eleanor telling me not to panic, that Jack was in hospital – he had to get stitches in his head.

Two minutes later we were in Damien's car and on our way to the hospital.

Chapter 24

The wet road unravelled like a black ribbon before us as we drove as fast as we could towards the hospital. We took direction from the girl on reception.

"I'll wait here," Damien said.

I almost ran to the children's ward.

Jack was lying on the bed. Gary stood beside it, while Eleanor sat on it.

"My little darling," I said and hugged him close to me.

"Careful," Gary said.

I glared at him coldly.

"Mammy," Jack said, "hurt head."

I kissed his head.

"He's got five stitches – the doctor is just after giving him the all clear."

"How did it happen?"

"It was an accident," Gary said defensively.

"How did it happen?" I demanded in a self-righteous voice.

Eleanor took Jack by the hand. "Aren't you a brave boy?"

"Treat!" Jack said.

"I promised him a treat," she explained.

"I see." I was so grateful that he was all right.

"Brave little boys deserve a treat," Eleanor said.

I looked at Gary. Eventually he turned and looked directly at me.

"I need an explanation," I said, calmly.

"He hit his head against the side of the kitchen table."

I remained silent, waiting for him to continue. He looked from the bed towards the window. "We were playing chase."

"Can we leave now?" I asked him.

"Yes, the doctor said he's fine," he said in a measured voice.

"We were just waiting for you," said Eleanor.

Gary shuffled from foot to foot. I picked Jack up and held him in my arms.

"Would you like to come to the shop with me, Jack?" said Eleanor, taking his little hand.

Gary and I stood at the bed and watched our son walk down the polished floor with Eleanor.

"I'm so glad he's okay," I said, my voice filling up with remorse.

"Me too." He turned to me. "Where the hell were you?"

"None of your business."

He smirked. "And don't blame me for Jack's accident – if you were bloody looking after him properly it wouldn't have happened."

Gary walked purposefully out of the ward, leaving me to collect Jack's teddy and bloodstained shirt. I smelt his shirt, breathing in my baby's smell.

"Thank God you're alright," I whispered.

The little girl in the bed opposite looked at me with big sad eyes.

"Hello," I said as I walked over to her. "I'm Jack's mum."

Her mother sat on a chair beside her bed. She looked pale and tired.

"Hi," she said.

"Is Jack going home?" the little girl asked.

I nodded, unable to speak.

The tiny line of her mouth trembled. "It's not fair," she said.

Her mother hugged her fiercely.

I walked away with a sense of relief and guilt all mingled into one.

Gary was waiting outside the ward door for me. Eleanor and Jack had gone on ahead to the shop. We walked down the long polished corridor in silence, both of us retreating into ourselves.

"Look!" Jack said. He was holding a giant jigsaw box in his hands.

"I can't wait for us to do it!" I said.

Gary stood silently beside me.

The cold fresh air hit us the minute we walked outside. I saw Damien, standing nearby.

"Michelle, take tomorrow off."

"Thanks, Eleanor."

Gary looked like all the life had been drained out of him.

"Would you like us to go home with you?" I asked.

He squared his broad shoulders and said, "Jack is coming home with me. You suit yourself."

I held on tightly to my son's hand. "Fine," I said, irritated at Gary's childish behaviour.

"Daddy," Jack said, taking his hand.

We looked at each other across our son's head.

"Come with me if you like," he said.

"I'll follow you."

Damien was walking from his car towards us. Gary scooped Jack up in his arms and headed for his van.

"I'd like to spend some time with Jack," I said and tugged at Gary's sleeve.

"Get rid of *him*," he said through clenched teeth.

Damien stood beside me.

"I'll phone you, I need to be with Jack."

"Michelle . . ."

Gary had started to reverse his van.

I ran and waved at Gary to stop. I sat in and didn't dare look back at Damien.

I was swaying, slipping back into being Jack's mum and Gary's wife. I knew by the square set of Gary's shoulders that he was still angry. He was not prepared to forgive me, yet.

We needed to talk, I said in my head. I was rehearsing for Gary now. I turned and looked at my beautiful son beside me. He was pointing at cows in the fields. I took his small chubby hand in mine and held it.

I was silently promising my son that he would always come first. I didn't want his life dragged down by my stupidity. I wanted him to have the best childhood ever. That was my priority.

We drove to Longford in silence.

"Will I drop you off at your mother's?" Gary asked.

"I'd like us to talk," I said.

"We've nothing to say to each other."

"Gary, wake up," I said. "We have a son. This is not just about you."

We drove back to our house. I let him open the door and I followed him in.

"Gary . . ." I said. We stood in the hall. Jack picked up his new remote-control car and started playing with it. The car whizzed by my feet. My head ached and the noise of the car wasn't helping.

I walked into the kitchen. Gary stayed in the hall playing with Jack. The kitchen was a mess. There wasn't one clean cup in the place. I counted to ten.

He was still in the hall playing with Jack. I walked out and looked at them. My heart missed a beat. I was witnessing another one of those wonderful moments, which I would always cherish. Father and son playing, together. I looked on and felt pride and love and regret.

"Shall I go?" I heard myself ask.

"If you like," Gary said.

"Look, look," Jack said, pointing at the car as it sped around the hall.

I walked back into the kitchen and stood. I couldn't leave like this. I wanted to spend the evening with my son.

"Gary, please," I said from the kitchen.

"Just go," he said from the doorway.

"What if Jack wants me?"

"I'll be here for him," he said. He went back to Jack, leaving me alone. I slipped out the back door. I didn't want Jack to see me going – he might start to cry and then again he mightn't even notice. I felt I was wearing lead boots as I dragged myself up the road towards my mother's house.

Gary didn't want me anymore and it hurt. It hurt like hell. I should have known this would happen.

In town I stopped at Tesco. I picked up a basket. I bought a bottle of wine, Coco-pops and chocolate buttons for when Jack came tomorrow. I was hoping he would start crying for me and Gary would have to bring him to me. A trickle of hope was starting to drip into my brain, feeding me with the idea that Gary and I could get back together again.

The minute a Damien-thought entered my head, I ejected it.

My mother and I spent the evening sipping wine and staring at the TV. By ten o'clock I couldn't stand it any longer. I dialled our phone number.

Eventually, Gary answered.

"How is Jack?"

"He's asleep upstairs in his cot."

"You are bringing him here to me tomorrow?"

"That's what we agreed."

"Would you mind bringing up the rest of his clothes – you'll find some in the hot press and some in his wardrobe."

"See you tomorrow." He hung up before I got the chance to find out what time he'd arrive at. What was the point, I reasoned. Even if he gave me a time he'd never stick to it.

I poured myself another glass of wine and drank most of it down. I couldn't bear being separated from my son. I wanted him here now. Damn you, Gary, for doing this to me!

* * *

"He's ringing the doorbell downstairs," my mother said, shaking me.

I sat up in the bed, trying to get my bearings. I was in my mother's house; I had finished the bottle of wine and opened another that my mother had. My head was heavy. I pulled my feet out of the bed and onto the floor.

The doorbell rang again.

"Okay, damn him, I'm coming." I thought of Jack's smiling face, my ray of sunshine. I couldn't wait to see him.

"I don't want him here," my mother said, her voice piercing.

I looked at her, baffled.

I pulled on my dressing-gown and went downstairs. I opened the door to find Damien standing there.

"Damien . . ." I pushed strands of my tossed hair off my face. "This is a surprise . . . what are you doing here?"

He grinned and shook some keys at me. "I thought we'd drive to Westport for the day."

"I'm expecting Gary to arrive with Jack at any minute."

"Great," he said, planting a kiss on my cheek. "We can take Jack with us."

"Damien, I left a message on your mobile last night. Didn't you get it?"

"Yes, I did."

My mother was in the kitchen making a lot of noise, her way of protesting as she tided up after me.

I heard a van and looked down the road, hoping it wasn't Gary.

"Damien, let me get dressed. Why don't you go and sit in your car?"

I looked at his flashy red sports car. It would be like a red rag to a bull if Gary saw it. Last night's wine was too much for my system this morning. I wanted him to go, but I didn't know how I was going to get rid of him.

217

"Damien, please, let me get dressed!" He looked like a tourist in his bright orange T-shirt and white jeans.

"So we're going."

"We'll talk," I said and attempted to close the door in his face.

"I'll wait for you."

"Damien, please –" I paused mid-sentence as I watched Gary drive up in his old van. He was dressed in his work-clothes.

"Oh no," I heard myself say.

"What?" Damien said, looking around him.

Gary drove off again at speed.

I leaned against the wall. "That was Gary," I said, my voice nothing more than a whisper.

"Sorry . . ." Damien said.

"Damien," I snapped, "please, just go! I have to sort this out with Gary."

"Michelle, let me stay with you!"

"I'll get dressed," I mumbled and closed the front door in his face.

Upstairs, I opened the curtains to let some light into the room. It was only then that I noticed the sun was shining. I pulled on a blue T-shirt and shorts. I ran my fingers through my hair and tied it up.

"That sounded like Gary's van," my mother said, when I came downstairs.

"It was," I said. "I have to go and see him."

"Don't bring himself," she said and nodded her head towards the door.

"I wasn't going to," I snapped at my mother. Then I added a hasty, "Sorry."

I walked down the cement path towards Damien's car.

"I'm sorry," he said and looked at me with big pleading eyes. "I've made things worse for you."

"I need to see Jack."

Damien said nothing.

"I'm Jack's mother, I'm worried about him."

"Do you want me to go?"

He looked disappointed when I said. "Yes."

Damien was used to getting his own way. He ran his hand though his hair and grinned at me. "I think I'll go back to Dublin and let you sort things out here," he said softly.

I nodded.

He attempted to kiss me, but I moved away.

"Ring me," he said as he got into his car.

"He's gone," my mother said as I walked into her kitchen.

I switched on the kettle. "Yes."

After I made a coffee I dialled Gary's mobile number.

"Gary . . ." I said and paused. My tongue was stuck to the roof of my mouth. "Can I see Jack? I'm worried about him."

"No bloody way! I'm not having my son around you and that bastard."

"He's not here, he's gone back to Dublin."

Gary grunted and then the phone went dead. I dialled again, but he had switched his mobile off.

I sat down on the bottom step of the stairs, motionless. I had lost my family.

"Michelle," my mother said.

I looked up at her. I was aware she was talking to me, but I couldn't make sense of it.

"Why don't you lie down?" I heard her say from a distance.

"What have I done?" I asked my mother.

I felt her help me up off the stairs. She led me into the sitting-room. I sat down on the sofa and felt myself slowly unravel like an old jumper.

"I have to go and see Gary," I said.

"First, you have to get some rest. You're in no fit state to go and see anyone."

"What about Jack?"

"I don't think you are up to looking after Jack today," she said softly to me, her voice almost motherly.

"But he needs me."

My mother put her withered hand on top of mine. "I know he does, but trust me on this. Give Gary time to calm down – he's bound to be furious when he saw *him* here."

I nodded my head as if I was agreeing with her while inside I knew I had to see my son or else I'd die.

Chapter 25

We sat at our kitchen table. It was like old times only my father and Vincent were missing. My mother had made soup.

She tutted.

"What?" I said.

"Nothing." She looked at my bowl. "You've hardly touched it."

"It's lovely, but I'm not very hungry."

She was looking out her kitchen window. I knew by her face something was wrong.

"What is it, Mammy?"

"That bastard of a magpie is back again."

"Mammy, he's always been there!"

"No," she said, shaking her head knowledgeably. "For the past while he was on Skellys' wall."

"You mean Eleanor and her family could be having the same bad luck we've always had?"

A look of pure malice flickered across her face.

"Wouldn't it be nice for someone else to have it for a change?"

"Are we cursed?"

My mother grunted. "I don't know – look! Puss is back again!"

There, sitting on the widow-ledge, was my mother's black cat. It was a delicate balancing act my mother had going.

I buttered some bread and ate it. I moved the spoon around the bowl. I don't like mushroom soup. I longed for a glass of brandy, something to numb the hell that was going on inside my head.

We were washing up when the doorbell rang.

"I'll get it," I said, dropping the tea towel.

I opened the door. "Eleanor!" I couldn't keep the disappointment out of my voice. I'd been hoping it was Gary with Jack.

"Is this a bad time?" Her voice was soft and full of apology.

"No, no," I said, as I attempted to smile. "Not at all."

"How is Jack?"

I hugged my arms around me. A new anger was drumming inside my head.

"Come in," I said.

"You look exhausted." The words were spoken with sincerity.

"I am. Gary won't let me see Jack."

"Oh Michelle! I'm so sorry."

"So am I. I've made such a mess of everything."

"Would you like me to go? Maybe you'd prefer to be on your own."

"I just want to see Jack, I really need to see him, but –"

"Is there anything I can do?"

"I don't know."

Eleanor handed me a tissue. "Here," she said, "have my last one."

"Thanks," I said and attempted to laugh.

We sat down on the front doorstep like we used to do when we were children.

She looked crisp in her shorts and matching navy and white T-shirt, in contrast to my creased state.

"You look nice," I said.

"The day I went shopping with Rosemary, this was the one thing I liked so I bought it. That damn dress that she insisted on me buying for the wedding cost a fortune and I'll never wear it again."

"Hello, Eleanor," my mother said, sticking her nose out the front door. "I thought I heard someone talking."

"Hi!"

"Nice day," my mother said, stepping out past us.

"It's lovely," Eleanor said.

My mother walked down the path towards the gate.

"The magpie has moved back," my mother said.

"Oh," said Eleanor, pretending she knew what my mother was talking about.

My mother chuckled. "The magpie was on your mother's wall – now it's back on mine again!"

"Oh dear," said Eleanor. She put her hand over her eyes to shade herself from the sun.

"But you've still got your black cat," I said, determined to remain positive.

"A fat lot of good he'll do." My mother looked up at the blue sky. "It's going to rain," she announced.

"Don't say that," said Eleanor.

"You know Mother – she always predicts the worst," I said under my breath.

My mother turned to look at us. "Time flies," she said, her eyes dreamy. "It's only like yesterday that you two were little girls sitting there playing with your dolls." She walked back up the path towards us. "How do you like your new house?"

"It's grand," Eleanor said.

I remembered sitting on this step, my mother in the kitchen on autopilot, my father asleep on the sofa after spending the past few days on the drink, the heavy silence that weighed down on us as we all crept around afraid to make a sound. That's why I loved going to Skellys' – their house looked exactly like ours but it was so different. Now, as I sat on the step I wanted to cry. I didn't know why I wanted to cry, but I did and I was afraid to.

"Would you like me to talk to Gary?" asked Eleanor when my mother eventually retreated into the house.

"It's complicated . . ."

"I'll go," she said, sensing my need to be alone.

"Bye . . ." Then I added for good measure, "See you tomorrow."

I waited all day for Gary to phone, but he didn't. There was nothing for me to do but wait. My mother caught me looking at the kitchen clock and two minutes later at my watch.

"Stop walking around! Sit down. You're making me nervous!"

I threw myself down on the sofa. I wanted to tear my hair out and my mother's just so she would suffer as much as me. "Mother, please! You're not helping!"

"I suppose I'm not. We should do something to pass the time."

"Like what?"

"I don't know." She lit a cigarette. "You don't have to snap my head off with everything I say."

"Why won't he ring? Doesn't he know I love Jack too?"

"Why? How often I asked that self-same question."

I looked across at my mother and for the first time in my life I saw her sadness, her regret at a life wasted.

"I suppose there is an answer if we knew where to look," she said.

"Will I make us some tea?"

"I suppose."

So I made tea. We sipped it and continued our vigil. I attempted ringing Gary's mobile and our house. No reply. I hadn't the nerve to ring his parents' house.

Thin clouds of silver smoke rose from my mother's cigarettes and clung to the ceiling. The white paint had turned to grey and in places to black.

When I got tired in the house, I went outside. As darkness fell, the moon bathed the garden in metallic light. Eventually, I went to bed. Gary didn't phone.

I had lost my family; the one thing I held dear was gone. This was the one thought that filled my head. I woke to hear the phone ringing downstairs. I jumped out of bed and ran to answer it.

"Hi," he said.

"Damien," I said, hoping my disappointment didn't transmit itself down the line.

"Yes, who were you expecting it to be?"

"Gary won't let me see Jack. I haven't seen him since Sunday and I miss him so much."

"Go see a solicitor. You have rights," Damien said with authority. "You shouldn't have to take that crap."

I closed my eyes as a new exhaustion swept through me. The day had only begun.

"Michelle, look, I'm really sorry," he said. "I should be there for you –"

"No, no, it's fine, I'll sort this myself."

"Michelle, don't let him bully you."

I thought of Gary, my childhood friend. He was never a bully. He was always strong and protective towards Vincent and me.

"Thanks for calling," I said softly. I could hear my mother's footsteps on the stairs.

"I'll phone you tonight – bye, Michelle, I love you!"

"Bye." I put the phone down.

"Who was that?" my mother asked.

"Damien."

She grunted. "He's up early."

We walked into the kitchen. My mother switched on the kettle. Already she was irritating me and she had only got up.

"I'll have a shower and get dressed," I said.

"It's early."

"I know but I –" I stopped mid-sentence not knowing what to say next. My throat was full of unshed tears.

She nodded her head and turned her attention towards the window.

I drove down to my home. There was no van parked in the drive. My heart sank even lower. They'd spent the night in Gary's parents' house. The Kennys had re-shuffled themselves and made space for them. This was no more than I deserved.

There was only one thing for me to do, and that was end my relationship with Damien.

* * *

"Hi," Rosemary said. She was testing the water to see what state I was in.

"Hi," I said. The word was dead heavy, not a drop of good cheer in it.

"How are you this morning?" Rosemary was wearing a white linen blouse and khaki trousers.

"I like the outfit."

"I bought it last year." She pulled up her trouser leg. "What do you think?"

I looked down at the sandals. "They're really nice."

"I got them in Paris – they were ridiculously expensive."

To my relief the phone rang and our day began.

Eleanor and Rosemary danced around me, afraid to ask, yet curious as to what was happening. I said nothing, hoping my silence gave the right signals that things would work out and Gary and I would be a family again.

I stayed after work and rang Damien. It had to be done and it was better do it now and not think about it.

"Is something wrong?" he asked.

My tone was serious. "Damien, I'm missing Jack so much. I've got to see him."

"Get in contact with Gary – tell him he can't do this."

"Damien . . ." I paused. I was trying to find the right words. "I can't see you again."

"Michelle . . . please."

"I'm so confused and –"

"Michelle, I'll come back. In fact, I shouldn't have left – you need me."

"No, Damien, please . . ."

"I'm coming –"

"Damien, please, listen to me," I said, cutting across him. "I'm sorry, I hate saying this, but I need to sort this out with Gary."

"Are you saying it's over between us?"

"Yes," I said and put down the phone before he could reply.

After I left work, I drove by our house, hoping Gary's van would be outside. It wasn't. I drove up to Kennys' house and saw it parked outside.

Inside the house was baby Jack. I wondered if he was crying for me. Did he even miss me? I couldn't bear it, yet I couldn't bring myself to get out of the car and knock at their door. I sat and waited, hoping Gary might come out. I grew tired waiting. Eventually, I drove home and tried ringing his mobile. It was switched off.

In desperation, I rang Eleanor.

"Would you go and talk to Gary for me? I need to see Jack! Please?"

"Of course I will," she said. "You stay at your mother's and I'll phone you back when I see him." Her soft voice reassured me.

My mother was in the garden weeding.

"Hi," she said. "Isn't it a lovely evening?"

"I'm missing Jack."

She nodded. "I know." The evening sun was warm and filled the garden in a rich light.

"Your garden is lovely." I looked around at the disciplined beds filled with flowers.

She took this compliment with an awkward nod of her head. "Why don't you sit out for a while?"

I sat down in my mother's sun-chair and felt the sun lick my pale skin with its warm light. I hated being on my own. I hated my own company. I could only conclude that I didn't like myself very much.

"The phone," my mother shouted out the kitchen window.

"Hello?" I was breathless when I reached it.

"It's me, Eleanor."

I waited for her to continue.

"I was speaking to Gary . . . he's very upset. He doesn't want you to see Jack. I'm sorry, Michelle."

"But I have to! I need to see him and Jack needs to see me."

"I know, Michelle. I tried to explain this to Gary, but he's so angry – he's in no fit state to listen to reason." Her voice was calm and diplomatic.

"Thanks," I muttered and put down the phone.

I turned and saw my mother standing at the sitting-room door.

"That was Eleanor," I said. After the bright sunlight the sitting-room felt cold and dark. "It's no good. What am I going to do?"

"Give him time."

"I need to see Jack," I snapped back.

"I know! I'll go and talk to Gary."

"You can't do that – you'll only make matters worse."

"Michelle, if *you* go you'll make matters worse."

"I'm not so sure it's a good idea."

"I'm your mother, Michelle, and I can't bear to see you suffering. I'm going to Kennys' to talk with them."

I fell onto the sofa.

"Why don't you go outside? The sunshine will do you good."

I looked at her in amazement. My mother had just developed another self. I had never seen her so decisive in my life. For some strange reason I felt she would come back with a result.

And she did. I could pick Jack up from Kennys' the following evening.

Chapter 26

After work, I went to Kennys' house to pick Jack up. Gary's father came to the door when I rang the bell. He didn't invite me in; he went inside and came back with Jack in his arms and his baby-bag.

Jack was all excited when he saw me. I kissed his lovely face and he wrapped his arms around my neck and squealed with delight.

"Jack, Jack," I said over and over. "Thanks," I said.

"You're welcome," Gary's father said, his face impassive.

As I walked down the drive I felt Gary's mother's eyes on me from an upstairs window.

I trudged up the path towards my mother's house.

"Well?" my mother said, the minute we walked in the door.

"Well, Granny," Jack said.

"Well what?" I said, my irritation showing with her.

"What did Mrs Kenny say?"

I switched on the kettle. "She wasn't there."

My mother snorted. "Silly woman, always fussing," she remarked as she opened the fridge door. "Look what I got for you," she said to Jack and took an ice cream out of the fridge.

My temper had suddenly evaporated. At least I had Jack back.

The bright sunshine was teasing us, inviting us out to play. I would have preferred to stay indoors. I wanted it to rain. I longed for grey sky and dark days.

"Come on, Jack, let's go outside," my mother said.

Jack ran to the back door and banged on it.

"Wait a minute! You're just like your mother – you have no patience," my mother said.

I wanted to scream at her to stop picking on me. "Mammy," I snapped.

"I was only teasing," she said and smiled to herself. "Lighten up, as Vincent would say."

They walked out, hand in hand, to the garden and left me in the kitchen on my own.

I looked around at the dirty walls and grey ceiling and decided I would start to clean it. First I attacked the walls with soapy water. Every time a panicky thought entered my head I shoved it out. I had no time to think. I put all my energy into washing the walls. Tomorrow I would paint them and the ceiling.

Outside, Jack was helping my mother water her flowers. Bees hummed as they stole nectar from her summer blooms.

"You don't have to wash the walls," she said.

"I know, but I have to do something." I sat down on the grass beside her and Jack.

"Thanks for going to see the Kennys."

232

"Jack needs you and he needs his father." She leaned back in her sun-chair and I noticed how old and wrinkled she actually was. "You can't halve him so you're going to have to share him. I said that to Gary and I'm saying it to you."

I sat up and looked at my mother with new interest. "What did Gary say?"

She looked down at me. "Nothing much."

"How is he?" I asked anxiously.

"Angry, very angry. It's a terrible thing that you have done."

"I know, I wish I could change things."

"Well, you can't," she said in the dead-pan voice that always irritated me. "So you'll have to make the best of it."

I was furious with her and with myself. I headed into the kitchen and started to wash the ceiling.

It was after eleven o'clock. My mother had just gone up to bed. Jack was sleeping in my bed. I had finished my second glass of wine. All evening as I washed the ceiling, a thought kept coming into my head and every time it did, I blocked it. I was going to go and see Gary, tell him that I had finished with Damien. I kneaded the thought like it was dough. I twisted it, turned it, shaped it and hoped it made sense and the more I thought about it the more sense it made.

I could see myself getting into my car and driving down to his house. He never locked the back door. Excited by my own reckless thoughts, I tip-toed upstairs. I had a quick shower, changed my clothes, put on some make-up and stole out of my mother's house.

When I arrived at Gary's house it was in darkness. His

van was parked outside. I sat in my car and stared up at our bedroom window. Gary was up there.

I whispered his name; all around was still and quiet.

The distance between us was growing; every day that passed I felt I was losing him. Soon we would be strangers. I shook my head and told myself that was not going to happen. I had parked my car under a streetlight. A pool of orange light lit the car, making it easy for me to fix my hair and put on some more lipstick.

I was smiling to myself. Already I was dreaming up the scene. Gary was in bed, naked to his underpants. I could see myself creeping up the stairs, opening the bedroom door.

I found myself wanting to giggle. I pulled my face into serious lines.

I went into the house.

I had almost reached our bed when he said, "Michelle, is that you?"

I giggled and fell onto the bed laughing.

"You're pissed," he said.

"No, I'm not."

Gary switched on the bedside lamp. "I hope that Jack is okay?"

"He's asleep, and my mother is in the house."

"Well, go back to them," he said and turned his back to me.

"Gary," I said, tapping his back. "Please, Gary," I was hoping I sounded nice and seductive.

"Michelle, go home."

I hit him on the back a little too hard. "Sorry, pet." I kissed him. "Gary, come on, we're good together."

Before I knew what was happening, I felt myself being lifted off the bed and carried downstairs.

"Gary, please, don't do this! Let me stay, I need you, I need you so much!"

"Go home," he said dumping me outside his front door. I heard him turn the key in the lock.

I stared at the door, feeling ashamed of myself. Slowly, I walked back to my car. It felt like my life was over.

Chapter 27

Next morning, we all slept late. Jack, my mother and myself. When I had come back from Gary's house, the place that I once called home, I had finished the bottle of brandy. I needed it for comfort. I had to anaesthetise myself against the pain.

"Wake up, Michelle!"

I felt my mother shaking me.

"Go away," I muttered. I didn't want to rouse myself, I didn't want to face the day.

"You're late for work!" my mother shouted a little too loudly in my ear.

"Jack," I said, sitting up.

He was still asleep beside me. He turned and gave me a sleepy smile.

"Michelle!" my mother shouted at me. "Look at the time!" She put the clock in front of me.

"Oh no!" I threw back the covers. "I'll ring her and explain!" I ran down the stairs.

Twenty minutes later, I was walking quickly down the corridor towards our office.

"Can I have a word?" Eleanor said, stopping me in my tracks.

I walked into her office and sat down opposite her.

"Michelle," she said.

She was probably counting to ten before she spoke. Eleanor looked smart in her cream tailored suit and no-fuss white blouse. I looked creased and faded in my white shirt and navy trousers.

"Michelle, you're late again. This is a serious matter."

"I know," I said. "I couldn't sleep last night."

"Neither could I, but I still managed to get into work. You're not the only one with problems."

Inwardly I sighed. I thought it best to say nothing.

"I'm afraid I can't let this go." She picked up the letter off her desk and handed it to me.

I could tell it was an official warning. My hand trembled slightly as I took it.

"I'm sorry that I have to do this," she said.

We eyed each other across the desk.

"Eleanor, you don't have to do this," I said. My chin tilted defiantly.

"Michelle, I would like to think that I treat everyone fairly here," she said in her diplomatic voice. "I don't have one set of rules for you and a set for everyone else. If you have personal problems then you'll have to deal with them in your own time."

An awful weariness crept up on me, seeping into me, pulling me down with its weight. I felt detached from her and what she was saying.

"Michelle," she said quietly, "are you alright?"

"You're taking sides." I spoke the words as I thought them.

She laughed with forced brevity that confirmed what I had said was right.

"I'm not taking sides. What goes on between you and Gary is your business."

"He's talked to you," I said.

"Yes, he has."

"But you've never heard my side."

She suppressed a smirk.

"Well, you can stuff your stupid job," I said.

She looked at me in amusement and said, "You can't afford to quit. How are you going to support yourself and Jack?

"That is none of your business," I shot back.

"I suppose you'll run back to Damien. You've never been on your own – you couldn't stand it, could you?"

I glared at her and she looked away. This was the first row we'd ever had.

I walked out of her office, taking the letter. I was fuming. At my desk I scrawled my resignation on a piece of paper. I ignored Rosemary when she tried to speak to me. I marched back into Eleanor's office without knocking and handed it to her.

She scanned it and said, "So you're handing in your notice."

"That's right."

"Michelle, you can stay, you don't have to do this."

"I should have done it a long time ago." My body temperature was rising – now I started to count: one, two, three . . .

"I don't want us to fall out." Blotches of red trailed up her neck and onto her face. "You're overreacting." Her serious face softened.

I stood with my arms folded across my chest. "Can I leave today?"

"You don't have to. You can work out your notice."

"I'd rather not," I found myself saying. It felt like someone else was in my head speaking for me.

* * *

Rosemary's mouth dropped open when I told her my news.

"You can't," she said.

I laughed nervously.

"Oh, Michelle, what are you going to do now?"

"Guess what, I have no idea!" Instead of feeling panicked, I felt relieved.

The phones started to ring.

"Would you like me to call around later?" she asked.

"If you like," I said.

I answered a call and took a message. Rosemary was busy, dealing with a customer. I took my box of tissues and my diary off the desk and put them in my bag. I dumped all my unfinished paperwork in the in-tray. Then I picked up my photograph and avoided looking at my son or his father.

Two minutes later, I was in the carpark driving away.

"I've quit my job," I said to my mother.

She was standing at the sink peeling potatoes. Her eyes widened, almost in horror. She pulled out her chair and sat down on it.

"Michelle, what have you done?"

"I've quit my job," I repeated and laughed with a gaiety that I didn't feel.

"You had a good job, Michelle, and you gave it up," she said slowly.

"Mother, it's not the end of the world."

My mother rubbed her hands together. "Michelle, you're so hasty. Did you think this out?"

"No, not really, but I hated that job anyway."

"Are you going to go off with that fellow?"

"You mean Damien?"

She nodded. I could feel the warmth of the sun coming in the kitchen window and hitting my cheek.

"I don't know what I'm going to do."

"Nothing to do and the whole day to do it," my mother said.

My face burned with embarrassment when I thought about Gary. I poured a glass of water and drank it. I felt really hot. Jack was outside playing with the new tractor that my mother had bought him.

My mother followed me out to the garden.

I wanted to tell my mother to go away, to leave me alone. Knowing her, she was going to take it on herself to worry on my behalf.

"Don't worry I'm going to buy some paint and finish the kitchen before I do anything."

Her brow was furrowed in lines when she said. "Michelle, I'm worried about you."

"I'll cook us a nice lunch and you sit here in the sun," I suggested.

Later, the door-bell rang. We looked at each other. How

easily you can slip into old ways. As a family we were unaccustomed to visitors. We could never predict if *himself* would be drunk or sober. So we never felt comfortable having friends around even after he'd died. We felt his ghost was still hovering around the place.

"Who could that be?" she asked.

We were in the sitting-room watching the news. Jack had had such an active day, he had fallen asleep on the sofa.

My mother looked around the tiny sitting-room. Jack's clothes were thrown on the sofa, toys were scattered around the floor. She liked to keep the sitting-room tidy – the saluting area, she called it.

"It's only Rosemary," I said in a loud whisper. Rosemary lived in a detached five-bedroom house in a exclusive estate with views of the golf course from her kitchen window.

"What does she want?"

"She's just called round to see me."

My mother tutted in disgust. Then she announced that she was off to see her friend Lil. I felt relieved. She was allowing me to have her house to myself for a while.

Rosemary glided in smelling of some new perfume that I couldn't put a name on. She looked radiant. I couldn't imagine why. I mean things weren't going well for her either. She never mentioned ovulation or her monthly cycle or sperm counts, so I presumed there was nothing doing in that department.

"Michelle!" she said, her greeting loud enough to wake Jack.

"*Shhh!*" I said as loud as I could. I wanted to vent my own anger. I couldn't understand why she was so damn happy, it was only Thursday. "You'll wake Jack."

I longed for Rosemary to go and yet having her there was saving me from spending the evening on my own. She sat where my mother usually sat at the kitchen table. I busied myself making tea.

"So how are things?" she asked. Her voice was tinged with a new lightness.

"Weird," I admitted. The kettle started to boil. "What have I done?" I shook my head miserably. "I never thought it would come to this."

"I know, you poor thing," she said. She looked at me with sympathy.

We made small talk for a while. In the sitting-room I heard the tune for *Coronation Street*. Down at our house, Gary was probably home now. I could picture my empty kitchen. Something tugged at my insides. Any minute now I felt I was going to be physically sick. It had to be her new perfume.

"Michelle, I have some news," she said almost solemnly.

I looked across the table at her.

"I'm pregnant."

"That's great news! Congratulations! See, I told you it would happen!" I said with as much enthusiasm as I could muster. I could picture the rest of my life, Rosemary playing happy families with Danny and the baby – and me separated, living here with my mother. The thought was enough to make me suicidal.

I hardly got a word in edgeways as she went on to give me a detailed report.

"I feel sick all the time and I can't drink tea or coffee."

I jumped up and switched off the kettle. Then I filled two glasses of mineral water because all the Diet 7up was gone, thanks to Jack.

Time was moving on and there was still no sign of her going. I was hoping to ring my house, to see if Gary would answer the phone. If I could only get him to talk to me, I felt we could get over this and get back together again. I was already planning what I was going to say when I phoned him.

"Michelle," Rosemary said, "Gary and Eleanor had lunch today."

I knew by her tone that she had drawn her own conclusions.

"They're both –"

I waited for her to continue. She didn't. I couldn't believe it: Rosemary was stuck for words. She made a face. "They're both after breaking up –"

"Rosemary," I said and shook my head, "Eleanor is helping Gary to get his business going. Gary is useless when it comes to accounts and she's helping him. They're friends and nothing more." My laugh was full of bogus merriment when it came. "I suggested that Gary get Eleanor to help him."

All this talking had made me thirsty.

A bluebottle hummed around. I wanted to track him down and beat the living daylights out of him like my mother would do if she were here.

"You read too much into things," I said.

"If you say so," she said and sipped some mineral water.

"Were they holding hands?"

"No."

"Was she rubbing his leg under the table?"

"Michelle, stop it," Rosemary said and giggled.

"Can you imagine? Gary with her!" I shook my head incredulously.

We took a well-earned break from talking and Rosemary looked around the kitchen and then remarked, "Yellow." Then she tilted her head. "But which shade would be best? I have some samples at home – I could go and get them."

"Rosemary, relax. I'll buy some yellow paint tomorrow."

"You can't just buy some yellow paint. You've got to try a few samples out."

My eyes narrowed as I looked across the table at her. "I'll get a nice bright yellow tomorrow."

She waved her hand in the air. "Not something that's going to glare at you. The sun comes in this window – you want something that's going to soak up the sun rather than glare at you."

"So have you started decorating yet?"

Rosemary looked at me sheepishly. "No, Danny won't let me – he said we might be tempting fate."

"This must be the first time in your life that you haven't everything planned and organised."

Rosemary nodded her agreement. "I don't mind – I couldn't give a damn."

* * *

The phone rang as I dozed in my mother's chair. It was Damien. I could hear the desperation in his voice.

He said all the right things: that he loved me, that he wanted us to be together again, that I was the one person that he truly felt at home with. All those things that should have been said five damn years ago, he had only got round to saying now. Then, the line went quiet. I knew I should hang up, but I couldn't bear to. I was holding on too.

"I need you, Michelle. Now that my father is gone I realise that I'm on my own."

I had to hang up. There was no point in torturing myself and nothing was going to be gained by letting him spill his heart out to me.

Heavy-footed, I walked back into the sitting-room after I took the phone off the hook.

* * *

The door closed. I knew they had gone. Gary had come to pick Jack up. Usually, he worked Saturdays, but not this one. He was taking it off to spend it with his son.

"They're gone," my mother said as she walked into the kitchen.

"I heard," I replied.

"I'll do some work in the garden."

My mother spent her day in the garden while I spent it painting. When evening came I felt like getting out of the house. I rang Eleanor, but she was going out with friends. Then I rang Rosemary, but she wasn't up to a night out. My evening dwindled in a haze as I drank wine and sat opposite my mother, both of us fixed solidly in front of the TV.

Chapter 28

It wasn't third time lucky, it was more like twenty-third time. Every time I tried to phone Vincent all I got was his answering machine. I didn't want to leave a message – somehow I didn't want my mess recorded.

Vincent chuckled to himself when I said this and then added lightly, "Sorry, sis."

I knew he wasn't sorry; he never was. He always said that, but he never meant it. I could hear someone else in the background.

"Did I phone at a bad time?"

"Ah, no," he said, and he coughed.

"Sounds like I did."

"I've been meaning to phone you," he said. He was walking around. Vincent always had to be moving.

"Could you sit down? You're making me nervous."

"Very funny."

I heard him flop down on a sofa or bed.

"What's going on?" he asked.

"What do you mean?"

"Mother's worried about you."

"Great," I said, the word dripping with sarcasm.

"She says you've quit your job and you've split up with Gary. What's going on?"

I waited for him to continue, but he said nothing more. He was waiting for me.

"I've finished with Damien, but Gary still refuses to see me."

"Gary can be so stubborn."

"I know."

Vincent laughed. "I'm glad you quit that job."

"Oh Vincent, I did it without thinking! I shouldn't have, but I can't do anything about it now. I should have stuck with it."

"Sis, it's probably for the best. Losing your job and Gary, they've all happened for a reason."

"Really," I said.

"You were stuck in a rut, admit it! You hated your job and I'm not sure you ever loved Gary."

"I did, I do," I said in protest.

"If you did, would you really have been unfaithful to him?"

"I suppose not. But we both love Jack and I want what's best for him."

"Michelle, be honest, who do you really love?"

"Jack," I said.

Vincent laughed. "And next?"

"I'm not sure. I'm just confused."

"Is there anything I can do to help?"

"Would you phone Gary and try to talk to him for me?"

"I'll try," he said and paused. "Gary has always loved you, Michelle."

"Oh Vincent, if he'd just give me another chance I would make it up to him."

"I'll phone Gary," he said.

* * *

The days strung themselves into weeks and still Gary didn't want to talk to me. Every time he came to pick Jack up he would only meet my mother. He said he didn't want to see me.

For every action there is an equal and opposite reaction, the first law of physics; so what Gary did to me I did to Damien. I felt it was for the best. I had to let Gary know that he was the one I wanted to be with.

I got myself a job stacking shelves in my local supermarket. It was just what I needed. I was earning some money and I had time to think or not to think.

"Where are the cream crackers?" a high-pitched voice asked. I turned to look at Rosemary.

"Hi," I said. I gave her a little nudge and said, "Find them yourself."

"How are you?"

"I'm fine, Rosemary, how are you?"

Rosemary was glowing. "I'm great."

"How is work?"

"Oh, don't ask, we're so busy – I've suggested to Eleanor that she should rehire you."

I laughed. "She'll never do that and I don't want to go back. I want to move on."

Rosemary dropped her basket. "Move on to what?"

"I have no idea and even if I had I'm not going to talk about it here."

"Please come and visit me, I don't want us to lose touch," she said.

I stacked some tins of beans on top of each other.

"So what's this place like?" she asked.

"It's fine, for now," I said.

"Eleanor seems to have got over Bob. She's going around like someone that's trying very hard to keep a secret."

"Believe me, no one can keep a secret like Eleanor."

Rosemary fixed her hair. She had changed her colour to auburn.

"Would it upset you if she was seeing Gary?"

Here we go again. Rosemary was determined to prove her theory right, that they were seeing each other. She always got things arseways. "I doubt very much if Gary is seeing her. He doesn't like her, he never has," I said and steadied the cans of beans on top of each other.

"I suppose you're right," she said.

"Rosemary, I am right."

"I'm sorry, Michelle. I don't mean to be a pain, but I'm just trying to help."

"It's alright. I just wish Gary would talk to me. If he'd just let me apologise and explain that nothing like this will ever happen again, I know we could get over this and be happy together again like we were."

"I know," Rosemary said and glanced at her watch. "Oh dear, I have to dash, ring me!"

Rosemary trotted up the aisle with her basket. Seeing Rosemary made me long for my old routine. I wanted to ring Gary. I went down to my locker and got my mobile phone.

Outside, I dialled his number. Soft rain was falling from a grey sky.

I felt my heart was in my mouth, but I had to do it. Every day I thought about doing it and today was the day that I had nudged myself down a little further into doing something.

I got a cold and indifferent "Hi" back to my "Hi." Still I was determined to keep going. This cold start was not going to phase me.

"It's me," I said and then added, "Michelle," just in case he didn't know who it was.

"I know," was his cold reply.

I gripped my phone tighter. My hands were sticky with sweat. I took a quick breath and then muttered something about wanting to see him. The line went quiet.

My forehead throbbed with pain. I massaged it with my hand and waited for his reply.

Finally, I had to ask him if he was still there. Two girls pushed past me on the way to the toilet. I could grow to hate this job if I put my mind to it.

"I am," he said.

"Can we meet?" I ventured to ask. My stomach rumbled.

"No, Michelle, I can't meet you."

"Please."

"No," he said and then the line went dead.

I felt myself wilt under his quiet rejection. It was almost two months now and he still didn't want to see me. I bit my lip and tried to hold back my tears. Two more hours of stacking shelves, then I could go home to my son and mother.

Chapter 29

"Damien."

He was standing at my mother's front door. "What are you doing here?"

Damien looked at me as if the answer was apparent. It was almost two months since I had last seen him. I was glad to see that he looked pale and drawn – at least someone was suffering with me.

"Michelle, I've tried to stay away, but I can't." His voice was low and hollow.

It was Saturday. Gary had Jack for the day. My mother had gone shopping – I was alone in the house.

"Damien, I can't talk to you."

I knew it was wrong to invite him in.

"Can I come in?" he asked.

"I don't think that's a good idea," I said.

His expression changed to something more vulnerable.

"Oh Damien, please don't make this any harder than it has to be!"

"Could we go for a drive?"

My mind was twisting and turning the idea over. To go with Damien would be fatal.

"I can't," I said. I was still hoping that Gary would take me back.

The corners of his mouth lifted into a weak smile. "We could drive to Westport," he suggested.

Rosemary had called the night before with a bottle of wine and some bad news. She suspected that Gary and Eleanor were seeing each other. I explained *again*, slowly and clearly, that Eleanor was helping Gary with his accounts. But by the time I had the bottle of wine finished I was beginning to think that she could be right. So, I rang Damien. I had to talk to someone. Thankfully, my mother had gone to bingo. I had daydreamed of taking Gary to Westport to show him the house. I had even written to him, but the letters came back unopened. Now I felt unsure. I was tired of waiting for him to forgive me. I was lonely. I needed someone to talk to. When Gary wouldn't answer his mobile I rang Damien.

"You could go in your car; I could go in mine," he said. His eyes never left my face. "No one has to know," he said softly like he was afraid to speak too loudly.

"Damien, I can't."

"What have you got to lose?" he said, raising his hands in the air.

"My marriage."

"But it's over. Gary doesn't want you."

Me and my big mouth. If Rosemary hadn't filled my head with ideas of Gary and Eleanor together. If I hadn't drunk the bottle of wine. If Gary had answered his mobile and we'd got talking. If only.

Damien stood waiting for me to make up my mind. He looked smug and it annoyed me. Old suspicions started to surface. I wondered what he did in his free time? Was there someone else? Someone more interesting than me? I stood in my mother's hall between two minds: stay or go.

"Wait there," I said to Damien. I ran up the stairs, taking two steps at a time.

I rang Gary. "Hi," I said, my voice feather-weight in lightness.

"Jack is fine if that's why you're ringing."

"No, I'm not ringing about Jack," I said. Gingerly, I sat down on my bed, afraid to ask the next question. I had to hear it from Gary. "Are you seeing Eleanor?"

There, I had said it.

After a slight pause, he laughed. "So that's why you rang! To have a go at me!"

"Are you?"

"It's none of your business."

This was not the response I'd been expecting.

I took a breath. My mind was racing as I tried to find an easy escape route.

"You thought that when I cooled down I'd want you back," he said.

Words failed me. I opened my mouth to speak, but nothing came.

Then he continued, "It was you suggested I get help with my accounts from Eleanor and I did and one thing led to another."

I felt my insides tighten.

"But we have a son to think about," I said almost timidly.

"We do," he said.

"So it's over," I said. I closed my eyes waiting for the words to hit me.

"Yes, Michelle, it's really over."

"Gary, I'm so sorry," I said.

"And, so am I," he said and then he added with a firmness that I never heard before. "I don't want you upsetting Eleanor, making her feel guilty."

"I wouldn't do that," I said, my voice raised.

"I know you, Michelle. You'd do anything to get your own way."

I hung up. I couldn't take any more.

Quickly, I changed my clothes, dabbed on some make-up, gave myself a quick spray of Allure and I was ready to go.

"I'm ready," I said, a little breathless.

His handsome face creased into a smile. "Great!"

We drove out of Longford. The day was neither good or bad, just another day of greyness.

I couldn't wait any longer. I had to ask him to pull over.

"Why?" he asked.

I kissed him on the lips.

"Mmm," he said and grinned. "Now I see why."

He pulled back his seat and I straddled him. We kissed eagerly and passionately. Damien's hand moved under my skirt. That was the reason I wore a skirt. His hand moved slowly up my thigh. I groaned with anticipated pleasure. His fingers touched me.

"You're wearing no knickers," he said, and I could feel his hardness under me.

His finger moved gently, stroking me, finding me and penetrating me with a sureness that was driving me wild. I undid his shirt buttons and kissed his nipple.

I hadn't had sex in weeks and I just couldn't wait.

"Damien," I whispered, my voice throaty – I hoped it made me sound sexy.

He moved his finger even deeper inside. His breath was hot against my face, our mouths teasing distance away from each other. Cars sped past, yet we were safe in our secluded spot.

We gazed at each other. We kissed, first gently, then we were tongue-deep in each other.

"That's nice, but it's not what I want," I said.

I lifted myself a little off him. My hands eagerly undid his belt and button and then his fly. He pulled his erect penis out.

"Nice," I said.

We moved into the back seat, Damien under me. He moved inside me. Our rhythm increased with each movement. I felt at that moment that we were one. We stared into each other's eyes, holding on, knowing at any minute now we were going to come.

"Michelle," he said. He was igniting me. I felt he had reached my inner being. I saw the expression change on his face. I knew we were moving together, bonding, as our journey approached its climax. Damien muttered my name again and then I felt him fill me.

I kissed his forehead. "Thank you."

"You're welcome."

He helped me fix my skirt and gave me some tissues to wipe myself. I took my sexy knickers out of my bag and put them on.

We drove on to Westport with the radio blaring. We didn't need to talk. We had communicated.

Later, Damien went into town to do some shopping. I rang my mother and told her I was in Westport and I was staying the night. My mother always felt she had licence to insult when she chose to and I was wondering what had happened when the expected smart remark wasn't forthcoming.

"What did you do today?" I asked.

"I went to the hairdresser's."

As usual, Vincent wasn't home when I rang him. I had lost track of time and I didn't care if he was up or not. I left a message on his answering machine.

As expected, we had a lovely evening. Damien cooked dinner and we ate by candlelight. We drank wine and made love almost in slow motion in a big four-poster bed. It was perfect. There was the occasional moment when I thought about my son.

Next morning, we sat opposite each other, the kitchen table between us. It was cluttered with dishes and newspapers. I felt the urge to move them. Why, I didn't know.

I was shocked. Damien wanted to go back to Australia. "Sell everything and move back to Sydney" were his exact words.

"What do you think?" he probed, when I didn't reply.

There was nothing that I could say. Damien was an only child in the habit of getting his own way. He never had to consider other people. He was asking my opinion and yet it was clear he had his mind made up what he wanted to do. I didn't know what to say so I said nothing.

Now I sat across the kitchen table and looked at his handsome face, saw the furrowed lines on his brow. I saw the child inside the man, the spoiled selfish child that wanted everything his own way.

"Sell everything," the words echoed in my ears. Even though it was raining outside I still wanted to go for a walk, to get away from Damien.

I had forgotten this side of him, how quickly he detached and if I complained he said he didn't know what I was talking about.

I knew now I was only fooling myself. I didn't love Damien. I looked at this accomplished man, that was always out of my league and I wondered if I ever really had loved him. He was capable of hurting me so much and being unaware of it. He'd done it in Sydney and he was doing it now. I had my son to consider. Jack had to come first. Yet, he never mentioned my son. He never even mentioned his name. I wanted to shout at him. To scream Jack's name over and over again. To tell him Jack existed. As a child I had always felt insignificant and the same thing wasn't going to happen to my precious son.

I saw a pair of wellies by the door. They looked like they belonged to a woman. They must belong to Nancy the housekeeper. I pulled my chair back and moved away from the table. He kept his head down, his eyes fixed on whatever article he was reading. I slipped into the wellies, hoping he would notice. He didn't. I pulled on my raincoat and left by the back door.

The air was fresh and I felt the cold wind slapping against my face. I started to walk, my speed building with each step. I wanted to get warm and clear my head. I should be an expert on rows – I witnessed so many when I was a child – but I'm not. I wanted to compose myself. I wasn't going to be reduced to tears by him.

I didn't stop to take in the view, I just walked. I wished Jack was there and we could walk into puddles together.

I can't go to Australia. Gary won't let me take Jack and I won't go without him, I said to myself and I meant it. My mother's words come into my head: you can't halve him so you'll have to share him.

When I returned, he had left the kitchen. I noticed he hadn't cleared the table, but I was not surprised. Old habits die hard.

I cleared the table. I wanted the place to look nice when I left. Coffee rings marked the table. While I was wiping them away, I thought of my schooldays and how I always managed to get everything wrong while Eleanor always got everything right.

I replaced the vase of flowers on the pine table. And looked around me. This house was *mine*, I thought. The next time I would bring Jack. We needed a holiday.

This was a big house in need of a real family. It needed children and a dog to fill it up with love and noise. The place was eerily quiet. Perhaps that was why Damien's father left me the house.

I walked into the sitting-room. Damien was lying on the sofa.

"Hi," he said.

"I'm going," I said.

He turned to look at me. "Did you have a nice walk?"

"Yes," I said. I sat down on the sofa beside him.

"I'm going home."

"Home?"

"Yes, Damien, home or back to Longford," I said. A thousand more words were lined up, waiting to be strung together to make my case. I knew it was no use, I was only wasting my breath. I knew Damien had made up his mind to return to Australia and nothing I could say or do would make him change his mind.

He reached out his hand to me. I touched it and smiled sadly to myself.

"Think it over," he said. "Don't just knock what I'm saying."

"Damien, I can't go with you. Gary will never let me take Jack out of the country and I can't go without him."

"We could get a good solicitor – I can afford the best," he said, his words full of fire and fight.

"I can't do that to Jack. He needs what I never had: a happy childhood." I was hoping my words would reach him in some way. "We could stay here, live in this house: you and me and Jack."

I heard the clock tick away the minutes.

"But we loved Sydney and we had a great life there."

"We had and we can have a great one here."

"Let's give Sydney a shot. If it doesn't work out we can always come back!"

I didn't reply.

I climbed the elegant stairs and thought of my mother's narrow one. Tonight I would climb it. Mechanically, I packed the few bits that I had brought with me. I had done this before; we had played this scene before. The morning that I had left for the airport, I had tried to tell him I was pregnant, but he wouldn't listen to me.

He would do nothing. He would lie on the sofa, ignoring the bang of the front door when he heard it. I felt relieved. He was letting me go.

My life would be much simpler. I would have to look for another job. The second step on the stairs creaked as I walked down. I went quietly, just like we used to do at home, when our father was sleeping on the sofa.

"Poor Mammy," I muttered and I was amazed at my own words. She was always trying to please him and keep peace in our house.

I opened the front door and allowed it to slam after me. As I walked I heard my feet crunch the gravel with each step I took. A slight breeze rustled through the trees.

I had almost reached the road when I heard him calling my name.

"How are you going to get home?" he asked. He was breathless after running.

"The bus," I said.

"What if there is no bus or train?"

I shrugged.

He pulled me close to him. "Why are we fighting? It was never like this when we were in Sydney."

"It might have been if I hadn't always been so eager to please you," I said frankly.

"Michelle," he said. He pulled back and glared at me.

"I've always tried to please you."

"You're all I've got, Michelle," he said and took me in his arms again. "I don't want to lose you."

"Damien, you have to understand I have a son, a little boy who needs me. I feel so responsible for him, I have to do what is right for him."

Damien nodded. "I know," he said. He took my hand in his. "Let's go back."

We walked up the winding avenue. The sun came through the leaves of the old trees and transformed the ground into moving patterns of light.

We sat at the kitchen table. Damien made tea.

I was glad he didn't want to make plans right now. For the moment it was just nice to enjoy this without planning out a detailed future.

Chapter 30

No matter how I tried I couldn't see us together. Something was missing and I felt that it was something in me that was missing. Damien was attentive to me – wasn't this what I'd always wanted? Wasn't I starting to sound like a spoiled brat? I couldn't fathom what was wrong with me.

With Gary it was different: we knew each other. He was comfortable to be with. There were no surprises: he was safe, predictable.

"Rosemary rang," said my mother. "When I told her you'd gone to Westport she told me you had to ring her the minute you got back."

"Mmm," I replied.

"Are you listening?"

"Yes, Mother, I am."

"Well ring her, I don't want her calling around here." She rubbed her dry hands together.

"What's up?"

"Nothing is up," she shot back.

"There is," I said.

"I just missed you and Jack. I thought it would be nice to have some time on my own, but I missed you both so much. I don't know what I'm going to do when you move."

"I wasn't thinking of moving."

My mother studied my face. "I'm not sure I believe that."

"Well, it's true."

She sighed.

"Gary doesn't want me," I said.

"So that's why you fecked off to Westport with himself."

"His name is Damien."

My mother tilted her head in disgust.

"Mammy, why are you always like this with me? You're always putting me down. How often did Vincent mess up and you wouldn't say a thing to him."

My mother sat upright in her chair and squared her shoulders. "Vincent is like his father. I had hoped you could have made more of yourself."

I was rendered speechless.

I wanted to ask her why she had never praised me or told me she loved me. I knew it was not my mother's fault that I was in this mess. And I didn't know why I wanted to ask her that but I did. And I hadn't the damn courage to.

The phone started to ring.

"I wonder who that could be?" she said.

"I have no idea," I said and went to answer it.

"You're back from Westport, tell me everything!"

"It's only Rosemary," I said to my mother.

Rosemary was like a ray of sunshine trying to break through the bruised clouds.

"*Only* Rosemary, thanks a lot," she said, and laughed.

She wanted a detailed account of my weekend with Damien.

"There is nothing to tell."

"We'll meet for lunch tomorrow," she said.

"What about Danny?" I inquired.

"I'm fed up meeting him for lunch. I want to hear all about your weekend."

"There isn't much to say. Only you were right, Eleanor and Gary are seeing each other."

"How do you feel about that?"

I could feel my mother's eyes on me. "See you tomorrow."

"Being pregnant is no fun."

She was ready for a marathon chat on the phone. I wasn't.

"Agreed."

"I'm tired all the time and I'm always hungry. I'm getting so fat!"

"I don't think you are."

"I am," she said, insistently.

"But you'll lose it all after the baby," I said, attempting another angle.

"I hope so."

"Bye, see you tomorrow," I said quickly before she started another conversation.

"The bistro is nice," she said.

"Fine, great, see ya then, at one." I hung up. I just couldn't listen to any more.

"She gets on my nerves," my mother said.

I looked around my mother's sitting-room and felt peculiar. It was only dawning on me that I might never live in my house again. I might never walk through the rooms. Gary and I would never share a meal or make love or do any of the things

264

that we had done together again. I flopped down on the sofa and felt the full impact of where my actions had led me.

Envy tightened my chest when I thought of Rosemary pregnant and so happy with her husband. Then, there was my so-called friend Eleanor. It had never occurred to me that Gary would be interested in her. She was dull and boring and my head raced as I tried to pick out words to describe her. Eleanor was also reliable; something I wasn't.

* * *

A few days later, I was kneeling down stacking biscuits when a familiar voice said "Hi" and I looked up to see Gary, looking down at me.

"This is a surprise," he said.

I looked at him blankly.

"You working here," he went on to explain.

"Ah, yes," I said and felt my stomach do a quick nervous rumble.

"So," he said as he shuffled from foot to foot, "how are you?"

I made a comical face. "How would I be, answering stupid questions all day? Where are the toilet rolls? Where is the checkout? You name it, they ask it."

"I think Jack has got all his teeth," he said.

"I hope so. By the way, that's a nice jacket you got him. Red suits him."

Gary looked embarrassed. "I'm afraid I didn't buy it, Eleanor did."

"Oh," I said and attempted to smile.

"Michelle, we've got to make the best of this situation."

"Yes, I suppose so," I said, eager to agree with anything he had to say.

"Let's make a deal," he said and looked directly at me. "Let's both try and do the best for our son."

I put out my hand and he shook it. "Yes," I said, "let's try and do that."

He walked away and I pretended to stack packets of biscuits on top of each other.

A chapter in my life had closed. I didn't want to stack shelves for the rest of my life. I didn't want to answer phones for the rest of my life. Yet, I didn't know what I wanted to do.

* * *

At least once a week Rosemary and I met for lunch. She said she wanted to be updated on what was going on in my life and I always got a detailed account of what was going on in hers.

I always felt reluctant when it came to meeting Rosemary. She was always so full of chat. Yet, at the same time it was good to talk and I needed to talk to someone.

She always asked how Damien was and I always responded that he was fine. This was never adequate and when I hinted that I didn't want to talk about him, she ignored this and pressed on anyway. Rosemary was an action woman; she always got what she wanted and she couldn't understand what I was doing. I explained to her that I was doing plenty. Her eyes grew bigger in her head and she looked at me in disbelief.

You've got to make things happen, was her current slogan. I wanted to ask her what magazine did she read that in but refrained. I didn't want to have an argument with my very last friend, especially today, as I wasn't up to it.

We both looked up at the same time as Eleanor and Gary

walked into the busy restaurant. They were standing at the self-service with trays.

"Would you like to go?" Rosemary asked.

I had just taken a few spoons of my vegetable soup and I hadn't touched my chicken sandwich.

"No, we'll stay. In fact, we could shuffle around a bit and let them sit with us."

"Do you think that's a good idea?"

I laughed. "Got you," I said.

Rosemary shook her head, "How can you act so bloody cool?"

I shrugged and looked stony-faced at her. I wanted to eat my lunch. I didn't want to be interrogated.

"I miss us working together. Sally is nice, but she's so quiet – she just works all the time."

"Well, come and pack shelves with me," I suggested.

Rosemary looked down at her bulging tummy. "Look at the size of me," she said proudly.

"You look great," I said.

Rosemary flashed me a bright smile and said, "I feel great."

Eleanor and Gary walked past. We all exchanged smiles and they hurried along as they tried to find two vacant seats.

"They're sitting down at the back of the restaurant," she whispered to me.

"That's great," I replied.

Rosemary shook her head. "Doesn't it bother you?"

"Sometimes," I admitted.

"Good. For a minute there, I though you weren't human,"

"Maybe that's it," I said and thought of what she said. I had learned from an early age to feel nothing. I glanced at my watch. "Gosh, look at the time."

Chapter 31

I was lying in bed. I could feel his long-limbed body close to me.

"Good morning," he said.

I moved lazily. "It's early, Damien," I said.

He picked at my earlobe with his mouth. "I know it is," he said, "but I've been missing you all week."

"You need a baby," I said, my voice still full of sleep.

Damien chuckled softly in my ear. "Let's make one," he suggested.

"I mean if you had a baby you wouldn't be so full of energy all the time," I said. My voice was sharp. I moved away from him.

"I'm tired too," he said, throwing back the covers and getting out of bed.

I heard him in the shower. Part of me wanted to go in and join him; part of me didn't. I took my mobile phone off the bedside locker and dialled Gary's number. I was worried about Jack. I didn't like leaving him and coming to Dublin.

"How is Jack?" I asked.

Eleanor answered the phone. "He's fine now," she said.

"What does 'fine now' mean?" I knew by her tone she was hiding something.

"We had to get the doctor last night. We were worried. We couldn't get him to settle." I could hear some noise in the background.

Then Gary got on the phone. "Jack is fine," he said reassuringly. "We panicked. I suppose he was missing you and I thought there was something else wrong with him so I phoned the doctor."

"I see. I'll go home today."

"There's no need – we're going to bring him to *Peter Pan*."

"But he might get upset tonight."

"If he does, we'll ring you," Gary said.

"I'd better leave my mobile switched on," I said.

Gary ignored what I said and continued, "Would you like to talk to him?" I was deep in a baby discussion when Damien got out of the shower. He had a white towel wrapped around his waist and rivulets of water ran down his chest. He was trying to ignore me.

"Bye darling, I love you," I said and blew some kisses into the phone.

Damien stood at his wardrobe. He had the door opened and he was looking inside.

"Sorry," I said softly. I got out of bed and walked over to him.

He turned around to me. "I'm sorry too."

"For what?"

He shrugged his wide shoulders, his eyes glazed. "For not

understanding what you're going through." He pushed me playfully down on the bed.

"Oh Damien," I said, my voice low and humble, "I'll do anything you ask."

He pulled my T-shirt off. "Love me, woman," he commanded.

He lay back on the bed and slowly I pulled the towel off him. I kissed his penis and felt it grow as I put it in my mouth. I waited for my own mounting excitement, but it didn't happen. Jack was okay, so why couldn't I relax?

Damien groaned. For some strange reason that I couldn't fathom the buzz was gone. I straddled him.

"Not so fast," he said. He gently pushed me over and started to work on my body. He kneaded my shoulders with his firm fingers and coaxed a moan of pleasure from me. At last I was starting to unwind.

He looked at me in admiration.

"Nice," he said.

"Oh Damien," I moaned. I wanted fast sex. I spread my legs. He got the message and entered me. He moved slowly, teasing me. Then, we started to move together, to find our rhythm, our speed increasing with each movement. I felt myself both surrender and dominate as we rolled over and back on the bed. Damien's face grew intense, he whispered something endearing in my ear. I clung to him and I felt us being swept away as we rode this great wave of passion. I arched myself into him and felt a sudden surge of pleasure inside.

I gasped for breath.

"Michelle," he said, his voice thick with emotion. We had reached a climax and slowly we had to climb back into ourselves. We snuggled up and kissed each other as was our custom.

We went into town and had a late lunch and did some shopping.

It was becoming a habit, me coming to Dublin every weekend to meet him. And somewhere through the day he slipped in the idea of us going back to Sydney. At the time I ignored it, I didn't want to discuss it.

As I returned home on the train I knew he wouldn't forget it. He would hold onto this like my father held onto a thousand grudges against my mother. Our union would ebb and flow, but it would never be constant.

I knew then I had to let him go. Yet, I didn't want to let him go. I, Michelle, was afraid of being on my own. I didn't like the idea of spending every Saturday night in with my mother. No man in my life . . . the idea didn't appeal at all. Yet, what was the alternative?

Without phoning I headed down to Gary's house. I felt like dropping in unannounced.

I had to admit I was a little taken aback when Eleanor answered the door.

"Come in," she said, her voice threaded with nervousness. She was dressed in faded jeans and a pale blue shirt.

"We were just watching *Bob the Builder* . . ." She folded her arms across her chest and looked at me nervously.

"That's nice," I said, trying to adjust to seeing her in my house, to wait for her to offer me a cup of tea.

"Mammy!" Jack said, his whole face beaming with joy when he saw me.

I picked him up in my arms and hugged him to me. "I missed you so much!"

She offered to make me tea or coffee. I refused.

"If you like I can go?"

"No, Eleanor. I shouldn't have dropped in unexpectedly like this."

"It's okay."

"How's work?"

"We're busy." She laughed nervously. "But we're always busy."

She got up off the sofa, picked some toys up from the wooden floor and put them in the toy box. I watched her doing the things I should be doing. I got up and helped her.

"How many times a day do you do this?"

Her shiny hair hid her face. "A lot of times, but I don't mind."

Jack took my hand in his, pulling me to go and see his new toy train.

"It's lovely," I said. "You're a spoiled little boy." I looked up at Eleanor. "I'll have that cup of tea if it's still on offer."

She smiled at me, relieved that I'd given her something to do.

"How was Dublin?" she asked, when she came back with my cup of black tea and one for her self.

"Fine," I replied politely.

We were dancing around each other, both of us afraid of saying the wrong thing.

"Did you have a nice weekend?" I asked.

"Yes, I had."

"How is Rosemary?"

"She's been off work all week."

"Is she all right?"

Eleanor visibly relaxed now she felt we were on safe

ground. "She's fine – they took her into hospital during the week, but she's out now."

"Gosh, when she didn't phone for our weekly lunch I thought nothing of it."

"Mammy!" Jack said, raising his arms for me to pick him up.

We rubbed noses. "I was missing Jack so much in Dublin, I decided to come home early. You don't mind if I take him now?"

"Gary is just gone to do some shopping." An awkward moment passed and then she said, "But I'm sure he won't mind."

She quickly collected his stuff and put it in the car.

"Give your Auntie a kiss," I said.

He gave Eleanor a quick kiss and then we drove off.

* * *

The next day after work I dropped off to visit Rosemary.

"How are you?" I asked.

"I'm fine, now."

She was laid out on her sofa, a pile of cushions built up around her.

"What happened?"

"I started to bleed and they thought it best if I went into hospital for a few days. It wasn't serious." She waved a hand in the air. "Enough about me. What about you?"

"You should have rung me."

"Believe me, if it had been serious I would have rung you. Now tell me what's happening with you."

"It's Damien's birthday in two weeks. Have you any ideas on what I can get the man who has everything?"

"Wrap yourself up!" she said. Her eyes sparkled as she suggested it. But we'd done all that. Summer was almost over, I could feel it in the air. Soon the leaves would take on the golden hues of autumn.

"Seriously," I said.

"A watch, camera, video recorder –"

"Slow down, I don't have that much money."

"Has he got a hobby?" she asked.

"He used to scuba dive."

Rosemary shrugged. "I can't think – usually I'm full of ideas."

"So what are you going to do with the house in Westport? It sounds magnificent."

"It is out of this world. But I feel it's not really mine."

"It is yours legally. I hope you're not going to move to Westport. I'm dying to see it."

"I know you are. But I'm not ready to show it off yet."

"I see," she said and sighed. We sipped tea and Rosemary ate three fun-size bars after each other. "I'm worried. I know the doctor has reassured me that everything is alright, but," she took out a tissue and blew her nose, "I want this baby so much."

"It will be alright," I said.

"I hope so," she said. "I don't think I could bear it if I lost it."

"I know," I said. "Would you like me to go?"

"Would you mind staying for another while? I hate being on my own and Danny won't be home until six."

She blew her nose. "And if he isn't you're going to have to go and drag him home."

"Me? I hope you're joking."

"I'm not," Rosemary said.

Sometime later Danny arrived home. I was glad to see him. We had spent the evening looking through glossy magazines featuring different types of nurseries and I couldn't take another cradle decked out in lace. I argued my point with Rosemary that they weren't practical. All babies did was throw up. She said they looked divine and would be perfect for her nursery. I agreed with her as she was set on getting it and who was I to disagree with a woman who knew her own mind?

I picked up my jacket. "I'll ring you tomorrow."

Danny loosened his tie and took off his jacket. He ushered me to the door.

"Thanks for coming," he said in a low whisper. I could smell alcohol off his breath. "I'm worried about her."

"She's going to be alright?"

He nodded and said cheerfully, "Of course she is."

"You've put those biscuits in the wrong place," Gavin said to me. I remembered baby-sitting him. He walked around the place like he owned it – well, he was the manager. He always knew when you were slacking and in the nicest possible way he would suggest to you to do something.

I bit my lip to stop my mouth from going off. I couldn't afford to lose my job; I needed the money.

"They go there," Gavin said and pointed down the aisle.

"No one told me, so I presumed they went here," I said. I just couldn't let him have the last word. Gavin was tall and wore a suit well. He was the first man I met that could actually do two things at once. He gave me a cheeky-boy look. I couldn't spend the rest of my life stacking shelves. There had to be an easier way to earn a living.

"When you've finished that I want you to go into the store and help Mike," he said.

"Right," I said and turned away from him.

His mobile rang and he moved a little away from me to answer it. Then he looked across, saw two girls having a chat and gave them that look that said get back to work. He walked purposefully away. We knew he was heading for his office and we could relax for a few minutes.

I took all the biscuits down and lined them up like little soldiers. Customers passed and wanted me to help them take down biscuits from the top shelves. My arms grew tired from stacking biscuits. I moved all the promotional stuff and the biscuits to the end of the aisle.

It was time for my break and I was delighted. I saw the assistant manager peep around the corner to see that I was doing it properly. If she had been brought up in Longford I probably would have baby-sat her. I bared my teeth at her. She thought I was smiling and smiled back at me.

I picked up a packet of chocolate-chip cookies and wondered if they were good value: buy one and get the second packet free.

Out of nowhere the word "ticket" came into my mind. That's what I would buy Damien. A ticket so he could go back to Sydney. He still had his apartment there and his friends. I knew he'd go. I didn't know if he would want to come back.

I couldn't possibly do it. Could I? Risk going out and buying him a ticket? What if he didn't come back? The thought was too scary to think about, so I dismissed it.

My mother liked chocolate cookies. I would buy them. I added another person to my love list: my mother.

In the distance I could see Eleanor walking around with a basket. This place was worse than the pub on a Saturday night. She was dressed in white tailored trousers and a pink top. She didn't look ordinary anymore; she looked slim and attractive. I found myself thinking about her in our bed. Eleanor and Gary. I ran down to the toilets. I just couldn't bear to meet her. Jealousy rose in my throat like bile; I had to swallow past it. "Stop thinking about them," I said to myself.

I ran some water over my flushed face to cool me down. I walked back towards my shelves and bumped straight into her. She was as surprised as I was.

"Eleanor!"

"Michelle! I didn't know you worked every day."

I laughed. "This isn't easy."

"No." Her neck was already blotchy with embarrassment. "See you," she said and hurried off.

Eleanor didn't take relationships lightly. She was an all or nothing woman – there was no halfway house with her. They had both found refuge and a safe harbour in each other.

* * *

It was that time of the week again that I had to meet Rosemary. We met in our usual café and got our usual spot by the window.

"You can't spend the rest of your life packing shelves," Rosemary said.

"Why not?"

"Well, for one reason you're getting too old."

"I know," I said. "Look at me, I'm hitting thirty and what have I got to show for it?"

"You've got Jack," she said, as she rubbed her round belly.

"Yes, Jack," I repeated.

"So," she said and flashed me a large smile, "have you made up your mind?"

She made a face when she saw my blank expression. "The birthday present!"

"Yes. I forgot I had asked you for ideas. Yes, I have made up my mind: a ticket."

"A holiday, nice one," she said.

"No, a ticket for Damien to go back to Sydney."

Rosemary's mouth dropped open. "You only bought one ticket!" She leant back. Her blonde bob wasn't as shiny as it usually was. "Why?"

"He loves Sydney, it's where he wants to be. He'd never have left it only his father was dying." I looked at my nails. They needed to be filed and shaped, but I couldn't be bothered. "It was his father who insisted on him finding me."

"I see," Rosemary said. "Poor Michelle. First you had two men and now you have none."

I thought for a moment and said, "Yes, that's it."

Rosemary resettled herself on the seat. "He might come back."

Chapter 32

I had bought a new dress, especially for the occasion. It was ridiculously expensive.

"This is a special occasion," Rosemary said.

I had brought her along to help me choose. It was a khaki/black animal-print dress, calf-length with a tie-neck. Rosemary said it looked great on me and she was the expert. She knew what was needed for the occasion.

I booked dinner for us in a local restaurant. I no longer had to weave around the situation, I was free to thread my own way. The fabric of my life had changed; things had turned from silk to cotton.

* * *

I turned to look at Damien. He smiled at me as the green landscape and stone walls whirled past us. He was driving too fast. I would have liked us to go at a more leisurely pace. We had the whole weekend – why did he have to rush?

My mother was taking care of Jack for me. Gary and

Eleanor were going away for the weekend. It occurred to me
as we drove along that I had never thanked my mother for
taking me in. Jack and myself had just dropped into her
quiet life and filled it with chaos. I had taken her for granted
just like my father had.

"You're quiet," Damien broke into my thoughts.

I smiled at him reassuringly. As if to say all was well.

He patted my knee affectionately, like a father might his
child. The touch felt like something more, like I was more
than a lover.

"I rang Nancy, told her that we were coming down," he
said.

"That was nice."

"Are you okay?" he asked, while taking a turn too quickly.

"*Jesus!*" I heard myself shout.

The car went out of control. I gripped the car seat,
grateful that I had my seat-belt on. In those few panicky
moments I heard myself call my son's name. Damien twisted
the steering wheel and tried to take control of the car. It
skidded as he put his foot hard on the brakes. We just missed
a van that was coming straight for us. Damien pulled in off
the road. I opened my window to let in some fresh air and
rid the car of the smell of fear and perspiration.

"That was close," he said, when he got his breath back.

I nodded. Somehow, I had felt something like this was
going to happen.

"Drive slower," I said. Surprised that I could speak. My
mouth was dry and I longed for a cold drink of water.

He turned on the ignition and pulled out without saying
a word.

* * *

Nancy had certainly done a good job. The house was looking wonderful. Fresh air drifted in the open widows. She had picked flowers from the garden and arranged them in old vases throughout the house.

I unpacked and hung my new dress in the wardrobe. I had paid for it with my credit card. After tonight I knew I would never wear this dress again.

"When he sees you in that dress he'll probably ask you to marry him," Rosemary had said in the shop.

I wanted to laugh when she said this, but I couldn't. It wasn't funny, it wasn't a joke, it wasn't going to happen.

I had the evening all planned. We would go to dinner and I would bring the ticket and birthday card with me. When we finished our meal, I would give it to him.

I rang my mother. I knew Jack was fine, but I had to talk, to reassure myself that someone still loved me.

"Everything is fine," she said, and added, "Enjoy yourself."

"I will," I said. "Thanks, Mammy." I hoped she understood that I was thanking her for all she had done for me. Suddenly, I felt very old.

An American appliqué quilt was draped over the old cast-iron bed, blues from the quilt picked up in the curtains and walls and lights. Someone had put a lot of thought into the room.

I took a long bath while Damien went for a walk, then I got dressed slowly. There was no hurry. I wanted to prolong this evening for as long as I could. I was afraid to face tomorrow, yet I knew it had to be done.

"You look stunning," Damien said, when he walked into the bedroom we shared.

"How are you?" I asked.

"A bit better. We could have crashed today." His face was drawn and pale. "We were this close," he said, showing a measurement with his finger and thumb, "to being killed."

"I know," I said. I hugged him and asked, "Would you prefer we didn't go out?"

"No," he said. "You look so lovely, I want to go out and show you off." He grinned, a lecherous look in his eye. "I want everyone to see you." He studied me for a moment and then said, "You look beautiful."

"Do I?" I said. "Would you like a drink?" I moved away from him.

"Mmm," he said, "that would be nice."

"Great," I said. I knew I needed a drink if I was going to get through the evening. There was never going to be a perfect moment to give him the ticket.

I went downstairs and strolled over to the window of the drawing-room. Damien and his father had never used this room. I never tired of looking out the old sash windows; every time I was moved by the grandeur and charm of the place.

Old paintings hung on the green walls, the colour reminding me of mushy peas that you had let boil for too long. The furniture was formal and elegant. I walked through the double doors and into the dining-room. I wondered what it would be like to eat here at night. What effect would the chandelier light have on the aubergine walls. Would I like the effect? Who would I invite to dinner?

Back in the sitting-room, I poured us two generous drinks. The pink roses were arranged in a crystal vase. I couldn't help but smell them. The delicate petals reminded me of Eleanor. Was she dressing up tonight, putting on sexy underwear so that my husband Gary could take them off? I shook when I thought of it.

I was surprised to find that I missed Eleanor. I'd always thought she'd be there in the background for me. Rosemary had tried to brush it off when I asked her how Eleanor was. "She's well," Rosemary said. Of course she was well – she had my husband to comfort her. I knew she deserved happiness – she had been disappointed with Bob and a string of others before him.

Eleanor always accepted disappointment gracefully. She adjusted herself, made herself flexible to suit the situation, but she never compromised herself.

Soon, I would be free, unattached, available – or 'on the shelf' as my mother would put it.

Damien came into the room and hugged me. "You're cold!"

"A little," I said.

I moved away from him and out to the hall where I had purposefully left my bag. His eyes were on me when I came back into the room. I was conscious of him watching my every move.

Van Morrison's 'Real Real Gone' was playing on the CD player.

"I got you a present," I said. My mouth was dry.

"I thought you'd forgotten my birthday!"

"Of course I haven't," I said lightly and handed him the envelope.

"It's not until tomorrow."

I finished my drink and felt I needed another, but stopped myself. I didn't want to get tipsy yet. I had a long evening ahead of me. We stood by the sideboard. I moved towards the open window. It was done. I had given him the envelope with the ticket. I hadn't meant to do it so soon, but something about the way he walked into the room – his assured step – had annoyed me.

Softy dewy rain fell and everywhere was hushed. I knew, after the rain the earth would smell fragrant and fresh. Already, I was aching to go for a walk.

Damien walked towards me.

"So we're going to Sydney," he said. His arms around my waist, his lips trailing slow lingering kisses down the back of my neck.

I attempted to turn to look at him; he held me firm.

"Damien," I said, and giggled – he was exciting me.

"You look so good," he whispered in my ear.

"My hair, it took me ages to fix it!" I turned around in his arms.

I could smell the sweet fragrance of the summer flowers from the open window. I looked out and saw the light rain had stopped. I could hear a cuckoo sing and I wondered to myself if that was what I was: someone who was too lazy to build her own nest and went to live in someone else's.

"I'm not going with you," I said. The words were out, the words that I had rehearsed in my head a thousand times. I had finally said them.

"I see," he said, and moved away from me. Two strides brought him towards the fireplace. "Why?"

"Because," I attempted to say, and I found I couldn't speak. I took a breath and then said, "Because of –"

He glared at me.

"Jack," I said. "I can't leave Jack."

"You still want to get back with Gary; so you bought me the ticket to get me out of the way so you can work on him while I'm gone."

I shook my head. "That's not true. Gary is seeing Eleanor! In fact, they've gone away this weekend together –"

"Yes, but you want him back!" Damien yelled at me.

"You want to go back to Sydney and I'm giving you the choice," I said, my voice raised to match his.

"Michelle," he said in a calmer voice. He walked towards me, his arms outstretched. "Come with me!"

"I can't go back there."

"But you loved Sydney!" I felt his warm breath against my skin.

"I know I did, but . . ." My words faded.

I turned and looked at the magnificent garden. I wanted to walk in it, to inhale the sweet fragrance from the roses. They stood tall and elegant, their last days of glory in the autumn light.

"Damn it, Michelle, I didn't know you were pregnant! If I could turn the clock back I would!" He had opened up the past again; broken through the cracks that I had carefully sealed up. Right now I didn't want to hear about that pregnancy, about that episode in my life. We had grieved and buried it. Speaking about it now would do no good.

He pulled me towards him.

"Damien, go back to Sydney."

"I want you to come with me."

"I can't."

He moved away from me. "I'm not very hungry." He walked out of the sitting-room. The front door slammed and

I stood staring out of the window, looking at the splendid garden. I couldn't bear to walk in it now.

I wanted someone to hug me, to wrap me in their arms, to whisper words of comfort in my ear. I was desperate; anyone would do. Anything was better than being on my own.

A panicky sensation swept over me. What was I doing? I was getting rid of Damien. And now I didn't want to. I walked around listening to my own footsteps on the wooden floor. I pumped up the cushions on the sofa. I looked around the sitting-room and felt a certain pride. Two cream sofas flanked the fireplace with a strawberry-coloured armchair at the end. A picture of Damien's parents on their wedding day stood on a small table. They were like silent spectators to all that was going on. I wondered if Rosemary would like this room? Would there be enough balance and harmony in it for her? Those were her new buzz words.

A picture of Damien and his father stood on the marble fireplace, their faces composed as they looked towards the camera, hair tossed. The front door was in the background. I knew this house so well. I had walked though every room and had taken an inventory. I felt at home in this old house beside the sea.

Night was closing in, shading everything in black. Across the lawn the big old trees swayed in the gentle breeze. I sat down in Tom's old chair in the conservatory.

It was here that Tom had probably sat and thought about me and wondered if he had a grandchild. A grey mantle of loneliness draped over me, blocking out all colour in my horizon.

I returned to the sitting-room. From time to time I

drifted off to sleep. A pain like period-pain filled the pit of my stomach.

It reminded me of having Jack. The pain of labour was almost unbearable; I'd thought I was going to die. It gripped my stomach like a massive claw and squeezed at my insides until I felt dizzy. And yet it passed; now it was a memory. After the hard pushing, the endless agony, the fear of something going wrong, after all that I got my reward: my beautiful son. I remember taking him in my arms and thinking, "I will always remember this moment." And looking up at Gary, his face full of love and admiration for me and his son.

"He's beautiful –" Gary had managed to get the words out before his throat contracted.

I took my husband's hand in mine and squeezed it. "He is," I said, feeling elated and exhausted at the same time.

Now, that precious memory was tainted.

Later, Damien returned. I was lying on the sofa, a blanket around me.

"Fancy some fish and chips?" he said. He picked up my hand and kissed it. "We seem to do nothing but argue."

"We've both changed," I said. "Things are different now."

He opened the two bags of fish and chips and placed them on the table.

"Can't we compromise?" he said simply.

If words were a colour chart, his was black and white.

"You want to go back to Sydney, I don't," I said. My words were tinged with an angry red.

"That's not true," he said. He paused. I waited for him to continue.

He said nothing. We sat in the muted light, both of us lost in our own thoughts.

"These are good," I said.

Our knees touched as we ate in silence.

"Let's go to bed," I suggested when we had finished.

"Michelle," he whispered, as he took me in his arms, "I love you. I'll go back, sell my apartment and come back." It was all said with calculated ease. I felt we were circling each other now, neither of us sure.

I nodded, too exhausted to say anything more.

We climbed the stairs and went to bed as the birds started to sing.

Chapter 33

It was with me all the time, the one thought. *I was going to be on my own now.* I tried to put it out of my mind, like dust in a corner, but it sat there. At odd moments the thought would slip back into my mind. There was no getting rid of it.

I couldn't bear the thought. Me, on my own. This little bit of information had to be logged in that part of my brain that held my pin number and other useless information. It was something I was going to have to get used to.

I tried desperately to reassure myself, but the ugly fact glared at me like a coffee stain on my best blouse. I had no friends. Gary and Eleanor were gone. I had managed to get rid of my two best friends in the one stroke. Now, I was the odd one out.

Rosemary was caught up with Danny and pregnancy. She didn't want me around shadowing her blissful life.

I was back to where I was before Gary came and picked up the pieces.

Damien's parting words were, "*I'll ring you.*"

I had weakly replied, "Please do."

Fear gripped me. For the first time in my life there was no one there for me. Ahead of me there was nothing. I realised in that instant that I too, like so many other people, was disposable.

Damien had packed early that morning, taken the ticket and left. I stood at the window at the top of the stairs. Tears blurred my vision as I watched him drive away.

Would he ring? Something told me he wouldn't; another voice inside my head said of course he would. The house fell silent except for the sound of my feet on the steps of the stairs. In the kitchen I forced myself to make tea. I had to do something. My thoughts raced. A lot had happened; over the past few months my life had changed entirely. I had no job, no husband, no lover – all was gone.

I walked down the drive and crossed the road. Every time I walked down to the sea I felt it looked different. Flossy clouds drifted across the sky, spreading shadows across the sea.

I wondered how many people had stood and looked at this scene. Immigrants home on holidays wishing they could come back here to live. People, weighed down with personal pain, might have stood here staring out at the sea and hoping for the gods of the universe to hear their prayer.

A man was walking along. He stopped a little distance from me and said hello. I didn't respond. I didn't feel like talking. He moved a little towards me.

In the distance I could see a family; a mother and father holding hands, children running on ahead, buckets and spades in hand. Squeals of excitement as they ran in and out of the cold water.

"Nice day," the man said.

I turned to look at him, annoyed that he had disturbed my thoughts. "Yes," I said.

He looked to be in his mid-forties or older.

"You live over there?" he said, nodding towards the gates.

I frowned. "Why?" I asked.

He walked a little closer. He was easy on the eye, too damn easy. Looking at him was like opening a box of Pringles. You just tasted one, pledging not to have any more, and before you knew it you had half the box eaten.

I turned my back to the sea and moved away from him without uttering a word. "*In my new life I'm travelling light, eyes wide open . . .*" I sang in my head. It was all of the Neil Young song I could remember.

There was no use putting it off: it was time I went home. I couldn't wait to see my son, yet I hated bumping into Gary and Eleanor. I felt this weekend would seal their life together.

I heard a slight tap at the kitchen door. I was looking for the keys. Nancy put her head around. "Where is Damien?"

"Gone."

She looked at me, puzzled, as she walked into the kitchen closing the door behind her.

"I think he's gone back to Australia," I added and smiled to let her know I wasn't bothered.

She paused for a moment and then said, "I'll go so."

I wanted her to go. I didn't feel like talking about anything. And that's what we would end up doing.

"Are you going to sell?" she asked.

"What?" I asked.

Nancy looked at me oddly. "The house?"

"I haven't thought about it."

She was standing in the centre of the kitchen floor.

"I'm looking for the keys, so I can lock up," I said as I moved around the kitchen. Damien had left them on the worktop last night.

"Tom loved this house," she said, her voice tinged with sadness. Then, she smiled and added, "I loved it too."

"It's lovely," I agreed.

"Damien isn't drawn here like his father was; he doesn't feel the magic of the place."

"He loves Sydney," I said. "Got them," I added.

"If you do decide to sell I'd appreciate it if you'd let me know."

"I will," I said.

Nancy fixed the mugs back on the old dresser.

We stepped outside and I locked the back door. She took a piece of paper out of her coat pocket and handed it to me. "My phone number."

"Thanks," I replied.

Every nerve-ending in my body was alive, every brain cell urged me to go. Inside my head, tears were congregating, waiting to be shed. I didn't want to go home yet. I felt I needed a bit more time here – all I wanted to do was sit here and wallow in the peace.

Chapter 34

There was nothing left for me to do. I had to try once again with Gary. The more I thought about it the more I thought it was the right thing to do. I wanted to talk it over with someone, get a second opinion – but who?

I rang Vincent. He knew Gary as well as I did.

"Remember how stubborn Gary is," Vincent pointed out. He went on to reminisce about when we were children and he broke Gary's gun. Gary was so upset, he wouldn't speak to Vincent. Eventually, Vincent had to buy him a gun to get Gary to be his friend again. When I asked Vincent where he got the money to buy the gun, he confessed that he had stolen the gun out of the shop.

I feared rejection. And I knew the odds were stacked against me. Gary found it hard to forgive and forget.

"Phone Gary. Talk to him, please," I said.

Vincent sighed. "I did phone him before for you, remember?"

"But I've got to try. I don't want us to get divorced."

"Of course I will, but I can't promise anything, sis, so don't get your hopes up."

I had it all planned.

Location – my mother's house.

Time – Saturday morning.

Players – Gary, Jack and Myself.

The stage was set. All I had to do was wait for the main player to come and then the performance could begin.

"Are you ready to go?" Gary said to Jack, when I answered the door to him on Saturday morning. Jack was in my arms in his pyjamas. I had sent my mother off shopping.

"Sorry," I said, "we're running late." This didn't count as a lie – it was part of the plan. "Come in."

He walked past me, his hands shoved into the pockets of his old jeans. I was wondering if Vincent had rung him. I hoped he knew that Damien had gone back to Sydney.

Gary stood with his back to the fireplace. Jack put out his arms for Gary to take him. I passed Jack over to him.

Gary kissed him on the lips, nose and forehead. "Hello, son."

"Go in van," Jack said and pointed his finger.

"In a minute," Gary said. "We have to get you dressed first."

"Would you like a coffee?" I asked.

"No, thanks."

Jack whinged impatiently. "Stop it, Jack," I said a little too crossly. "Sorry, pet," I added and rubbed his head. "Come on, let's get you dressed."

"I'll do it," Gary said, taking his son's clothes. I sat down in my mother's armchair and watched helplessly.

I tried to compose myself, to shape the words in my mouth and then to verbalise them, but nothing happened. All I heard was the sound of my son laughing as Gary attempted to dress him.

Jack stole the show. I had to bide my time, I told myself, as I watched father and son make their grand exit.

* * *

Rosemary was no help. I wanted to whinge to her and here I was listening to her. "I'm not looking forward to Christmas," she confided.

We didn't sit at the window, like we always did when we met for lunch. We were huddled in a corner.

Rosemary hardly touched her toasted sandwich. "Why does he do it?" she asked me.

I looked at her in bewilderment. I didn't know the answer; in fact, I had more questions than answers. Her husband had gone drinking last night and had crawled in the door at four that morning.

There was nothing for me to say. I took a small bite of my sandwich. "Selfish bastard," she muttered. "I hardly slept last night. I'm exhausted today and I'm pregnant."

"I mean," she leaned back in her chair, "he can't continue to do this when the baby comes."

I nodded my agreement. I noticed black roots were beginning to appear in her hair.

"Did you hear from Damien?"

At this stage he had been gone two weeks – or sixteen days to be exact.

"Yes," I said.

"And?" she inquired like I knew she would. Because

she had made inquiries last week and I had been evasive.

Now she had pinned me down and was looking for a reply. At that moment I wished it were Eleanor who was sitting across the table; she would never ask. She would wait until I was ready to volunteer the information.

"Rosemary, can we skip the subject?"

"That's your problem, Michelle. You never want to face things – you wait for it to go away."

"Yes, he phoned," I said. "Twice," I added, knowing she hadn't heard enough information. Then, I warmed to the conversation. "It was strained."

I heard the crunch as she bit into her cheese and tomato toasted sandwich. Two people walked past. I looked up, fearing it was Gary and Eleanor. I was having a grey day. Seeing them together would surely make it black. I smiled, relieved it wasn't them.

"He's supposed to be selling his apartment. It's a really nice apartment with magnificent views of Sydney harbour. He'll have no trouble selling it, but I don't think he wants to sell it. He sounded very –" I paused and searched in my head for the right word. It was there, I just had to say it.

"Happy, sad, pissed off, lonely – which one?" Rosemary prompted.

"Happy," I said. Suddenly I had lost my appetite. I left down my sandwich and looked at the crumbs around my plate.

"You did buy the ticket – you wanted him to go," she said tentatively.

"I know," I said.

"So what's the problem?"

"Me, I suppose."

"What now?" she asked.

I shrugged. I wanted to tell her that I didn't want to meet her for lunch anymore, but, if I did that, I would have no friends at all and at this point her company, no matter how irritating, was better than my own.

"Michelle, I guess you haven't met him yet."

"Him?"

"Yes, Mr Right, The Man Of Your Dreams, Your Soul Mate . . ." she said, her hands outstretched.

A man passing by knocked the sandwich out of her hand.

"What did you do that for?" she asked, her face turning an angry red.

"Sorry," the man said.

"Hi, Bob," I said. This was the man that Eleanor had fallen in love with.

He looked at me. I could tell he was trying to put a name to the face.

I wanted to ask him if he was missing Eleanor? Did he want her back? Could we construct a foolproof plan and execute it to get the desired effect?

Rosemary coughed.

"Ah, now I remember," he said and reached out his hand to shake mine. "Michelle –"

"Excuse me," Rosemary said, butting in. "I have to go back to work."

"Oh dear," Bob said. We all looked down at the mess of tomato and cheese on the floor. "I'll order you another." His voice was full of apology. He bent down and started to clean up the mess.

"No need, I've suddenly lost my appetite."

"Bob, ignore her," I said, bending down to look at Bob whose head just came up to the level of our table.

Rosemary's eyes bulged with rage. "Thanks a lot!"

I helped Bob pick up the sandwich. His eyes were so pale they were almost transparent. He left the mess down on the table.

"Where is he gone now?" Rosemary asked, as we both watched him walk purposefully away.

"To get a sandwich?" I said.

A few minutes later we watched him weave his way through people as he made his way down to our table.

"Sorry," he said. He put the brown-paper bag down on the table, unaware that he put it on top of the messy sandwich.

"I have to rush – an emergency," he said as he backed away from us.

"He's mad! No wonder Eleanor dumped him," said Rosemary before he was out of earshot.

"Rosemary!"

His mobile phone started to ring out in the pocket of his raincoat. He struggled to take it out while almost knocking an old lady over. I couldn't help but laugh. I guessed he was having a grey day too.

Chapter 35

When do you give up? When do you realise you've lost? Damien was right; I wanted him out of the way. I thought if he was gone that Gary would want me, but he didn't. He didn't want to talk to me, let alone have me back in his life.

It was Christmas Day. We sat in my mother's sitting-room. Jack was playing with his toys.

"It's present time," Vincent said.

I felt my eyes grow bigger as I looked from Vincent to Gary and then my mother.

"Gosh, I didn't do much Christmas shopping," I said.

"Me either," Gary said and looked embarrassed.

Vincent laughed. "Then, it's a good job I did!"

He handed me an envelope. "For you, sis," he said. "And this is for you . . ." He presented my mother with a large gift-wrapped box.

"Vincent," she said, her face flushed. "You shouldn't have."

He placed the box on her knee.

"What's in it?"

"Open it and see," he urged.

Jack ran over to help. We all looked at my mother as her withered hands fumbled with the ribbons.

"Help me, Michelle!"

I got up and helped her open the box. Inside was a set of six crystal wine glasses.

"Oh, Vincent, they're beautiful!"

"They're Waterford Crystal," I whispered to her.

I looked from my mother to Vincent. We were being transported in time to another Christmas day when my father smashed all her good glasses. My mother used to keep them in a glass case in the sitting-room. She always took them out at Christmas: it was the only special occasion in the cycle of our lives.

He got up around three, I remember, because we always had our Christmas dinner around that time. Vincent and myself always referred to him, as *him*. We couldn't bear to call him Daddy or Dad or Pops.

"He's your father, call him by his name," our mother would say. But no matter what telling off she gave us, we were not prepared to call him our father.

He must have got out of the bed the wrong way because he pounded down the stairs and into the sitting-room where we were watching telly.

"Is the dinner ready?" he asked. His voice full of fight. He smelled of the pub, that horrible mixture of cigarette smoke and beer and sweat.

I sat as though paralysed and watched *him* sweep his hand across the table that my mother and I had set with our old cutlery and a white linen tablecloth that my mother had got along with the glasses from her mother. The four glasses toppled from the table onto the linenoum floor and broke. After this display, he seemed calmer. He moved Vincent and me off the couch and lay down. We sat huddled together in the single armchair that our mother sat on and watched in fearful fascination as she cleaned up his mess.

Later, when he went out to play cards on Christmas night, we watched our mother cry silently for her precious glasses.

"When I'm gone, Michelle, these can be yours," she now said, her voice a mixture of pride and sadness.

I touched them and gently took one out.

"They're beautiful," I said.

She squeezed my hand. We didn't hug; we never had. One cannot break the rules of a lifetime, just because it's Christmas Day.

Jack reached to take the glass from me.

"No, darling, these are Granny's," I said.

"Me, me."

I let him touch the glass.

"Let's use them, let's drink from them," Vincent said, a new buoyancy in his voice.

"Be careful with them," my mother said with authority as I took them from her.

I handed my mother a small gift. She opened it and slipped on her glasses.

It was a Barbara Vine novel. My mother wanted to know who she was. I explained that she was Ruth Rendell using a pen name.

She looked at me baffled. "What's wrong with her own name?" she wanted to know.

Vincent threw a present in Gary's direction. He opened it to find another shirt, same as last year. They laughed at this. I opened my envelope and was surprised to find he'd given me a gift cheque of money.

"I'll just wash these," I said, picking up the glasses. I felt the need to leave the room. Suddenly, it had become smaller.

Gary hadn't got me a present and I felt disappointed.

"I'll help," Gary said.

My spirits lifted, maybe he was going to give me my present in the kitchen.

We walked into the kitchen together. I felt the urge to say something, but nothing intelligent came to mind.

I wanted to ask him if he minded being here? I wanted to ask him if he was still seeing Eleanor? (I knew he was – I had already got Vincent to ask him.) I wanted to ask him if he had any feelings for me? I knew the answers – but it was Christmas and I wanted to pretend that we were still together.

"Jack seems pleased with his toys," he said. "I'm glad we got that train set."

I noticed the way he said *we*. I wondered if this was a slip of the tongue or if he was thinking of us getting back together.

He had spent the morning putting the train set together, which meant he didn't have to make small talk with me.

"So am I," I said. I felt the need to puncture my trail of thought by saying something. "So," I said, as I gently placed the glasses into the soapy water, "how are you?"

I concentrated on splashing water on each glass, then rinsing with cold and putting them on the draining-board. He stood close to me. I felt he was going to give me my present at any moment.

I turned to look at him. His face broke into a smile.

"I'm fine," he said, as he picked up a glass and started to dry it with the Santy tea towel, "under the circumstances."

I shook the suds off my hands. Gary was here because he wanted to share Christmas day with our son and Vincent had helped to persuade him come.

I felt irritated and I longed to lift one of the glasses and hit him with it. As usual, I was kidding myself. He had no present for me.

"Thanks for coming," I said and looked at his honest face.

For the first time I saw a glint of something else in his eyes. We walked back into the sitting-room with a bottle of chilled white wine and four of the glasses.

"Let's pour some wine," I suggested.

My hands shook a little as I filled the four glasses with wine.

"A toast to our mother," Vincent said.

"To Mammy!" I said, raising my glass.

"To Granny!" Gary said.

I turned to look at Gary. He had Jack sitting on his knee. I felt gutted. Here in this tiny sitting-room that was full of haunted memories of my past, was this man who had loved me for me, and I was too stupid to see it. The furniture had been shuffled around in the room, we had decorated, yet I still felt it was full of my father's presence. I could feel he was looking on at us, laughing at our attempts to forget about him.

"This is the best Christmas I've ever had and it's thanks to you all," my mother said. She wiped the tears away and attempted to say thank you, but the words were lost.

"I'm starving," Vincent said.

"Well, dinner won't be ready for another hour," my mother said. She had regained her composure again. "When I wanted to do a fry this morning you wouldn't let me."

"We could eat the starters now," I suggested. I needed to get out of the room; I hated having to spend Christmas here.

My mother looked at me, horrified. "What will Gary think of us?"

Vincent punched Gary affectionately on the chest. "Gary is probably starving too."

"Well, I wouldn't say no to one of those bacon rolls that you make," he said.

My mother loved all this attention and jumped up to get them some.

We all looked at Jack. He seemed to be the only one that was enjoying himself.

"Any wild plans for next year, Vincent?" Gary asked.

He made a comical face and said, "As a matter of fact, I have."

"Oh what?"

"I'm going to get married."

"Who's going to get married?" my mother asked as she walked back into the sitting-room.

"I am," Vincent said and paused.

We all waited, wondering what he was going to say next.

"You're joking," I said.

"Why didn't you bring her home with you?" my mother asked uncertainly.

Vincent looked poker-faced around at us all.

"Is she Irish?" I asked.

"Is she Catholic?" my mother asked.

"Is she rich?" Gary asked.

Vincent laughed. "We've nothing planned but we're engaged."

"Engaged," my mother said. "Why didn't you tell us?"

"So when's the big day?" I asked.

"Like I said we have nothing planned."

An audible sigh of relief came from my mother as she slumped into her armchair.

"Any beer?" he asked.

"In the fridge," I said sourly.

"Why the face, sis?"

"Why couldn't you tell us you were engaged? Why the big secret?"

"Because I like teasing you," he said shortly.

"Ha, ha – you're such a happy-go-lucky . . ." I stopped myself from finishing the sentence.

"Go on," Vincent urged, "finish it."

"You can be such a shit," I said.

"And who are you to talk?" Vincent replied before leaving the room.

"These are nice," Gary said, taking one of the bacon rolls.

"Vincent, come in and have some before they get cold!" my mother shouted after him.

"I'm just getting a beer. Gary, do you want one?"

"Yes, please."

Vincent returned with three cans of beer.

"Sorry, sis," he said and handed me a can of beer. "Sometimes, I can't help myself."

I nodded, knowing he was cloaked with the same past as me and sometimes it crept up on us and we found ourselves acting in ways we couldn't explain.

We ate dinner, all of us, including Jack, on our best behaviour.

Gary took Jack in the afternoon to see his parents. My mother sat dozing in her armchair. I was left to do all the washing-up. Vincent had gone for a walk. He said he would help me do it when he came back, but I didn't believe him. There seemed to be no end to the amount of dishes. I refilled the sink twice and wondered how many other fools like me were left to do the washing-up.

I thought of the kitchen in Westport. I thought of Damien. I thought of all the people in the world that had sat down to a solitary Christmas dinner on their own. I wanted to cry. My mother was right: Christmas was overrated.

When Vincent returned from his walk, he saw me sulking and wanted to know what was wrong. Nothing, was my sharp response. I should have gone for a walk with him, but I didn't want to walk by other people's windows and see fairy-lights winking out at me from Christmas trees. I'd know they were having a better time than me.

The phone hadn't rung once all day. I had expected Damien to call. When no one was looking, I sneaked out to the hall to check if it was still connected. Jack liked to pull it out of the wall.

I had told Vincent that Damien had gone back to Sydney to live. So I couldn't start whinging to him that I was disappointed that he hadn't phoned me. Everyone I knew was in a relationship. The only people who weren't were my mother, her best friend Lil and me.

When the phone did ring, I let Vincent answer it.

"It's Gary for you."

I took the phone and felt the news wasn't good. "Jack

has fallen asleep on the sofa," he said, the words slurred.

"He's going to be upset when he wakes up, you've no bottle for him." I said hurriedly. I needed to see Jack. I just couldn't bear the idea of not seeing him all evening. I could hear Gary's mother in the background.

"My mother has bottles here," he said.

"Gary, I'd like you to bring him back here to me tonight," I said. I was gripped by panic; I needed my little son's warm body to snuggle up to tonight.

"Tomorrow," he said.

"Gary, I want him back here tonight and that's final," I almost yelled down the phone.

Vincent was standing by my side. "How about us picking Jack up first thing tomorrow morning," he suggested.

"We'll collect him . . ." The words faded in my throat. I handed Vincent the phone.

"Gary, we'll collect him in the morning – is that alright?"

I shot dagger-looks at my brother. 'Is that alright?' I mimicked in my head.

"It's Christmas bloody night, I'd like my son here with me," I said.

"What's the racket all about? Surely you two are not fighting on Christmas Day?" my mother shouted from the sitting-room.

We exchanged knowing looks, both of us on the ready to list other Christmas Days when there were plenty of rows.

"See you in the morning, Gary," Vincent said and put the phone down.

Vincent hugged me and I was glad of it. I could feel my nothingness. "He's punishing you," he said.

"Fuck him! I don't care about him, I just want Jack here with me."

"I know."

I was trying to hold it together at this stage, trying to pretend that things would work out. My mother waded past us, in her slippers. She was on her way to the kitchen to make yet another cup of tea. I didn't want to go for a walk when Vincent suggested we should. But it was better than sitting in the kitchen with my mother.

Outside the air was fresh and crisp, a thousand stars twinkling down at us from the night sky.

Vincent wanted to hear about the house in Westport. He was trying to stop me from sinking into total despair. I tried to talk about it, but I couldn't warm to the subject so we just strolled along, trying to pass an hour before we went back to eat some Christmas pudding.

I wanted to talk to him about me, but I could see he would lose interest in the complications of it all. Vincent had a short attention span. He was so unlike Eleanor. Now, Eleanor and I could quite happily spend the evening looking at all the angles and all the possibilities. We probably would come up with no solution, but we enjoyed the process.

"I miss Eleanor," I confessed.

Vincent put his arm through mine. "More than you miss Gary?"

"No, not more – probably the same amount."

"But you were always giving out about her."

"I wasn't," I said, indignant, and I found myself taking my arm out of his.

My step increased. Vincent could be such a smart-arse. Lately, a lot of home truths had come home to roost.

Vincent caught up with me and said, "I'm going back to Dublin tomorrow."

I was shocked. "Vincent, you can't leave me to spend the rest of Christmas with my mother in that house!"

"Sis, I have to. I've promised Nicola I'd meet her tomorrow."

"Why didn't you bring her here for Christmas."

"I thought about it and I'm afraid I decided not to."

"Tell me about her," I urged.

"There isn't much to tell."

"Where is she from?"

"Ireland, Dublin, Stillorgan. Any more questions"

"And what does she do for a living?"

Vincent sighed. "Michelle, all these questions are doing my head in."

"What is it with you? Why are you so bloody secretive?" I knew I was spending too much time with Rosemary and this was the proof of it.

"I'm not," he said defensively.

"Well, if you love her and you're thinking about marrying her, then why don't you want to talk about her?"

"We're not sure about marriage. It's a big commitment."

"Why not?"

"Because," he said and turned his head up to look at the night sky, "I'd probably fuck it up."

"Oh Vincent," I said.

We both started to laugh and we walked on.

Chapter 36

In the morning when I woke I didn't want to get out of bed. I wanted to lie there, my eyes closed and feel the comfort of my duvet around me. I heard noise downstairs. I knew my mother was up, having her first cup of tea and cigarette for the day.

"Are you awake?" Vincent asked as he put his head around the door.

I groaned. I was enjoying the slumber too much.

He walked heavy-footed into the bedroom and landed with a thump on my bed.

"Do you have to make so much noise?"

"It's nine thirty, sis."

"So?" I said.

"I was wondering would you drive me to the train station?"

I pulled down my duvet. "I thought you were leaving this evening."

"Ah sis, I –"

"Vincent, please stay! At least come with me when I'm collecting Jack!"

"I have to go. Nicola wants me to go and I can't say no."

"Ask her to come and see us," I suggested. At this stage I was sitting up in bed and I was ready to argue my case.

"I'm going to see Nicola and that's the end of it."

"Have you told Mammy?" I asked. My eyes narrowed to slits.

Vincent tilted his head and gave me his pleading look. "No, I haven't told her."

"Well, you can because I'm not doing your dirty work for you."

"So you'll drive me to the station?"

"Will do. Can we go and collect Jack first."

Vincent glanced at his watch. "The train leaves at eleven."

"Go and tell Mammy you're leaving and I'll be ready in a few minutes."

"It's never a few minutes."

"This time it will be. I want you to do some dirty work for me for a change."

I could hear him whistling as he packed. He was happy; he was looking forward to seeing his girlfriend. I felt both envious and happy for him. My brother had been bitten by the love-bug.

He ran down the stairs like he did as a teenager. Already I was missing him. I could hear him talking to my mother in the kitchen.

I fixed my hair, slapped on some make-up, pulled on my new jeans and jumper that my mother bought me for Christmas.

"He's going today," my mother said when I walked into the kitchen.

"I know," I said.

"He comes all the way from New York and all he can spend with us is a day."

"I was here Christmas Eve and –"

My mother cut in. "Ah, away with you and enjoy yourself."

I looked at him and felt only love for this charming bastard of a brother of mine.

"Let's go and get Jack," I said.

"Right," he said, glad to make a quick exit.

My mother stood at our front door and waved at him.

"Happy New Year!" she shouted after him.

"Happy New Year!" he shouted back and waved.

He exhaled loudly as he put on his seat belt.

"Mission accomplished," I said.

"Something like that," he admitted.

"I have to spend the rest of Christmas with her."

"Michelle, you don't have to. Haven't you got friends that you could spend a few days with or can't you go to the house in Westport?"

I mumbled something about the long drive and the icy roads and what would I do with my mother.

We drove in silence. Neither of us had the appetite for small talk.

"Ah, we're here," he said, looking out at Gary's house. "I hope they're up, it's still early."

I grinned to myself. "If I know Jack, they're up."

"Michelle, maybe it's best if you stay in the car and I go and get him for you."

"Is there something you're not telling me?"

"Michelle, just sit here. I'll get Jack."

I watched Vincent walk up the drive. He rang the doorbell and stood with his back to me. A few minutes later Gary arrived with Jack in his arms. My heart missed a beat. I didn't know if it was for Jack or Gary or for them both.

Vincent walked inside. I started to bite my nail. I was eager to go in and yet I knew I was not welcome. Snow-white clouds drifted across the pale sky. Cars were parked outside every house in the estate. No one was up. I tapped the steering wheel – I was losing patience. I looked at the clock, switched on the radio, tuned it into a station, attempted to listen to a Christmas carol, looked at my watch. Nothing happened. I waited five minutes and still nothing happened.

Eventually, I got out of the car, and walked up the short drive towards the house. I opened the door. I could hear voices in the sitting-room.

Vincent came out to the hall, as I was about to go in. "We're ready to go," he said.

"Where is Jack?"

"Wait outside. We'll be out in a minute."

I walked outside. Vincent followed with Jack in his arms.

"Gary and I were good mates. We just had a chat," he explained as I put Jack into his car-seat.

"Did he say anything?" I asked.

"No, Michelle. I'm afraid not. I think Eleanor is going to move in with him." He squeezed my hand gently. "Hang in there."

"Ah, well," I said as I started up the engine. "You'll miss your train if we don't hurry."

"And you'd hate me to miss my train," Vincent said as he lolled back in his seat.

Jack and I waved him off. I couldn't bear the thought of going back to spend the rest of Christmas with my mother.

"What are we going to do now?" I looked at Jack for inspiration.

He smiled at me.

"Have you any ideas?" I tickled him and he started to laugh. "Let's go for a drive while we think." I hugged him and kissed his chubby cheek. "It's so good to have you back again. I missed you sleeping in my bed last night."

* * *

There was nothing else to do but return to my mother's. We had driven for over an hour.

"Where did you get to?" my mother asked the minute we walked in her front door.

"I just fancied a drive," I said, knowing this would only fuel her temper.

"I see."

I felt my stomach muscles contract. I felt like I was a little girl again and everything was my damn fault.

"Mammy, if you're having a bad day stop taking it out on me."

Our eyes met across the sitting-room. She turned away and said something under her breath.

"What did you say?"

"Nothing."

"What did you say?"

"I said nothing," she repeated, her voice like an echo from the past.

The swell of my own failure and disappointment filled my chest. I realised how limited my life was. This was it, my uneventful life, set by me. In that instant I decided I had to do something about it.

"Look, it's time myself and Jack got our own place. We're only going to get on each other's nerves if I stay here much longer." Now I was standing beside her. She headed for the kitchen. I followed. She filled the kettle with water and switched it on.

"Would you like a cup of tea?" she asked.

"No, thanks."

"I don't want you to leave, I like having you here," she said. Her tone had changed. Suddenly she sounded defeated.

"Would you like me to make the tea?" I said, my voice soft and soothing as if I was trying to reason with Jack.

She nodded and retreated to her chair in the sitting-room.

I came in with a cup of tea and sat down on the sofa. Jack was in the hall playing with the box his train set came in.

"I worry about you, I worry about Jack, I worry about Vincent, I'm tired worrying," she said by way of explanation.

"I'm sorry, Mammy."

"Don't make any rushed decisions. That's all I'm saying. Stay here until you're sure you know what you want to do."

We smiled at each other; we had reached a status quo for the moment, at least.

"What are we going to do today?" I asked.

"Nothing, what can we do?"

I shrugged.

I wasn't up to visiting Rosemary. As for Eleanor – we hadn't even exchanged Christmas cards. And now she was moving into the house that I once called home.

"We could go for a drive," I said.

"Where to?"

"Westport."

"Westport." Sometimes my mother was like a parrot.

"Yes, I have to get away for a few days. I can't bear it here any longer."

She looked at me. I could tell she didn't like the idea. A thousand "what if's" were racing through her mind.

"Mother, that's what we'll do: we'll pack the car and drive to Westport and we'll spend the rest of Christmas there."

"We can't do that," she said.

"Why not?"

"Well, what if he finds out?"

I flicked back my hair. "You mean Damien?"

"He mightn't like it."

I shrugged. "So what, it's my house."

"I'm not going," my mother said and folded her arms across her chest.

"They have a beautiful garden and the sea is only a stone's throw away."

"I'm not going," she repeated, her face set in lines of resistance.

"I'll feel safe with you there," I said.

She looked at me, a glint of amusement in her eyes. "What is there for you to be afraid of?"

"I don't know. It's a big old house."

She threw back her head and laughed. "I can't imagine you being afraid of anything."

You don't know me very well, Mother, I wanted to say. Instead I said, "I hate leaving you here on your own."

"I'll go," she said.

316

Chapter 37

When we arrived at the house, I opened the back door with my key. The place smelled damp and an icy air ran through the place.

We couldn't find the central-heating switch so I ended up having to ring Nancy. She told me she'd be round straight away. All I wanted her to do was tell me over the phone where the switch was and leave it at that, but she insisted.

My mother spent ages getting the stove to light and then she attacked the sitting-room fire. Then, Nancy arrived. It was on the tip of my tongue to tell her that I had no money to pay her, but she kept interrupting me, telling me how good it was to see me and this was her first Christmas on her own. I got as far as telling her I earned my crust stacking shelves, but she still continued to help out and I gave up after that. We invited her to stay and have some dinner with us, but she refused. We pushed the boat out and asked her a second time and she refused. I knew she lived on her own, but I didn't think I could cope with her and my mother for the evening.

"I'll call again tomorrow," were her parting words as she left.

"We'll never get rid of her now," I said and at once felt guilty.

"The only thing that's missing is a Christmas tree," my mother said. A big tree sat in our sitting-room at home, the smell of pine scenting the place.

We sat in the sitting-room watching *Coronation Street*.

"This place smells musty," my mother said and sniffed.

"Did you bring any of your books to read?"

"No, I hadn't time to pack them," she said.

I longed for her to be quiet, to just sit there and say nothing.

"There isn't much on the box, same stuff as at home."

I didn't reply.

"Jack's been very good."

"I think I'll go for a short walk," I said.

"Michelle, are you mad? You're not going out there – it's dark!"

"Mother, I'll just walk to the end of the drive and back. I just need some fresh air."

"What if Jack wakes?"

"Would you mind picking him up for me?"

"Don't be longer than ten minutes and make sure you lock all the doors before we go to bed. No, I'll do that myself."

I turned and headed for the door. I needed a break from her chatter. In the hall, I turned and looked up the stairs. I heard our laugher and saw our entwined bodies. A memory, a happy one to be stored in the album of my head.

Outside it was dark. I walked down to the sea. The smell

of salty air was refreshing as I breathed it in. I regretted coming out, yet I didn't want to return. I needed a break from my mother. My feet crunched against the gravel, slowly my eyes adjusting to the dark.

Next morning we woke early. My mother surprised us both by getting the stove to light on her first attempt.

"Would you look at what's coming?" she said.

I looked down the drive to see Nancy driving up.

"You're up early," Nancy said.

"Early risers, that's us," my mother said as she eyed Nancy suspiciously.

"I just came to see if you're alright."

"We're fine. Would you like to come in for a cup of tea?" I asked, hoping she'd say no.

"That would be great."

"I'll take Jack for a walk," said my mother.

"Did you sleep well?"

"We did, thanks," I said as I filled the kettle.

Nancy started to clear the table.

"Oh leave that!"

"Very well," she said and sat down.

"How are you, Nancy?" I asked as I placed a mug of tea before her.

"I miss him," she said. Nancy pulled a tissue out of her sleeve and started to dry her eyes. "He was such a good man and he loved this house."

"I know. Is there anything here you'd like to take?" I asked quietly.

I noticed how red her eyes were when she looked at me.

"No, just sitting here is nice." She wiped her eyes. "He

told me everything. He was terrible disappointed when you told him that you hadn't his grandchild."

"I'm surprised he still left the house to me."

"Damien wanted him to, said there would be other children." She smiled to hide her embarrassment. "Is there anything you'd like me to do?" Her brown eyes almost pleaded with me to suggest something.

"Nancy, I stack shelves, I can't afford to pay you anything." I knew by her face this was not what she wanted to hear. "I have no problem with you coming here," I found myself saying.

"I'd like to call in on you," she said and then added, "now and then."

"We don't mind, we'd be glad of the company," I said, not meaning a word of it.

"Such a shame! This house needs to be lived in."

"It's lovely. I could get used to living –"

My mother burst in the back door. "Michelle, you'd better follow Jack! I can't keep up with him, he's gone down the drive!" She gasped for breath, her hand on the door for support.

I ran out the back door and legged it down the drive. I could see him making for the road.

"*Jack, Jack!*" I screamed at him. He turned and laughed at me, then started to run. A sharp pain ran through my chest. Jack was at the gate heading for the road.

"*Stop, Jack, stop!*" I ran and grabbed him just as a car whizzed past. "Oh Jack, my baby," I cried and hugged him close.

"Mama," he said, and laughed.

"Bold Jack! Look at cars on road."

He pointed his little finger towards the sea. I noticed how chilly it was now that I had stopped running. I shivered with cold – I was only wearing a denim shirt.

"Look," he said, pointing at the sea and pulling me to go with him.

"Yes, pet. Let's go back to the house and get a jacket for me and then we'll go down to the sea."

It was later that I found out my mother had invited Nancy over for dinner that evening.

"What are we going to cook for her?" I said, alarmed at how my evening peace was being undermined by my mother. "She's a brilliant cook."

"Are you saying there's something wrong with my cooking?"

"No, but we don't have the ingredients."

My mother folded her arms across her chest. "Oh, do we not now? I know Nancy likes nothing better than a nice bit of steak with chips. Now could there be anything simpler than that?"

"No, but where are we going to get the steak?"

My mother grinned. "The freezer," she said, and tilted her head towards the sink where she had meat thawing. "And I'm going to make a trifle or something for dessert," she added.

"Mammy, why are you doing this?"

"Because, dear child, I want to."

I raised an eyebrow.

My mother took the mugs off the table. "Is Damien coming back?"

"I don't think so."

She stopped, a dish-cloth in hand. "Will you miss him?"

I looked at Jack who was sitting at the table eating a sausage. "I love Jack so much and he has to come first and Damien didn't understand that. He never asked me about him or he never wanted to get to know him. I just knew he'd never love Jack like a real father would. Like Gary does."

My mother turned abruptly away from the table. She busied herself washing the dish-cloth in the sink. She sniffed quietly to herself for a few moments and, when she had composed herself, she came back and wiped the table.

"Why did his father give you this house?"

I pulled out a chair and asked my mother to sit down. "Tom, that's Damien's father, thought I had his grandchild."

My mother's eyes bored into me. "And have you?"

I shook my head. "I was pregnant when I left Australia, but I lost it."

My mother nodded. She was in recall mode. "I was thinking at the time that you might have been pregnant, but I was afraid to ask."

"Tom was disappointed," I added.

"I can imagine," she said.

* * *

"They never ate in the dining-room," Nancy confided.

My mother frowned.

"Always here in the kitchen. He was a very ordinary man."

Nancy's eyes twinkled with excitement. She was enjoying herself. It was written all over her face.

I sipped my wine. Outside the wind howled and rain rattled the window-panes. It was like there was some monster out there trying to get in.

Nancy was guzzling down the wine like it was her last supper. Belts of air came from under the door and sent a shiver of cold around the kitchen. I fed the stove more turf. Nancy and my mother never commented on the storm that was brewing up outside.

"Red wine was all he ever drank," Nancy said.

"It's supposed to be good for you, a glass every day," my mother said. "Isn't that right, Michelle?"

"Oh, yes," I said.

"Check those baked potatoes," she said to me.

"I see you did them in the electric. I always use the stove," Nancy said.

"Ah, we're not used to the stove," my mother said sweetly as she poured more wine into Nancy's empty glass.

"Had you a nice Christmas?" My mother was an expert at small talk.

"Ah, no, I spent Christmas with my sister. To tell you the truth, I would have rather spent it here."

"You're always welcome here, don't you know that?" my mother said.

I poked the potatoes with a fork. "These are done, Mother."

"Surely you can serve it out to us," my mother said.

"Would you like me to help?" Nancy said and in a flash she was standing beside me.

I took the warm plates out of the oven.

"This looks good," Nancy said. Her voice had lost its crispness and slipped into something more homely.

"Thanks," I said.

"Ah, we haven't much practice at entertaining," my mother said.

I put the vegetables on a dish and left them down with a slight thud on the centre of the table.

"They look great, like something you'd see in a magazine," my mother said. "She's not a bad cook, if I say so myself."

"You're lucky to have her," Nancy said.

"I am, Nancy."

To my surprise my mother raised her glass, "To Michelle," she said.

"To Michelle," said Nancy.

I could only laugh. I felt safe and warm in the kitchen while a full-throated storm was raging outside.

"Terrible night," my mother said.

"I've heard worse," Nancy said confidingly.

Just then we heard glass breaking.

"That'll be the conservatory," Nancy said, as she moved from the table. "I'll go and check it."

I picked up the tongs and followed her.

She looked at me with amusement. "What are you going to do with that?"

"Just in case someone has broken in."

"I see." She walked on like she was following the footsteps of Grace O'Malley, who once was the pirate queen of these waters.

Nancy switched on the light and immediately saw the broken glass, high up on the roof. "There is nothing we can do until morning."

I felt myself shiver with cold. My mother came along with old cloths and a basin. She kept moving the basin until she got it exactly where she wanted it. Drops started to tap-tap into it.

"I'll get someone to fix it tomorrow," Nancy said.

I felt redundant; she was taking over, doing what I should be doing. I folded my arms across my chest and clamped my mouth shut. I was afraid to speak. There was a good chance I'd say the wrong thing.

"Let's eat our dinner before it gets cold," my mother said, as we made our way back to the cosy kitchen.

"Yes," I agreed eagerly.

"Nancy, you can't go home in that – stay the night," my mother said.

"Yes, stay," I said. They hardly heard me. Nancy and my mother had bonded. I should have been glad, but I wasn't. Who was going to be friends with me?

Next morning, we woke to calm. Jack was up with the birds. He was all excited in this new house with plenty of rooms for him to explore. I made breakfast for us both. At seven o'clock in the morning the day seemed long and uneventful. I had no idea how I was going to spend my day or the rest of my life for that matter.

If I was at home in Longford, I could be getting up for work now, rushing around the place, trying to drink my mug of coffee and feed Jack his breakfast. Gary would be gone to work. Now, our house in Longford was still, no rushing around. Gary didn't doss around in the morning: up and out. I felt like someone had vacuumed my insides out. I missed my family life so much.

"Gary," I whispered to myself.

An hour later Nancy and my mother got up. They walked around the house surveying the damage done. Jack and myself tagged along after them.

In the sitting-room, my eyes were drawn to the photograph

of Damien's parents. I felt their spirits were still in the house. Wafting through the place, flying high. Somehow I found this image comforting. I felt they wanted me here.

"I'll get Jimmy to come and do the repairs," Nancy said.

"Jimmy, who is he?" I was attempting to put my stamp on the place, to let her know this was my house.

"Is that alright?" she asked.

"I suppose so. Is he who you always get?"

Nancy nodded as she slipped into her brown quilted jacket. "It is."

"I might go with you for the drive," my mother said.

"Me drive," Jack shouted.

"No, pet, you stay with me," I said.

I looked out the window: grey slanting rain was beating down from a dark sky.

"We'll bring him. The drive will do him good, get him out," Nancy said, and she started to tickle him. All this cheer so early in the morning was getting me down.

"He needs to be in his car-seat," I said. My voice almost shrill with annoyance.

"I can do that," said my mother.

"Great." I hated the thought of being in the house on my own.

I could always go for a walk and get soaked.

But I had something to think about, something to contemplate doing.

It was night-time in Sydney. The phone calls had become less frequent. It seemed like the right thing to do, to dial Damien's number.

In the background I heard laughter.

"Hi," he said.

It was definitely a woman's voice in the background.

"You're enjoying yourself," I said. Instantly I regretted it. The words were full of unsaid accusations.

There was a pause, like it had taken a few moments for my words to travel down the line to him.

"Michelle, hi . . . how are you?" he said, his voice light and happy.

The line went quiet, each of us waiting for the other to speak.

Eventually he did. "It's lovely to hear your voice. I miss that."

I twirled the phone-line in my hand.

After another quiet pause, I said, "I'm in Westport."

"Ah, nice," he said.

"Yes, it's lovely. It would be perfect if we had a Christmas tree."

"Yes," he said.

I waited for some words of love from him, but none came. I felt disappointed, but what did I expect? I had bought the ticket, I wanted him to go. I didn't love him and he knew it.

Over the past few months all our conversations had become strained; it was time we said goodbye to each other.

"I just rang to wish you a Happy New Year," I said.

"Thanks, Michelle," he said. The words sounded thin and hollow.

"Bye, Damien."

"I wish you were here –" he started to say as I put the phone down.

Our paths had crossed because his father had made them cross, not because of love. We had come to the end.

I saw Nancy drive into the yard. I rushed to the back

door and opened it. A man was standing at the door, just ready to knock.

"Jesus," I almost yelled.

"Sorry, I'm Sean," he said, extending his hand to me.

His handshake was firm and almost vice-like. I pulled my hand away and looked up at his ruggedly handsome face.

"We met before," he said, and smiled.

I didn't respond.

"Down at the beach," he said.

I heard my mother and Nancy and Jack coming towards the house. They were talking.

"Ah, Sean," Nancy said, "how are you? You're welcome." She led the way into the kitchen and he followed.

He sat down at the table and Nancy proceeded to make tea. This was something I was going to have to get used to, Nancy taking over. Yet part of me didn't mind.

"Sean used to live around here," she went on to explain.

I sat down at the table with Jack on my knee and listened to Nancy and Sean reminisce. I could imagine him as a young boy, with wellingtons and old clothes, eager to do anything for some pocket money.

"I'm coming back to live," he said.

"You can live anywhere you like – haven't you done well for yourself?" Nancy said with pride, like she was speaking about her own child. "Sean has worked all over the world."

"Oh," my mother sat up straighter in her chair. "Doing what?"

"Engineering – he has his own company," said Nancy smugly.

"Do you still bake?" he asked her.

"I do indeed." She sat down beside him.

"I could fix those broken windows in the conservatory," he said.

Nancy looked at me for approval.

"That would be great," I said and kissed the top of Jack's head, "but I'm sure you have more to do with your time."

Sean looked directly at me. "I don't mind. I used to help my father do odd jobs here when I was young."

"That's right," Nancy said, nodding her head in agreement.

* * *

My mother's friend Lil came down to visit and brought the black cat. She had some letters for her also, most of them bills. She handed me a letter. I recognised the handwriting. It was from Vincent and it was a week old. I ripped it open and scanned through it. I was worried that some terrible bad luck had befallen him.

He just wrote that he was giving up on acting and he was going to go back to school to study law. I knew he'd look good in a suit and he could always argue his case. Next summer he was coming home to get married. I re-read the letter, afraid I had missed something, I hadn't. He was fine and that was all that mattered.

I went into Tom's study. I looked around for a pen and paper. I was going to reply to Vincent's letter. After I wrote the "Dear Vincent" bit and scribbled a few lines congratulating him on his plans to get marred, I wished him luck with his career move and then I was stuck. I felt I should tell him that I too had plans, but I hadn't any. I told him that I was thinking about moving to Westport. I stopped writing when I thought about Gary. I picked up the phone and dialled his mobile. He didn't answer. I didn't leave a message. I had nothing to say.

Chapter 38

A few days later Rosemary arrived. She looked exhausted and it was contagious. My mother and I decided to stay on for a while. I rang the supermarket and told them I wouldn't be back. I knew why Rosemary was here; she didn't have to say. I could guess Danny had gone drinking. It was madness what she did, driving on her own and she so pregnant. We sat at the kitchen table.

"My back is killing me," she said as she stretched herself. "All the reception rooms you have and we end up sitting in the kitchen."

"Would you like to go into the sitting-room?"

Rosemary shook her head. Her hair was honey-coloured and it brought a sense of calm to her face.

"I like your hair," I said.

She looked at me. "Why the compliment?"

"Because it's a nice warm colour. It suits you."

She made a face. "You realise that's the first time you've ever complimented my hair?"

"Gosh, I didn't realise you were counting!" I put my hands up to my face pretending to be shocked.

"This house is lovely. No, lovely is not the word. This house is magnificent."

When she arrived early that morning, the first thing she did was go to the loo to have a pee and then she gave herself a full tour of the house. I caught up with her as she was going upstairs.

Nancy had taken my mother and Jack for a drive and I was glad. I couldn't cope with them and Rosemary.

"Sean says a lot of work needs to be done."

"Sean," she said. Her face had fleshed out over the past few months and it gave her a deceptively innocent look.

"A neighbour," I said and picked some clay from under my nail. Yesterday, my mother had me cleaning out plant pots in the conservatory. The day had passed without me noticing. I had found something that I liked doing.

"I see," she said.

"Are you hungry? Would you like some lunch?" I had to do something, I just couldn't remain sitting.

"I thought we might go into town for lunch," she said.

"That might be a problem. I don't have a lot of money left."

Rosemary frowned. "You're living in this beautiful house and you can't afford lunch?" Her voice high-pitched and irritating.

"I don't have a job, remember? All I was doing before I left Longford was packing shelves."

"So you're not coming back."

"No, what's there for me?"

"What's here?"

"Maybe a new life, if I could get myself a job. But I'll need something more than packing shelves if I'm going to keep this house."

"You certainly will. You'll need to find another rich boyfriend and this time you better keep him."

As I looked out the kitchen window, I could see Sean standing looking up at the roof, a puzzled look on his face. He had volunteered to do the repairs in turn for me letting him store some office furniture. Nancy told me he was relocating his business to Ireland. Jack was missing all the drama this morning; he would love to be here helping out. I wanted to invite Sean in, but I couldn't bring myself to do it, not with Rosemary here. She'd definitely drive him away.

"Is this Sean fella nice?" she asked. She had an uncanny way of reading my thoughts.

"He's okay."

Rosemary got up and strolled over to the window. "Is that him?"

I nodded and felt myself holding my breath.

"Why is he here?" she asked.

"Fixing some slates that came off the roof."

"A handy man," she said to herself.

I busied myself washing out the blue teapot, like Nancy did. I poured boiling water into it and then let the tea brew on the warm stove.

"Are you not going to invite him in for tea?"

I ignored her question, pretended I didn't hear, a trick my mother often used.

"I bet he'd love a cup of tea and I'd like to meet him. He looks interesting."

"Rosemary," I found myself saying, exasperated.

I walked over to the dresser and took down some cups. I didn't want her talking to Sean. The next thing she'd be filling him in on my life story. I could just see him sitting at the kitchen table, his eyes mocking me.

"Nancy has made some vegetable soup," I said with my back to her. "Perhaps you'd like some later."

"Sure," she said. I heard her fill a glass with water. She didn't turn the tap off properly and it started to drip.

I heard his light tap on the back door. He walked in casually, like he owned the place.

"Can I see you later?" he asked, looking directly at me. "I'd like to talk about some repairs you'd need to get done."

"Sure, no problem."

"You can do it now," Rosemary said, her eyes bright with curiosity.

"No, this evening's fine," he said.

"See you then."

Rosemary's eyes followed him as he left. "Well, he's not my type, but he's attractive and very charming and he seems interesting."

I noticed the way she dragged the word interesting along. A smile must have flickered across my face because she said, "So tell me what's he doing here?"

"He used to live here, or near here years ago. He's worked all around the world and now he's back."

"Is he single, seeing someone, separated, divorced, gay . . ."

I was losing patience with her. "Rosemary, I have no idea."

"He's probably got a child or two. He looks like someone with a few notches on his belt. What do you think?" When

I didn't reply she smirked and said, "He looks like Yul Brynner only he's got hair."

"I haven't really looked at him."

She smirked again. "Is your mother going to stay here with you?"

"It looks that way. When she gets on my nerves I'll go and hide in a cupboard like I used to do when I was a child."

We went for a drive out towards Croagh Patrick. Its conical shape looked magnificent in the grey light. We wrapped up and went for a walk on Bertra Strand. There she talked about Danny. They were rowing constantly about his drinking. She felt isolated; no one seemed to understand what she was going through.

We walked onto the beach determined not to let the bad weather defeat us.

It was on the beach that Rosemary told me that Eleanor and Gary had split up. The wind howled in my ears and I wasn't sure if I heard her right. I wouldn't let her say another word until we got back to the car.

"A week ago she came in to work and I knew by her that she had been crying. I went into her office to ask her a question about a customer – he was looking for a refund, you know the way she is about refunding. I caught her at a bad moment and she just started to talk."

I was willing her to hurry up, but I couldn't make her tell it faster. She enjoyed telling her story, filling in the details, having her audience captivated.

"She thinks Gary is still in love with you, that he doesn't really love her."

I listened to the words: *Gary is still in love with you.*

"Are you sure? I mean this happened a week ago. Maybe

things have changed since," I said. I had to be sure. I didn't want to get my hopes up for nothing.

"Well, she looks miserable, has done all week."

"But they could be back together again."

"I doubt it."

"But they could." I was taking no chances.

Rosemary sighed. "Maybe I shouldn't have told you; but if it was me I'd bloody well want to know. Maybe you should make a move."

"I suppose you have some suggestions?"

I opened the buttons of my jacket. The heat of the car was getting to me.

"Your house is in need of repairs. Why don't you get Gary down to have a look at the place?"

"He'd never come." I started the car. I had to move. I couldn't sit still with this news in my head.

"He might," she said and smirked. "You could use some of your charm."

"Very funny."

"I'm starving. Any chance of us going into town and getting some real food?"

"What do you call real food?"

Suddenly I felt rich. I was going to treat her to lunch – she'd just made my day.

"Burger and chips."

"Rosemary, your standards are slipping!"

"This little monster will settle for nothing else," she said, rubbing her rounded belly.

When we got back from having our burgers and chips in town, the kitchen was full. Jack came running to greet me.

Sean was sitting at the table. Nancy was filling bowls with soup. My mother was slicing brown bread. They filled the kitchen with their chatter. Jack was sitting on Sean's knee. Nancy talked to Sean about this and that. My mother and Rosemary talked civilly to each other. Either Rosemary had gone up a rung in my mother's estimation or else my mother had climbed down one. The easy conversation was nice.

I wondered if the sprits of Susan and Tom were looking on. Did Damien ever look out at the horizon and think of me and this house or had I slipped into some compartment in his head like I had five years ago, to be left there to get dusty?

Chapter 39

Later, that evening, when Rosemary had gone home, I
dialled Gary's number. I couldn't help myself – I just had to
talk to him. I counted the number of times the phone rang
and then my heart sank as I heard the answering machine
come on. I didn't leave a message. I'd keep on trying;
eventually he would answer.

Nancy and Sean were in the kitchen. My mother was in
the conservatory. She was spending most of her time in
there, lost in a world of clay and plants.

"You wanted to talk to me," I said to Sean.

"Will I go?" Nancy asked.

"There's no need," I said. Jack was cycling an old tricycle
around the kitchen. Sean had found it in the barn.

"I'd like to buy this house if you're willing to sell," he
said.

"I wasn't thinking of selling." I saw the look of
disappointment in his face.

He wanted this house, I wanted my husband back.
Would either of us get what we wanted?

"If I do sell, you'll be the first to know about it," I said.

"I'd better go," he said.

Looking at his determined face gave me an idea. Tomorrow I was going home to see Gary.

We got up early, myself and Jack. My mother didn't want to come; she told me she was in the middle of re-potting plants.

By lunch-time we were in Longford. I rang Gary on his mobile and asked him if he would like to come to my mother's house for dinner that evening. He accepted when he found out that my mother wouldn't be there and Jack would.

I couldn't wait to see him again.

Jack and I bought flowers for my father's grave. I was always ashamed of my father – after all, he was a drunk. When he died our neighbours sympathised with us, but not to the same extent as they did with the Brady family when their father died of cancer. It seemed people were better able to sympathise with the Brady's than us.

It's history now. Time has moved us all on to another place.

Gary arrived late.

"Sorry," he said. He had changed his clothes, his hair was damp and he smelled of shower gel.

I put the bottle of wine he had brought in the fridge and started to dish out our dried-up dinner.

"It's not great," I said.

"It's fine," he said.

Jack threw some carrots across the table and said they were yuck.

"Stop it," I said. He was really testing my patience.

"Good boy," Gary said and patted him on the head. I

wanted to ask him why he was praising Jack, but refrained under the circumstances.

"Are you busy?" I asked.

I tried to eat some chicken, but it was too dry. I noticed Gary was playing with his food and not eating it at all. This wasn't like him. He always cleared the plate no matter what concoction I put in front of him.

My stomach turned. I felt I was in very rough waters. I attempted to smile, but it was more like a grimace.

"Had you a nice Christmas?" I asked.

"We spent it together, here," he said. I felt he was holding out on something – it was the way his chest expanded and then went flat again.

"Oh, yes," I said and laughed nervously. "I mean, had you a nice New Year?"

He nodded.

I turned to look at Jack. He hadn't eat anything.

"Come on, Jack, you have to eat something," I coaxed.

"Perhaps he's lost his appetite," Gary said.

I put down my knife and fork and sipped some wine. The tension in the kitchen had reached a high voltage. I felt at any minute one of us was going to suffer a shock and I knew it was going to be me.

After I cleared away the plates I made some coffee. Gary went into the sitting-room with Jack. I heard them playing together. I was hurt he had left me all the washing-up to do.

I felt he wanted to hit me.

I brought a mug of coffee into the sitting-room to him. They were sitting on the floor, putting a jig-saw together.

"So, what's the occasion?" Gary said, looking up at me.

"No occasion," I said limply.

"Help," Jack said, pointing to me. I sat down on the floor and we made the jig-saw between us.

Gary got Jack dressed for bed and read him a story. I sat on my mother's chair pretending to read a magazine. Eventually Jack fell asleep in his father's arms.

"Shall I put him up?"

"No," Gary said and kissed his son's head. "I just want to hold him for a while."

I had forgotten how good they looked together.

"Gary," I said softly.

He glared at me.

"I don't want us to separate," I said.

Gary moved himself on the sofa, then gently laid his son down beside him.

He said nothing, so I continued.

"We both love Jack. Can't we try again?"

"No, Michelle, I could never trust you."

"Gary, for our son's sake. Look, I'm sorry about what happened, but it happened and we can put it behind us and move on." My voice rushed on ahead of my thoughts. "I'm sorry, nothing like this will ever happen again, I swear. Please Gary, could we not try?"

Gary shook his head.

"Damien's gone back to Sydney. He's not coming back, I don't want him back. I want you, I want us to be a family."

"I can't," he said.

I watched him stand up.

"Is it Eleanor?"

Gary shook his head. "No, it's not Eleanor," he said, and then added as if it was an afterthought, "I believe she's seeing Bob again."

I said nothing; there was nothing more I could say. The fire needed more coal, but there was no point putting some on. I knew Gary was about to leave.

"I'm going back to Westport in the morning," I said.

Gary nodded. "I miss my son," he said.

I wanted to shake this stupid man and tell him stop being so stubborn and move on.

"You're welcome to come to Westport any time," I said.

"Thanks." He slipped into his old denim jacket. "Thanks for dinner." Then he left.

I had to phone Rosemary. I had to talk to someone.

"Gary doesn't want me back," I said, when she answered the phone.

"Why?"

"Because he's a stubborn stupid man," I said, glad to have an ear to verbalise all that was going on in my head.

"I'm sorry," she said.

"How are you?"

"Fine. Going to Westport for the day put the wind up Danny. He was so worried when he didn't know where I was." She laughed mischievously. "Perhaps he thinks I have a lover."

"Oh, no, Rosemary, that's the last thing you need! Look at the mess I'm in! All because I couldn't say no to Damien."

"You have to admit you had fun – it broke the monotony of work."

Chapter 40

Outside the kitchen window I saw Sean talking to my mother. Jack was cycling around them on the old tricycle. Nancy told me that Tom had been going to convert the old building into holiday homes. She and my mother had got Sean up for a second opinion. They had been on about this for weeks now, sitting at the kitchen table trying to get me interested, but I couldn't care less.

I had lost interest. Gradually, the real cold of winter had left the earth. My mother was busy planting. I had given up hoping that she would go home. She never suggested leaving and I hadn't the heart to ask her. Besides, I had got used to her company, had come to accept her as part of the package like Jack was. Come to think of it, like Nancy was – she practically lived here.

I had also given up hope on Gary forgiving me. He came every second weekend to take Jack for the weekend. He drove him to Longford and drove him back on the Sunday evening. I tried to get him to stay with us, but he wouldn't.

It came as no surprise when I got a letter from his solicitor saying he was looking for a divorce. Vincent had phoned me, to tell me.

I just functioned. My mother took over and did all those things that needed to get done. It was my mother who remembered to put frozen peas in the freezer for when Jack fell. She paid the bills and told me she was selling her house in Longford, so she could help out. I agreed with her, though I didn't really know what she was talking about. She was there making everything seem normal while I absorbed the fact that Gary was divorcing me.

I had got myself a job as a receptionist in one of the local hotels. It paid for our groceries and it got me away from my mother and Nancy for a few hours.

Over the past few months I had come to accept that Gary didn't want me back. Yet, every morning when I woke my first thought was of Gary. I would look at the clock and try to imagine what he was doing.

Rosemary told me Eleanor and Bob had moved in together. Rosemary found her throwing up in the toilets and told Eleanor that she was pregnant before it had dawned on Eleanor what was wrong. Poor Eleanor. I'm sure she could have strangled Rosemary like I had often wanted to.

Gary was seeing no one. How Rosemary could be so certain was beyond me – I think she was trying to protect me. Keep me in my fantasy bubble believing that we were going to get back together again. I knew better.

Daffodils were starting to grow again. I loved to walk up the avenue, with Jack beside me, cycling his bike and this mass of daffodils swaying gracefully in the wind.

* * *

When I woke up that morning the first thought on my mind was what seeds I would sow. Gary divorcing me was my second thought. I'd made progress. It was my day off. I didn't wash my face or comb my hair. The morning passed by without me noticing.

I opened the door when I heard the gentle tap and found myself looking into Sean's sincere face.

"Your mother and Nancy want me to talk to you about these holiday homes," he said.

He had drawn up some plans. He'd shown them to Nancy and my mother. When they had discussed it in depth, they decided it was time to tell me. I was unsure. I didn't want tourists around. They reassured me that we'd never see them. I knew I had to do something. I couldn't afford to run the house on what I was earning.

"I'm a mess," I said, almost apologising.

"You look fine to me," he said.

I laughed, and felt I had inched myself out of that dark hole of despair where I had taken up residence for the past while.

"Come in. You make the coffee and I'll have a shower."

Upstairs, I took out a new white T-shirt to put on with my jeans. Sean was a nice man and he liked Jack and more importantly Jack liked him. I couldn't help but wonder was he, like me, available.

The End.